I0699627

# PRAISE FOR EUGENE LINDEN AND HIS BOOKS

## DEEP PAST

"An excellent thriller with real meat on the bones . . .
makes you think as well as sweat."

—LEE CHILD, #1 *NEW YORK TIMES*–BESTSELLING AUTHOR OF
THE JACK REACHER SERIES

"An extraordinary novel on so many levels . . . One of those rare novels
that bends (if not blows) the mind with deep and compelling ideas about
consciousness, intelligence, and our place in the world."

—DOUGLAS PRESTON, #1 *NEW YORK TIMES*–BESTSELLING AUTHOR OF
*THE LOST CITY OF THE MONKEY GOD*

"A fascinating thriller . . . Linden does a masterly job of integrating
intriguing speculative science into a page-turning plot."

—*PUBLISHER'S WEEKLY,* STARRED REVIEW

"An immersive tale that is both intellectually enlivening and genuinely
entertaining."

—*KIRKUS REVIEWS*

## THE PARROT'S LAMENT

"Wonderful, humane, touching. You cannot read it and remain unmoved."

—JEFFREY MOUSSAIEFF MASSON, AUTHOR OF *WHEN ELEPHANTS WEEP*

## THE FUTURE IN PLAIN SIGHT

"May well be the most important book of the decade."

—*ROCKY MOUNTAIN NEWS*

# THE WINDS OF CHANGE

"A lucidly written guide to the near future and a provocative manual of public policy."

—EDWARD O. WILSON, BIOLOGIST AND AUTHOR

"*The Winds of Change* is fascinating—a tour de force. Linden has accumulated a greater comprehension of paleoclimatic and oceanographic issues than all but a very few scientists. I have nothing but admiration for this book, which is just what we need right now."

—GEORGE WOODWELL, FOUNDER OF THE WOODS HOLE RESEARCH CENTER AND FORMER PRESIDENT OF THE ECOLOGICAL SOCIETY OF AMERICA

# SILENT PARTNERS

"Mr. Linden knows the minefield well and guides us through it with intelligence and unfailing good humor . . . A great display of science as snake pit, and those who liked *The Double Helix* can get the same evil glee from it."

—URSULA K. LE GUIN IN *THE NEW YORK TIMES BOOK REVIEW*

"The ultimate fate of a group of primate research animals in *Silent Partners* poses deeply disturbing questions about science and society. Eugene Linden's handling of this important material is poised, compassionate, and insightful."

—BARRY LOPEZ, AUTHOR OF *ARCTIC* AND *OF WOLVES AND MEN*

# RESURRECTING BART

# RESURRECTING BART

## A DEEP PAST NOVEL

EUGENE LINDEN

*For my old (meaning longstanding) friends. I can't name you all (as I wouldn't know where to stop), but I will name those who have maintained our friendship for a long, long time:*

*Bill Adams, Jeff Brenzel, Jim Bennett, Earnest Abrahamson, Stephen Evans-Freke, Tom Kehler, Tully Friedman, John Tierney, John Paul Newport, Ralph Schmidt, Susan Babcock, Spencer Bebe, Tom McNamee, and Eric Konigsberg. You have all challenged me and enriched my life, and I'm a better person for having the privilege of your friendship over many years.*

# RESURRECTING BART

*Nine years old, he was still discovering the breadth and depth of his powers, and how they separated him from others, even his family standing close by. He was intimately tuned to the rhythms of the rainforest, and now he sensed a disturbance, an intrusion several miles away. He knew instantly they had come for him. He had the power to do the intruders great harm, but he also knew that if he did so, he would embark on a path from which there was no turning back. Vivid panoramas unfurled in his mind of what his future life would be like based on what he did now. Even though he had not yet reached adolescence, his family treated him with deference, some even with reverence. Yet, he knew he would have to make his decision alone, and soon. At last, a solution proposed itself. While not perfect, he knew it would buy him time.*

# EX NIHILO

# 1 A MEMORIAL AND A REUNION



THE GROUP MET AT HELEN HAYDEN'S SPRAWLING PACIFIC lodge–style estate on Vancouver Island in British Columbia. All seven people in the group had played a role in bringing to the world's attention an extraordinary find that had sent shock waves through a host of scientific disciplines two years earlier.

The occasion was the third anniversary of the death of Fletcher Hayden, Helen's father. The elder Hayden had been a board member of Transteppe, a Canadian-Kazakh mining concession in the northern steppe land of Kazakhstan, and he had provided protection and financial support for Claire Knowland's efforts to bring the extraordinary discovery to light when all other backers had stepped away. Hayden's death was traced to a Russian oligarch, who had ordered his murder to clear the way to control of Transteppe as part of a plot to launch a Crimea-style Russian takeover of northern Kazakhstan. Claire's husband Sergei had foiled that plot when he brought to light the role of a hired assassin in Hayden's murder, and the assassin's connection to the oligarch.

Claire dutifully attended memorials on the anniversary of Hayden's death out of a profound sense of obligation to a man who saved her career. Still, she had another purpose in attending this gathering; it provided a pretext for meeting with this select group, whose assembly in other circumstances might have aroused unwanted interest and speculation.

After the other attendees had departed, this select group of seven gathered in what had been Hayden's study. The room had half-timbered walls and a high-vaulted ceiling. A fragrant fire of Douglas Fir warmed the room and lessened the bite of the marine layer that had rolled in. Ever the considerate host, Helen invited the group to partake of the single malts and digestifs arrayed on a drinks trolley. "Most appreciative," mumbled Willem Keerbrock. A world-renowned geophysicist, he had also played a role in bringing Claire's discovery to light. He ambled over to pour a shot or two of a vintage Red Breast Irish Whiskey into a heavy crystal tumbler. Others followed.

As she wandered around the room, Claire thought back to the discovery that had started them on this journey. After she had taken over an archaeological dig near the concession of Transteppe, she'd had a surprise visit from Rob Rebolet, the chief of security for the concession. He told her about some strange, exceptionally large bones that had been found in a remote corner of the concession by Sergei, who was then Transteppe's chief geologist. The bones turned out to be elephant ulnas, dating back 5.3 million years. Even more intriguing, they appeared to have been arrayed in parallel. But by what, and for what purpose? Expanding the dig, they had uncovered an elephant cranium, but it had a pronounced forehead, and the team had taken to calling the mystery elephant "Bart" because the shape of the skull reminded them of the animated character, Bart Simpson. Mischievously, the team retained the reference to Bart Simpson when they gave the formal name *Simpsoniensis* to the newly discovered species.

The mystery of the bones was compounded when another member of the group, Katie Segal—a grad student working at the dig— uncovered a mysterious piece of jadeite in the rubble when they had unearthed the ancient bones. Shaped like a yam, the stone had extraordinary properties. One of the most intriguing being that humans could hold it only for a few seconds before a powerful field emanating from the stone made it too uncomfortable to hold.

Katie had guessed that the field might have been created with the expectation that an animal with the body mass of an elephant would be picking it up, so she had brought the stone to an elephant sanctuary where it subsequently had a remarkable impact on the animals that touched it with their trunks. The elephants had become excited, gathered in a circle, and began rhythmically swaying together. Some had even picked up sticks and tried driving them into the ground with their trunks.

*Why had they done that?* Claire thought quietly to herself, but her reminiscence was interrupted by Helen, inviting her to speak. Claire stood up and surveyed the group. Besides Keerbrock, there were Sergei—now Claire's husband—Katie, and Rob Rebolet. Also present, but not at all interested in the conversation at hand, was Sofia, Claire and Sergei's eighteen-month-old toddler, who was fast asleep in a bassinette that Helen had rustled up.

Also present was Zoe Taylor, who had founded Boisbeaux, a sanctuary in southern Louisiana for formerly captive elephants, and the place where Katie had introduced elephants to the jadeite. Zoe had never met Helen's father, and was puzzled when she received the invitation, a first-class, round-trip ticket from New Orleans to Vancouver, and a note from Helen saying that Claire hoped her schedule would permit her to attend. Zoe was rough around the edges and felt uncomfortable in this grand setting, but she had witnessed firsthand the extraordinary impact the jadeite had on the elephants at the refuge. The others in the group also had noted the presence of Zoe, and wondered about the significance of her being there.

Claire raised her glass and turned to a portrait of Fletcher Hayden that hung over his desk (Helen had it installed after his death; he never would have allowed it during his lifetime). "First a toast to..." she halted. She still couldn't say his name without choking up. "... to your father. He was always there." She trailed off. The others raised their glasses in silence.

"Actually, all of you were crucial to bringing our discovery to light, and Dr. Keerbrock, proved indispensable in helping us publish our findings."

Keerbrock shook his head, remarking, "Whenever I hear the word indispensable, I think of Charles de Gaulle, a man not known for his modesty, who when told he was France's indispensable man, remarked, 'The cemeteries are filled with indispensable men.'"

When the laughter died down, Claire continued. "OK, you're probably wondering why this little gathering." She nodded at Zoe. "We all remember those magical sessions with the jadeite and the Boisbeaux elephants."

Keerbrock peered at her intently. He had a global reputation for the ferocity with which he protected scientific rigor. As he put it, "If you're going to theorize about *why* something had happened in the past, the first step is to be damn sure you know exactly *what* happened." He had made his endorsement of Claire's research conditional on her publications' not over-reaching what was justified by the data. At the same time though, his curiosity had been profoundly piqued by his observations of the elephant reactions to the jadeite, and he had encouraged Claire and Katie to continue exploring the properties of the jadeite and the messages it seemed to convey.

Keerbrock chuckled. "I was hoping that tooth would someday gnaw its way to the surface." The others looked at each other in confusion. He waved at Claire. "Go ahead, explain."

Claire smiled gratefully. One gate passed, but there would be many others to get through. "There's something I've been hiding for the right moment."

"The husband is always the last to know," said Sergei with a laugh that was joined by the others. All of them knew about the storm of innuendo, disinformation, and character assassination, which had accompanied her efforts to describe the discovery in a scientifically credible way, and none of this group begrudged her resulting tendency to limit disclosure of anything controversial until it was absolutely necessary.

"Sorry Sergei," she said. "I did tell Dr. Keerbrock about it, just to be sure of its significance."

Sergei gave an amiable shrug. "It's good to know where I stand in the pecking order."

"Here's what happened," said Claire. She went on to describe how she had come upon a softball-sized salt crystal during her last days on the mesa where the ancient elephant bones were found, and how on returning to Rushmere—the university where she was a research affiliate—she had dropped the crystal during a wave of nausea brought on by her pregnancy. The salt crystal had shattered, revealing the edges of a tooth embedded inside. She had immediately protected it by placing it in a buffer of phosphate solution chilled by liquid nitrogen, where it had remained untouched for two years.

"A tooth?" asked Katie, looking around to see if others were equally confused.

"It's not just that it was a tooth," said Keerbrock, jumping in, "It's that it was encrusted in salt. Between the fact that it was encrusted in salt, the extreme aridity of the circumstances of its encapsulation, and that the surrounding dental material might give further protection to the root, which itself was isolated from blood and tissue, raises the possibility of mummification rather than petrification."

Zoe and Rob still looked confused, but Katie got it. "Full strands of preserved DNA? Full set of chromosomes?"

"… and the possibility of bringing one of these ancient elephants back to life. With that came the possibility of understanding what message that ancient species was trying to pass on to those in the future, as well as the possibility of encountering an extraordinary and utterly different type of intelligence." Claire spelled it out.

There was stunned silence in the room.

After a moment, Katie spoke. "Why didn't you bring this up earlier?"

"There was so much to think through, and if word got out, events would likely have gotten out of our control," said Claire quietly. "There were practical considerations of how to do it, how many people would have to be brought in, where it might be done." She nodded at Zoe, who seemed deep in thought. "Then there were the ethical conundrums. Would we be playing God? This resurrected, intelligent being would be completely at our mercy and could conceivably live for many decades. How could we protect it, and give it a good life?"

"All very good questions," said Katie evenly, "And you found answers?"

"Maybe," said Claire. "For me, the answer *is* the jadeite. Five million years ago, as Kazakhstan roasted during the Messinian salinity crisis, those ancient elephants knew the end was nigh. Maybe the jadeite contains a record they made for posterity so that some future intelligent creature would know who they were. Perhaps they wanted to leave an account of their time on earth, and it's not a stretch to then assume that they would be overjoyed if they could know that future intelligent beings could bring them back to live again."

"Well said," remarked Keerbrock, lending his imprimatur to the venture.

Claire looked at the others, all deep in thought. "This is not something we're going to decide today, and I can't and won't do this without you. Think about it, and let's all confer again, or individually. We'll figure out how. One thing I'll ask though, because I know I can trust every one of you, is that only we seven can know about this. Agreed?"

They all nodded, and then Katie spoke up. "If we do decide to go ahead, we have to bring in more people, right?"

Claire was secretly pleased—she'd been worried about Katie. "Right, but only very few, and others we might need to work with don't have to know the significance of what they're doing. Please, all of you, think hard about this and what it might mean."

Rob, who had not said anything, finally spoke up. "I suppose the fact that we're all here means that you think it can be done."

Claire nodded. "There are a lot of ifs involved, but the answer is yes. If we can recover a full strand of DNA, it's all execution. It's called nuclide transplantation—you irradiate modern elephant eggs to destroy the nuclei, and then introduce the recovered and replicated DNA. We share ninety-nine percent of our DNA with chimpanzees, from whom we separated more than five million years ago. It's likely that the similarity between the ancient elephant DNA and a modern elephant will be something like that, similar enough that a surrogate mom could bring an embryo to term."

She paused for a moment and then continued, "One more thing." She took a breath. "One thing I've thought a lot about is—if we go ahead—how it should be done." She looked around the room. "Given what happened with the discovery of the bones, imagine the freak show that would descend on us, if we publicly announced that we were trying to resurrect a five-million-year-old animal." There were nods around the room, but nobody said a word. "And then imagine the life the baby would have given the spotlight that would be on it every minute. It would be a nightmare, and the baby would be like some Caliban put on display in Elizabethan England. So, I'd like all of you to agree that utter secrecy starts now. If we're successful—big if—things will get a lot harder." She paused to let that sink in. "We'll have to maintain utter secrecy for years, maybe decades. So, please consider that as you make your decision. If we succeed, the satisfaction of having brought this noble species back to life will have to be sufficient. There will be no glory, no grandstanding, and no publication. At least while the elephant is alive, which quite possibly may be longer than any of us will live."

Claire paused. "I know it's a tough ask."

Claire looked each of them in the eye, one by one. All present nodded assent.

Rob broke the silence. "Lot to think about. I'm afraid I've got to catch a plane." He turned to Helen. "I truly admired your dad. He was a man in full."

Helen blinked away a tear and nodded. Then, as the rest of the group got up to leave, she cleared her throat. "One last thing. Claire and I spoke for a minute before this meeting. If you decide to be a part of this, you've got funding."

As the group broke up, Claire paid particular attention to Zoe who looked uncomfortable and concerned. If this was going to happen, Zoe had to be on board, and clearly Zoe knew it.

# 2 BOISBEAUX

Claire's concerns were justified. Two months after the meeting in Hayden's study, Claire got a message from Zoe. "Flo's learned a new trick."

The group communicated by a supposedly secure encrypted messaging app, but they still took pains to use bland messages—Flo was one of the Boisbeaux elephants—to make any arrangements. Zoe was saying they needed to talk.

"Love to see it," Claire texted back, "Can I bring a friend?"

"Sure."

So, Zoe wanted Claire to bring Katie and for Katie to bring the jadeite. That was good news.

Only the seven people who'd met earlier in Hayden's study were aware of the near magical properties of the jadeite. The story of how Katie got the stone to the elephants at Boisbeaux was complicated. The stone had been uncovered at Transteppe alongside the arrayed and petrified elephant bones. Katie, who Claire had designated as chief investigator of the stone, cleaned off encrustations and discovered its mysterious energy field. A former animal activist with a long history of working with elephants, Katie had gone rogue and taken the stone to Boisbeaux, the elephant preserve that had been started by Zoe, another former animal activist. When Katie presented the stone to some of the elephants at the refuge, their hypnotic rumbling and swaying made it clear that there was some sort of message in the jadeite that the elephants received and at least partially understood—a message that had been encoded more than five million years earlier. Subsequently, Katie had a rapprochement with Claire and demonstrated the stone's effect on the elephants to Claire, Helen, and Keerbrock.

Over the days and weeks since the Vancouver meeting, Claire heard from the others. So far, all had given the green light. Keerbrock had signaled his assent even before the Vancouver meeting when Claire first told him about the tooth and her misgivings. Rob knew the project would be a security nightmare, but, after some back and forth with Claire, he came to accept that the stakes justified the effort. Sergei struggled for a while. He completely understood the value of the undertaking, and he agreed with Claire that the jadeite itself meant that Bart's long dead forebears would endorse the effort. But he also knew that if news of what they were doing leaked, the publicity would tear apart their lives. When Sergei returned to Transteppe (he still intermediated between the mining concession and the archaeologists on the dig), Rob and Sergei had several long conversations about the various risks and the practicalities of maintaining secrecy during the pregnancy and birth of the world's largest land animal.

"So," said Sergei during one conversation. "We need to make an elephant disappear."

"That's about the size of it," agreed Rob.

"Obvious answer," said Sergei.

"Which is?"

"David Copperfield did it. Hire him."

Rob laughed. Sergei was in.

Katie took her time with her decision. She still retained the spirit of her days as an animal activist. Her looks had made it easy to get jobs at roadside zoos (usually owned by men), where she surreptitiously documented the awful living conditions of elephants, tigers, and other animals. Freeing the animals was one thing, finding a home for them was another, and once Zoe had secured the funding for Boisbeaux, they teamed up with Katie providing the documentation for shutting down the zoos, and Zoe providing the refuge for the freed elephants. A volunteer network helped them find homes for the other freed animals at refuges and sanctuaries around the country.

Katie quickly earned a reputation as someone who would go the limit to rescue abused animals. Unfortunately, that reputation extended beyond the animal activism community. After a couple of years, word got out among the private zoos and Katie was blown as an on-the-ground operative. She also found herself being sued by a number of zoo owners whose operations she shut down. Burnt out at twenty-five, she'd enrolled in a graduate archaeology program at Rushmere, the university where Claire was an adjunct professor of anthropology. Katie got a position on a dig looking for evidence of ancient domestication of horses by the Botai people of Northern Kazakhstan, the dig that Claire had taken over after the principal investigator got sick. The research took a radically different direction after Rob brought Claire the news that Sergei, had found what appeared to be ancient bones of an exceptionally large animal protruding from the ground in a remote part of the concession. Katie enthusiastically joined the new direction of the research, which had rekindled her passion for elephants.

Still, her fascination with ancient elephant intelligence was tempered by her deep conviction that those elephants living today should be treated with respect. So, back at Rushmere, she found Claire in the lab.

"Since you invited Zoe, you're thinking Boisbeaux, yes?"

Claire guessed where this was going. "Yeah," she said slowly. "And you have a surrogate in mind?"

"Yeah," also slowly.

"Who?"

"Flo."

Katie looked down uncomfortably, but then looked up curiously. "Makes sense." She knew that Claire had known Flo from her early research at an elephant park in Florida. She shook her head. "But we don't have the right!"

Claire put a hand on Katie's shoulder. "I know, but what if she gives consent?"

Katie looked confused. "What, have her sign a document with her lawyer present?"

Claire laughed. "That would be best, but maybe we can figure out whether she wants a baby."

There was a long silence. Katie drummed her fingers on a table. "Okay, that works for me."

Claire breathed a sigh of relief.

"But will it work for Zoe?"

Claire nodded. "That's where I'm going to need your help."

# 3  MBEMBE

AFTER DRIVING OVER THIRTEEN HOURS ON I-95, ENROUTE FROM New Hampshire to Boisbeaux in Southern Louisiana with only stops for gas, both Claire and Katie were getting saucer eyed. They had decided to drive because they couldn't risk taking the jadeite through an airport metal detector. They hadn't talked much, mostly taking turns driving while the other slept. Claire had called Sergei a couple of times to break the monotony, and he put Sofia on the phone who gave an exhaustive, babytalk, account of a playdate with three other girls at her friend Monica's house. Just before they got to the border between North and South Carolina, Katie roused herself, and glanced at the sign for an upcoming exit. "Hmm, Lumberton. Maybe they have a diner with pies like in *Twin Peaks*."

Claire had other ideas. "Yeah, or a bar with a double martini like in *Mad Men* or *Gilmore Girls*. I'm fried." She looked at the navigation screen in her Kia. "We're about halfway. Let's find a meal and a motel."

As they drove along Lumberton's main drag, they spotted a honky-tonk with a parking lot full of pickup trucks. Katie raised an eyebrow. "Looks lively."

Claire glanced at Katie, who, as usual, was looking languorous and irresistible in jeans and a rugby shirt. "Might be better to find a family restaurant that serves alcohol if we don't want to start a riot." Katie chuckled.

Just down the road, Claire spied what appeared to be a small restaurant. She slowed down and peered inside.

"Cool, it's loaded with families and has a bar."

The restaurant was redolent of 1950s, middle America. Formica tables, bright fluorescent lighting, plastic menus, and the din attended to lots of children of all ages, scattered around the room with their parents. Claire liked the din—it meant they could talk freely. They settled in a booth and both ordered double vodka on the rocks, which elicited a disapproving look from their just-past-middle-aged server. But it hadn't stopped her from taking their drink orders, which she soon returned with. They then placed their food order, both choosing meat loaf and mashed potatoes (under the logic that it was hard to screw up meat loaf, or mashed potatoes for that matter). As the server turned and left the table, Katie nodded toward the retreating woman. "I guess the gals of Lumberton do their drinking at home."

Claire jerked her head in the direction of the shit-kicking bar they had passed. "Or down the road." She raised her glass. "Here's to a successful launch."

Katie turned serious. "Do you think Zoe's going to go along."

Claire thought for a second. "My guess is she's already made up her mind. I'm thinking she wants to see a session with the jadeite one more time just to confirm her decision."

"Yeah, I hope that's right anyway."

A few moments later, their server returned, with two hot plates in hand, dropping them in front of each of the women with a loud *clank*, and then turned and walked away without a word.

There was a pause while both women picked at their meat loaf. Claire glanced at Katie and wondered, as she often did, to what degree Katie took her looks for granted. Katie was an accident of genetics that produced something of a miracle, and yet, so far as Claire knew, Katie had never pursued any of the obvious career paths on which her looks would have opened doors. Indeed, she had done something of the opposite, going into animal rights and then academia, and for the past several years a secret project that required the equivalent of monastic vows.

Claire noticed that Katie was studying her. "What are you thinking?" Katie asked.

Claire felt herself blushing. "Actually, I was wondering what you look for in a man."

Katie laughed. "As you know, these days that's a theoretical question." She cocked her head. "A question that brings me back to the days when I had imaginary friends."

Claire instantly regretted asking. "I'm sorry Katie, I didn't mean to open a wound, especially since I'm the one responsible for your having to resort to imaginary friends."

Katie waved this off. "My choice . . . but lemme think . . . to some degree that question is context dependent . . . has to love animals, especially elephants, can keep their mouth shut, loner, not interested in bros, someone with values, courage, a mind, and a sense of humor—I'm sounding like the perfect *Cosmopolitan* subscriber, aren't I?"

Claire laughed. "I doubt you'd be interested in that thing they always have on the upper left corner of the cover, 'Tricks on how to drive your man wild.'"

Katie was still pondering the question. "Most of all, trustworthy. If you're going to open yourself up, it's like a dive into the void. Trusting someone with your heart is the hardest thing I can imagine doing."

Claire was *fascinated* with this. Was she saying it had never happened? She thought about Sergei, and felt a warmth rise within her. She trusted him completely.

Their conversation was interrupted by the return of the server, only this time instead of looking disapproving, she looked discomfited. She was carrying two tumblers of vodka and as she approached the table, she subtly shook her head and then briefly turned her eyes up to the ceiling. "The two gentlemen at the bar bought you a round."

Claire was confused, but Katie got the message. She got up, taking the two glasses. "Thanks, I'll handle this."

Claire started to get up too, but Katie waved her down and headed to the bar.

Claire watched as Katie approached the bar, and had a brief conversation with the two men. The men looked a bit agitated. Katie came back to the table after getting the bill from the server. She didn't sit down, but paid the bill in cash, leaving a generous tip. "Time to go," she jerked her head toward the door.

Once they were back on the road, Claire asked, "What just went on? What did you say?"

"I said thanks, but we couldn't drink anymore because we were headed to church—the one next to the police station. I suggested that they give the drinks to a couple with three young kids who looked like they needed them. That's when they got agitated, and that's when I knew they'd put roofies in the vodka—which, by the way, is what the server was signaling."

Claire shook her head. "Not easy being Katie Segal, is it?"

"A few of these encounters and a girl could get cynical about human nature." Katie looked out the window. "But then there was the waitress who did the right thing."

Claire drove past the motel where they'd planned to stay for the night. "Given the situation, we should keep driving, yes?"

"Yup, four-hour shifts?"

They arrived at Boisbeaux at eight the next morning. Boisbeaux consisted of an isolated, 2,000-acre expanse of bayou and bottomland in Southern Louisiana. Both Claire and Katie knew it well. It was to Boisbeaux that Katie had absconded with the jadeite back when the stone's strange properties first became apparent. She'd gone rogue because she thought that Claire and Keerbrock would never give permission to test her hypothesis that the ancient elephants had encoded a message into the jadeite that only an elephant, with its extraordinary sound processing capabilities, might decipher. Since Keerbrock had ruled out publication on speculations about the nature of the stone without evidence to back it up, Katie had felt that she had nothing to lose. After Claire and Keerbrock tracked her down to Boisbeaux, and witnessed the impact the stone had on the elephants, the three reconciled. For her part, Zoe, though fiercely protective of the elephants, recognized that the jadeite brought out extraordinary and positive reactions from the giants under her protection.

After Claire and Katie had settled in, they went to sleep, waking just after the staff had departed for the day. With only Zoe and Claire in attendance, Katie started another session with the jadeite. A jumble of elephants had already assembled in the fenced area where they had held their earlier sessions—by this point the elephants seemed to eagerly anticipate the opportunity to touch the rock. They formed a circle around Katie and Claire of their own accord. Zoe hovered just outside the circle. Each elephant patiently waited to touch the jadeite with their trunk. Then they started swaying in synchrony and emitting ultra-low rumblings that could be felt as much as heard, and as more elephants joined, the chant—for that was what it seemed—built, driving out all other sensations.

Even though Claire, Zoe, and Katie had no idea what images the jadeite aroused in the elephants, the impact on the humans was hypnotic, leaving them both exhilarated and drained as the ceremony wound down. The humans could not guess what the elephants were experiencing, but, clearly, the stone had become something of a sacred object for them. Actually, it was becoming something similar for the humans.

After the spell was broken, Claire looked at Katie, "We've done this what? Eight to ten times? I still don't know how to describe it."

Katie smiled, looking off in the distance. "Losing yourself?"

Claire nodded, "Something like that. We're getting it second hand; we're feeling the power of the elephants' reactions, not the stone itself. Imagine what they're feeling."

"I don't know," said Katie, "I get these dream-like, amorphous images floating at the edge of consciousness, just out of reach. Maybe I'm part elephant?"

Zoe, stocky and weather-beaten, looked at the stunning auburn-haired young woman and snorted. "Of course! How did I miss it?" Zoe looked down and kicked some dust. "I know why you're here." She jerked her head toward a female elephant walking away. "Flo?"

Claire nodded.

It turned out that Flo was something of a doting aunt to the few young elephants at the sanctuary. It wasn't a stretch to assume that she would want to have a baby of her own. Not that there weren't issues that Zoe had to work through: The sanctuary had a policy of keeping males and females separate when the females were in estrus or the males in musth, a policy driven by Zoe's conviction that she did not want to add to the captive elephant population. She struggled to find the resources to provide for the herd as it was, and there were many captive elephants that would benefit from the better life at Boisbeaux. Zoe was also uncomfortable about the idea of bringing a baby elephant into a life of captivity. Given Helen Hayden's expression of support, however, Zoe knew that this baby would have a dowry and devoted protectors.

And then there was the jadeite. Zoe knew that if this baby survived and turned out to be as intelligent as its ancient ancestors seemed to have been, it would not only transform science, but it might also galvanize people to protect the world's fast disappearing wild elephants.

So, getting Zoe's permission to use Flo as a surrogate mother was not the hard part. That came later as the three women were sitting on Zoe's veranda, and Claire walked her through the steps that would be necessary to maintain secrecy and safety once Flo was impregnated.

The even harder part would be actually implementing those steps. For one thing, these steps involved somehow securing the frozen remains of a stillborn elephant fetus. Then there was the matter of moving Flo to Africa during the twenty-two-month gestation period.

Claire had spent years thinking about this. She'd approached the issue from three angles. First were the ethical considerations of whether the project was justifiable. Despite the assurances she had given the others in Vancouver, she had lingering doubts. She could hardly ask a priest or moral philosopher about the issue, so she had turned to Keerbrock as he was one of the very few people who knew about the tooth.

She recalled their earlier conversation about the tooth vividly. She had arranged to meet with him during one of his regular trips to Boston. They found an isolated booth in a deli near the port, and far from the many campuses where they might be recognized.

As she waited in a booth for the great scientist, Claire had thought back on their long history, which dated back to her days as a graduate student. Her first encounter with Keerbrock had been traumatic and almost destroyed her career before it began. She had been planning her thesis in comparative psychology on metacognition in the great apes, and, for reasons that only later became apparent, the chair of the department had invited Keerbrock to sit in on the presentation. Keerbrock, a hard scientist (geophysics, oceanography, and evolutionary biology) had systematically pointed out the violations of Occam's razor embedded in her approach to the subject. The thing was that Claire later realized that Keerbrock had been right—that if she were to venture into positing consciousness for non-humans, she had to be absolutely bulletproof in her approach and data collection. She also later realized that the chair, a hard-core behaviorist, had invited Keerbrock, a stickler for protocol in the hardest of the hard sciences, because the chair wanted to nip this type of investigation in the bud. Years later, after the discovery of the elephant bones, she had reached out to Keerbrock because she knew that he had long wanted to do a deeper study of the relationship between climate and the evolution of intelligence, and evidence of an ancient, non-human intelligence might be just the thing he was looking for.

Now, she looked with affection as Keerbrock entered the coffee shop, and she almost laughed as Keerbrock's frown deepened as he looked around the dilapidated room. He sat down, ordered a coffee, took a sip of the viscous black liquid, grimaced, "This better be good to justify all this tradecraft."

Claire dove right in. "It's the tooth."

Keerbrock nodded, but said nothing.

"Here's the thing. I'm dead certain that resurrecting Bart would be honoring his extinct ancestors and an extraordinary boon to humanity and science."

Keerbrock raised an eyebrow, interested.

"But then I think about reports and my horror of hearing rumors that the Russians thought of seeing whether humans and chimpanzees could be crossbred. Humans and chimps have about the same evolutionary separation—five million years—as Bart and modern elephants."

Keerbrock shook his head irritably. "The baby will not be a genetic cross, but rather a purebred. The mother is a surrogate." He thought a bit more. "Also, I suppose the difference here is that Bart and his ilk were vastly more intelligent than modern elephants. Evolution doesn't care about that, but we sure do. Don't know if that would make a difference for an ethicist, though."

Claire turned that thought over. "That's kind of where I came out: a human-chimp hybrid would be a monster, and a freak—Bart would be something his elephant mother would be proud of."

Keerbrock offered a resigned smile. "There're about a million unsupportable suppositions in that statement, and you probably don't want to examine that too closely, but . . . yes."

"And then there's the issue that the mother will not know that she'll be carrying a baby from a long-dead species . . ."

Keerbrock opened his hands helplessly. He looked exasperated. "There's no way to tie this up neatly with a bow. We're already compromised in academic terms because—and I agree on this—the only way to go ahead on this is under complete secrecy . . ."

Claire started to say something, but Keerbrock waved her off. "Let me finish. We have to accept that to do this is, to put it bluntly, unjustifiable. Along the way, we can do the best for the mother and the baby, but let's be clear—we'd be doing this because Bart was one of nature's miracles, and there's so much we can learn from him. If you can't accept that justification, you should put the tooth back in a drawer. It's your decision, but I know what I'd do!"

Claire looked miserable. "I've got to think about this more."

Keerbrock got up from the booth. "You should. It's a binary decision, but there's a clock on it."

"What do you mean?"

"How much longer do you think we can keep our small team together?"

That conversation had taken place six months before the scheduled reunion in Vancouver. As they were leaving the coffee shop to get in separate cabs—more tradecraft—Claire turned to Keerbrock. "I'll let you know at Helen's."

Keerbrock offered a parting smile as he got in his taxi. "Oh, I think you had already made your decision when you asked me to meet."

Now in Boisbeaux, with her own doubts put aside—barely—and with Zoe's assent, there loomed the practical consideration of recovering DNA and then the insemination. But, even if the insemination worked, there was the issue of where mother and infant could live in relative tranquility.

After an intensive search of potential havens, while leafing through an old *National Geographic*, Claire came upon a reference to an isolated part of the Congo ecosystem called Mbembe. Claire had already ruled out protected areas. Most weren't that protected anyway, and, in the unlikely situation where she found a well-protected area that would accept a non-resident elephant, it would attract too much attention. Following up on Mbembe, Claire had discreet conversations with a number of explorers and conservationists, and with each conversation, Mbembe moved closer to the head of the line. It was completely surrounded by swamps and quicksand, and much of the forest itself was subject to flooding, which made it unattractive for loggers. Nor did the area have any gold or other underground resources that might attract miners.

This last bit was an important consideration since the Russian mercenary army—the Wagner Group—was active throughout the Sahel to the north, propping up strongmen in return for access to gold mining and other African riches. The mercenaries were known for their brutality and fighting skills. Claire shuddered as she remembered news reports of atrocities committed as Wagner established control, including beheadings and villagers buried to their necks under the scorching sun. The Wagner Group had also moved into the fringes of the Congo rainforest through its support for the leader of the Central African Republic. Claire thought about this—the last thing she needed was another run-in with Russians, especially these Russians. It seemed extremely unlikely that the mercenaries would show any interest, however, as there were far easier pickings to the north, and the swamps surrounding Mbembe provided a formidable barrier.

Mbembe seemed perfect. Instead of relying on institutions and people to protect Flo and the baby, Mbembe raised the possibility of nature and topography offering protection. Claire cast aside her doubts and confected an audacious plan. Because it was inaccessible and had little to tempt outsiders, logging and mineral concession rights to Mbembe might be bought on the cheap. Once the rights were purchased Mbembe could be converted into an elephant sanctuary (it was an increasingly widespread practice in central Africa for conservation groups to bid for logging concessions), whose first residents would be a few of the elephants from Boisbeaux. If Flo moved back to Africa with a few other elephants, the transfer could be done openly as only the team would know that Flo was pregnant. Hopefully, the Boisbeaux elephants could become self-sufficient over time, and hopefully they also might join with existing elephant herds (if the Boisbeaux elephants were females, this would be more likely). In this scenario, pregnant Flo would just be part of the crowd.

With that decided, all that remained to be planned and plotted was the not-so-tiny matter of getting Flo pregnant with five-million-year-old DNA.

# 4 ASSEMBLING THE TEAM

"WHY COULDN'T WE HAVE FOUND THE BONES OF A SUPER-intelligent rat?" Claire was exasperated and ready to give up.

Working with Katie and Zoe, Claire used a white board, actually a series of white boards, to outline the steps needed to extract the ancient DNA, replicate it, insert it in an irradiated, fertilized elephant egg, and successfully implant that egg in Flo's uterus. Complicating this was the need to do this without significantly widening their tight circle of participants, and the risk of attracting unwanted attention. They needed sophisticated lab equipment, but they needed it located where the work could proceed in secrecy. They needed to transport the egg without attracting attention. And they needed to implant the fertile egg in Flo without attracting attention. It would have been difficult to check all these boxes if they were working with a newt, but they were trying to do something on the sly with the world's largest land animal.

The workspace they currently occupied was as austere and no-nonsense as its owner. Zoe hadn't done much to the Louisiana farmhouse. It was a simple, gable roofed, two-story structure with a covered porch that ran the entire length of the front façade. The house had come with the acreage that was now Boisbeaux. She had set up the refuge office in a converted barn about one hundred yards from the main house. She gave over one of the upstairs bedrooms as a secure place for Katie, Claire, and the team to map out Bart's resurrection, though there was no evidence of the project in the room. There were no filing cabinets, and only a single white board.

One of the challenges presented by the need to maintain utter secrecy was that they could not leave to-do lists or problems to ponder on the board. Instead, it was required that the white board be erased and its contents redrawn and reconsidered every day (the repetition of which likely aided in thoughtful consideration and decision making). This everyday challenge was a simplistic example of the overall problem at hand: marrying the contradictory demands of maintaining secrecy within a small team engaged in a massive undertaking.

Frustrated with the complexities of the tasks ahead, Claire asked Keerbrock to make the trip down to Boisbeaux. Claire did not trust the security of virtual meetings or even encrypted calls, and as Keerbrock's foundation was responsible for a great deal of financial support to Boisbeaux, it was not at all uncommon for him to make the trip, nor to be seen around the locale.

Arriving two days later, the great scientist walked into Zoe's study just before Claire was wrapping up for the day. Upon entering, Keerbrock looked at the array of question marks that signified noted project vulnerabilities currently appearing on the day's version of the white board, and with a bright smile, said, "Well, this is fun."

Claire looked irritated, "This is definitely not fun."

"What you've got, is a classic trilemma," Keerbrock responded, framing the overall problem.

"And they are fun?"

"Not if you're in one. It's also called the Impossible Trinity—something where there are three necessary elements, but solving for any two of the elements automatically excludes a third element."

"That's us alright," said Claire, "How do you solve it."

"You don't," said Keerbrock, "that's why the word impossible is in the description. It's usually applied to monetary policy."

"Uh Will," Claire said slowly, "If you've come down to encourage us, you're doing a terrible job."

"Oh, don't give up; thankfully this is not monetary policy, so there's hope." Keerbrock assumed a more business-like tone. "Let's take a crack. How many extra people are you counting?"

Claire was looked at all the question marks on the white board. "Too many."

"OK," said Keerbrock, "Let's break it down further. Where's the real expertise required?"

Katie and Zoe put up their hands. "Don't look at us," said Katie.

Claire looked again at the board. "Probably the DNA extraction, the irradiation, the implantation, and then the impregnation?"

Keerbrock frowned. "Extraction, irradiation, and implantation can be done by one skilled biotech person. Then you need a highly skilled animal husbandry vet for the impregnation—though we can debate whether they have to know what type of egg they're implanting. That's two people, and maybe that's sufficient since Zoe and the team can support the vet."

Zoe looked troubled—she hated deception.

Keerbrock revealed a rare moment of sensitivity. He looked straight at Zoe. "I understand any ethical concerns you may be having at the moment, but this is not a procedure that can harm the mom elephant in any way. It'll either work or it won't, and vets do such impregnations all the time. And the one thing we all agree on is that this cannot become a circus, which is what it will become if word gets out."

Claire was dubious on practical grounds. "Really, that's all?"

Keerbrock thought a moment and then brightened. "I don't know about the veterinarian, but I've a thought on the cell biologist—Camilla Cohen. One of my brightest grad students switched from geophysics to molecular biology and is now head of research at an ag-tech company north of San Diego."

"Plant biology?" Claire was confused.

Keerbrock smiled. "When you get down to implanting DNA at that level, we're not much different than plants, neither is an elephant. Her lab would have the equipment you need . . ." Keerbrock trailed off and wandered away from the white board. He idly picked up a plaster Ganesh, an incongruously colorful item in the otherwise sparsely furnished room. Claire looked curiously at the great man. It looked like he was trying to make up his mind about something. *Indecisive? Keerbrock? This was something new.*

"And we could trust her?"

Keerbrock bristled. "I'd trust her with my life! I *did* trust her with my life!"

Claire looked at Katie, who looked back, saucer eyed; Zoe squinted at Keerbrock. All had the same thought: *Who was this woman and what the Hell had transpired between her and Keerbrock?*

Claire broke the silence. "OK, I had to ask. You know . . . the stakes."

Keerbrock waved her off mildly. "Of course. Yes, you can trust her."

Claire thought a bit more. "Logistics—seems like the back and forth between the West Coast and here might be a problem."

Keerbrock furrowed his brow. "I expect we can work that out. She does a lot of academic research as well. I'll find a way to fund some anodyne-sounding project that could provide cover. Maybe it could be done at a lab closer to here—Florida? I'll make the call."

Later, sipping wine on Zoe's porch, an uneasy silence fell over the group. Everyone was troubled by the question of how much the veterinarian should know. Claire had become something of an expert on slippery slopes, and Keerbrock's reassuring words notwithstanding, the distinguished scientist had spent decades building his impeccable scientific reputation. He sighed and got up. "I know what you're all thinking, but it's moot unless we get the vet an egg to implant. I'm going to call Camilla. No time like the present. Excuse me for a moment." With that Keerbrock walked down the steps and into the warm, moist evening air serenaded by a chorus of crickets, tree frogs, and other creatures of the gloaming.

As soon as he was out of sight, Katie and Claire whipped out their phones, but before either could type a word, Zoe said "Stop! Now!"

Claire realized immediately why Zoe had erupted, and felt embarrassed and stupid. If their communications were being monitored, the last thing either wanted to do was connect their names to this woman who might prove to be the key to bringing back Bart. "You're right," said Claire, looking at Zoe with renewed appreciation, "Thanks." At the same time, she resolved to google, "Camilla Cohen, Chief Scientist, ag-biotech, San Diego," on one of the shared computers back at Rushmere.

# 5 CAMILLA

CAMILLA COHEN WAS JUST FINISHING UP HER DAY AT THE LAB in La Jolla and looking forward to a quick parasail off the Torrey Pines bluffs when her phone buzzed. She only had limited time if she was going to get in a jump, so she was tempted to not answer. She looked at the number; it was vaguely familiar. Then she remembered. "Will? It's been years!"

"Too long," said Keerbrock, "My fault; lot going on. How are you?"

Camilla was puzzled; Keerbrock never called just to catch up; in fact, he never called at all—and that had hurt for a while. She decided to play it straight; Keerbrock would get to the point soon enough. "Quite well, thanks. The switch to molecular biology was timely; gene editing is the future of agriculture."

"So, I gather. How's Ben?"

Camila snorted. "Oh, I imagine that he and Becky—that's the lab assistant he ran off with—are quite happy, at least for now."

There was an uncomfortable silence. "I'm sorry, I didn't know."

"Don't be; it was inevitable, and the break was clean. At least I never stooped to interviewing candidates to be his assistant as all his colleagues insisted I should."

Another uncomfortable silence, then Keerbrock cleared his throat. He was perfectly comfortable calculating changes in the mass balance of the ice sheets, but he didn't do human relationships. "Um, I'm actually calling with an invitation. There's to be a big to-do at Proctor, celebrating the lab's various breakthroughs on climate science. It's September twentieth, a Saturday, and I'm very much hoping that you can come. You played a key role in some of my most important work. We'll fly you in. It's the weekend so it won't interfere too much with your work."

Now Camilla was totally confused. If Proctor wanted her there, a dozen other people could have called with the invite. But Keerbrock? Flying her in? She'd like to think her work as a graduate student back then was useful, but she could think of fifty scientists the lab would fly in before springing for a ticket for a student who didn't finish her PhD. Keerbrock must be picking up the tab. Something else was going on. "That's so nice Will, but it's tight. Let me see if I can work it. Can I call you back?"

"Of course, take your time, but I very much hope you can come. There's *a lot* to catch up on."

At the other end of the call, Keerbrock shook his head in frustration. He could only hope that she understood the semiotics of the fact that he, rather than someone else, had called with the invite.

She did. Clearly Keerbrock had a proposal of some sort, something so sensitive he couldn't mention it on the phone. One thing she was sure of—it didn't have anything to do with that fateful day in Punta Caleta, Cuba twelve years earlier.

Keerbrock and Camilla had been in Cuba to gather samples at the marine terraces east of Guantanamo Bay. Comprised of the remnants of ancient coral reefs, these limestone terraces looked like a stepped series of cliffs, with each terrace providing a record of past temperatures and sea level rise. Teasing out that record was fiendishly difficult as the scientist had to adjust for uplift resulting from plate tectonics and other factors, just the kind of problem Keerbrock loved. In fact, Camilla had never seen him so happy as he hung suspended along the cliff above the terrace at the part of the cliff face marking the last period between the ice ages of 125,000 years ago.

Camilla was standing below him, as Keerbrock had insisted that he could collect his samples and photos of the stratigraphy and then rappel down without her belaying him from the terrace. She thought she saw a tremor in the rope and squinted. The eyebolts that served as an anchor on the next higher terrace were on the flat surface, and not visible to either her or Keerbrock. She locked eyes with Keerbrock. Suspended seventy feet above the terrace she was standing on, his widened eyes told her that he'd felt the tremor. Then Keerbrock dropped about a foot as one of the anchors on the terrace gave way.

"Will, don't move!" She scanned the cliff face just above Keerbrock. There were several cracks where she could rig cams, pitons and other anchoring devices, but she needed to get to him in a hurry.

Cursing herself for anchoring Keerbrock to the eyebolts rather than belaying him from below, she envisioned how she might get him down. Camilla was an experienced rock climber (which was why Keerbrock had brought her along) and, working fast, she slipped on a bag with several cams, quickdraws, and other climbing gear. She paused briefly to remember the route she had taken to secure the anchors, and then quickly began climbing toward Keerbrock. When she reached him a minute later, she again paused briefly, saying, "I'm going to get you down." Keerbrock looked ashen but calm.

"I know," he said in a near whisper.

She nodded and then climbed about ten feet farther up to the crack she had noticed. She quickly inserted three cams and then cinched the ties together to equalize the pressure from the pulling direction—down—and then slipped a carabiner into the eye knot created by the cinch. She secured herself to the large carabiner, and then attached webbing that reached Keerbrock so that he could switch his weight from the failing anchors to the cams.

Once Keerbrock had attached the webbing to his harness, she said, "Do you think you can get off the rope and shift your weight to the cams?"

"I don't have much choice," said the Nobel Prize winner with a wan smile. Once he was secure, they both breathed a sigh of relief. She then slipped a climbing rope through the carabiner attached to the cams, tied another carabiner to its end and dropped it to Keerbrock. "Attach this but do not detach your direct tie to the cams."

She then turned her attention to another, much smaller crack about two feet parallel to the crack where she had inserted the cams. There she inserted and tapped in a series of copperheads, bugaboo pitons, and other small devices that, together, set another solid anchor. She attached herself to this anchor giving herself enough leeway that she could scramble and swing back toward the cams.

She grabbed a rope she had brought up and tied it to a carabiner, which she then attached to the eye she had created for the new anchor. She dropped the rope that was threaded through the eyehole attached to the cams, and using the rope attached to the smaller crack, quickly lowered herself to the ground. Without pausing she ran the rope attached to the cams through a braking belay device, which she then attached to her harness.

Keerbrock looked down. "How're we going to do this?"

Camilla furrowed her brow. "Best way is for you to rappel down the line I just came down. We'll keep you tied to me on the other line just in case. Can you snag it?"

Keerbrock pulled a rock pick from his kit and snagged the line.

"OK, you're going to pull up a braking belay device (she held one up), which you're going to attach to your harness and then run that line through, all the while leaving the line attached to the anchors. Got it?" Keerbrock pulled up the device and with Camilla giving advice each step of the way, ran the line through. "Done."

"OK, now you're going to rappel down. If anything fails (she thought of the sixty-pound difference in their weights), the worst thing that happens is that you get down and I end up dangling. I'll wave on the way up."

Two minutes later, Keerbrock was safely on the ground and Camilla sat on a rock shaking.

Keerbrock put a hand on her shoulder. "You saved my life."

Still shaking, Camilla looked up. "I almost cost you your life—I should have known that limestone was chossy. I should have belayed you from below."

"I prefer my version of the story," said Keerbrock gently.

Camilla looked up at the mess of cams, pitons, and rope still on the cliffside. "Back in a jiffy."

Using the ropes hanging from the cliff she scampered up to where Keerbrock had gotten stuck, and then carefully made her way to the top of the next terrace. There she saw one anchor bolt pulled from the crumbling rock and the other ready to come out. She pulled the bolt out easily, and shuddered when she realized the only thing that had prevented Keerbrock from a deadly fall had been the pressure of his weight that had wedged the bolt against a stone. Shaken anew, Camilla made her way back down, collecting the remaining equipment along the way.

Back on the ground, she looked at Keerbrock, "When this gets out, no one is going to climb with me again—justifiably."

"And no institution will let me go back into the field. Moreover, my wife will divorce me, and my kids will have me committed. So—no harm, no foul—this can stay between us."

And so it had, for twelve years.

Once she left Proctor for graduate work in molecular biology, she had almost no contact with Keerbrock. At least no direct contact, but she suspected his presence as some invisible force seemed to remove every roadblock that might come up as her career progressed. When she had applied for a post-doc position at Cornell six years earlier, she was quickly swept in. "I thought this would be touch and go," she said to the Dean as he welcomed her.

The Dean looked up surprised. "You don't know? You had an extraordinary recommendation; one we would not, and could not ignore."

She long suspected that Keerbrock had blessed her career, but if he wanted to remain in the background, so be it. And, yet now, he wanted to reconnect. *Whatever it is*, she thought, *it has to be big.* And whatever it was, she would listen.

# 6 THE PITCH

KEERBROCK'S IDEA HAS BEEN THAT IF CAMILLA CAME TO THE celebration at Proctor Labs, they could find time to chat without attracting any attention. Now he wasn't so sure. It was a warm September day, and the scientists and dignitaries were having cocktails on the lawn behind Proctor Hall. Camilla had attracted a cluster of scientists and grad students, peppering her about the switch from geophysics of gene editing.

"Well," she said, "Someone's going to have to figure out how to feed people in this new world; thought I'd give it a shot." She looked over at Keerbrock, who raised his glass. She made her excuses and walked over to him.

"I'm here."

"I'm glad. Let's take a walk."

Proctor Laboratories was a series of buildings, built on the Palisades on the west side of the Hudson River just north of New York City. Administrative buildings were interspersed with various labs housing the sophisticated equipment needed to interpret the ice cores, varve, ancient corals, seabed cores, and other proxies recording past climates. Keerbrock led Camilla to a bench overlooking the Hudson.

Out of earshot of the others, Keerbrock didn't waste time. "I'd have wanted you to come in any case, but there's a project I want to discuss."

"I figured—but why all the cloak and dagger?"

"It has to proceed in utter secrecy, and, before I go on, I need to know that you won't discuss this with anyone—even if you decide it's not for you."

Camilla frowned. "Is it illegal?"

*Good question!* "No, just extremely sensitive—it would cause a sensation if word got out, and that sensation would end the project."

"Did you contact me as a one-time, wannabe geophysicist or as a molecular biologist?"

"The latter, but more to the point, as a molecular biologist who I could trust to maintain absolute discretion."

Camilla's mind was racing. She began to see where this was going. "OK, I'll listen. Besides, right now, there's no one I could tell about whatever this is except my cat."

Keerbrock took a deep breath. "Remember those bones found in Kazakhstan that bespoke an ancient intelligence . . ." Speaking in short telegraphic sentences he quickly ran through the story, including the discovery of the tooth. "We believe that the tooth may have preserved sufficient DNA. W\e could recover it, replicate it, and do a nuclide transplantation. I think you have the skills to do the recovery and the transplantation."

Camilla gasped, speechless. Keerbrock realized what a bolt from the blue he had just delivered. "No need to decide on the spot, and I'm happy to have a longer conversation."

"Yeah," said Camilla slowly. "I definitely need time to think about this."

"If you're free, let's have breakfast tomorrow. I can fill you in on more details. There's a spot across the river in Dobbs Ferry where we're unlikely to run into anyone from here. That OK?"

Camilla nodded. "That works."

"OK then, let's get back to the group."

Camilla headed back first, followed by Keerbrock who split off to talk with an expert on marine heat waves. Camilla was peppered with questions from the cluster she had left to talk with Keerbrock: "What did he want? Are you coming back to Proctor?" A young post-doc with tousled black hair arched an amused eyebrow. "It must be nice to have Nobel Prize winners seeking your advice."

Camilla moved quickly to nip the line of questions in the bud. She smiled at the young man. "He wasn't seeking my advice, and I wouldn't have any to give him. We were just talking about why I switched out of geophysics."

The next morning, Keerbrock entered the small, Italian coffee shop. Two old men were reading an Italian newspaper at one of the tables, and, across the room, sat Camilla. Keerbrock ordered a cappuccino and sat down. The soundtrack from Turandot played in the background, and for once Keerbrock was happy for the camouflage of house music. He took a couple of sips, and looked at Camilla. "Before I go on, I have to reiterate that what we discuss here today has to remain absolutely secret, regardless of whether you decide to join us. That OK?"

The scientist's blazing gaze froze Camilla, even though she had known him for years. "You know me Will, I agree and will hold to that."

"OK, then." Keerbrock began by asking what she knew about the discovery of the bones. It turned out that she knew little beyond what had been covered in the press—the discovery, the controversy, Claire's vindication, and the curious absence of follow-up beyond the initial news that a new species of extinct elephant had been discovered in Kazakhstan that had an extraordinarily expanded cranium and which may have engaged in ritualistic behavior.

"Well, that's as much as was made public, but it's ten percent of the iceberg." Camilla's eyes widened as Keerbrock told her about the stone, the human and elephant reaction to it, and the discovery of the tooth.

"So," he said, "there's mounting evidence, not publishable, but still convincing, that these ancient elephants possessed extraordinarily higher mental abilities, even if those abilities were quite different than ours. There's evidence that they could encode messages that could be understood in some way by modern elephants, even after five million years. If such a mind could be brought back, it would revolutionize science, and open the doors to powerful technologies. This last point is one reason we insist on utter secrecy. If word got out, Claire would be besieged, and not just by those looking for the greater good. Another reason for secrecy is to protect the elephant itself, if we're successful."

Camilla was too stunned to speak. Keerbrock pointed to her coffee cup. "Refill?"

Armed with two new cappuccinos, he sat down and waited.

Camilla took a couple of tentative sips. "I don't know what to say . . ."

"No worries, let's start with the practical. Do you think it can be done?"

"That's what I'm wondering. The gating question is whether that tooth contains a full, recoverable strand of DNA. If it doesn't, the genomics of identifying the variances with any other elephant species and then making the edits would take years, if not decades. If there is a full strand, however, it's a matter of recovering the DNA, replicating it, irradiating a fertilized egg, and implanting the nucleus. That's pretty straightforward."

Keerbrock noted that she did not say that she could or would do it. "Could it be done in secret?"

Camilla frowned. "As a plant geneticist, I've got relationships with lots of universities and laboratories around the country." She thought a bit more. "If the expenses were covered, I could probably get the necessary lab time—as a commercial enterprise we're often doing projects under secrecy to protect competitive position." She squinted. "To avoid rousing suspicion, it might make sense to do different steps at different labs, which would shorten the time the project was at any one lab."

Camilla stopped for a second. "Why me?"

"That's simple," said Keerbrock. "One: you can do it. Two: I've first-hand experience that I can trust you, even when the stakes are extremely high."

She smiled. And then she had a thought. "Will, were you the mysterious stranger greasing the wheels of my career?"

Keerbrock frowned, "I don't know what you're talking about."

Camilla laughed. *That settled it. Of course, he was!* "OK, I'm in—but I have one condition."

"Yes?"

"If and when this can become public, I want a commitment that I will be lead author on a paper about how it was done."

Keerbrock smiled. This was what he had been waiting for—the woman had skills, and character, but now he knew she also had ambition, the secret sauce if she was going to make the sacrifices necessary for this project to succeed. "I wouldn't have it any other way—but keep in mind, and this is important, the day we can possibly go public might be very far off in the future."

Keerbrock waited a few minutes after Camilla had gone. The two old men were still at their table at the other end of the room. No one else had come in. With another glance around the room, the scientist got up and left.

# A CLOCK STARTS

# 7 RETIREMENT FUND



PETE ROZNIK HAD PUT IN TWENTY-FIVE YEARS AT THE FBI. IT had been a satisfying career—he was a surveillance expert—but he could see the writing on the wall. Surveillance technology was advancing so rapidly that the techniques he knew best, old-school standbys such as planting bugs and cameras, were archaic. As was he, he thought ruefully. He liked to believe his next chapter could be in the private sector, but he also recognized that most of the private firms wanted the same whiz kids the bureau was recruiting. He had secured a pension, but since he was still paying alimony, he recognized that he faced a dramatic downscaling. Such were his thoughts as he approached the building that housed the coffee shop that Keerbrock and Camilla had visited the day before.

"You're awfully quiet this evening," remarked his partner as he parked the van in a lot a block away.

"Just thinking what a waste of time this job was."

"No argument there."

It was 3:00 a.m., and Roznik entered the building from the back after picking the lock. Extracting night vision goggles from his rucksack, he made his way up the stairs from the basement, and, working quickly, gathered up the bugs he had installed in the room a month earlier. This part of the operation had been a bust and the judge had refused to extend the surveillance. The FBI had gotten the OK earlier because the coffee shop was a known haunt of the Carmezzo crime family, which had been extending their control over the restaurants in the increasingly hip river towns along the east coast of the Hudson. After retracing his steps and exiting, Roznik hopped back in his van, rejoining his partner who had been keeping watch. They then drove to the field office in White Plains to drop off the van and call it a night. Pete turned to his partner, "You go home. I'm going to check what happened over the weekend—Hail Mary, but you never know."

Once in the building, Pete fast forwarded through both the audio and video feeds, seeing nothing of interest. Then he saw Keerbrock, who looked vaguely familiar. Running his image through facial recognition software, Pete saw that the man was a world-famous scientist. That was interesting, as Nobel Prize winners did not fit the profile of the typical *habitues* of the coffee house. Intrigued, he watched as the scientist was joined by an attractive young woman at a table. Even more interesting. He was aware of privacy restrictions on monitoring surveillance product, but this was all going to be dumped anyway. So, he decided to check the audio.

Immediately, he realized that this was not an affair; nor was there anything illegal going on. *But, holy smokes!* Pete jotted down some notes. He was tempted to copy the conversation to a thumb drive, but he knew any copying would be noticed as a result of the strict chain of custody protocols and procedures at the FBI, and then questions would most certainly be asked. He knew that protocol required that he erase the surveillance, but he also knew that it was unlikely that anyone would follow-up to make sure that was done, since this was to be considered a failed mission. So, he simply saved the file, giving it an unconventional title so it was unlikely to pop up on any subsequent search. If necessary, he wanted to be the only one to ever open the file again.

On his drive home, he thought about the conversation he had overheard. The scientist clearly had gone to some lengths to try and keep their meeting confidential. Roznik chuckled as he remembered the old saw from his training in surveillance: "There's no perfect secrecy if the circle is larger than one." He let his train of thought continue. If secrecy was so important, that meant that the conversation could be extremely valuable to someone else. Retirement! But he realized that it was only valuable if he was the only one who knew about it; secrecy must be maintained. That meant no dinner table tales, no matter how tempting that might be. It also meant figuring out for whom that conversation would be most valuable. That could take a while.

# 8 KNOWING WHICH POND TO FISH IN

ONCE KEERBROCK HAD RECRUITED CAMILLA, EVENTS TOOK ON a momentum of their own. She had leased time at three different facilities, each with the equipment required for the various stages of DNA extraction and replication, egg irradiation, and then implantation. Camilla had come up with a routine investigation as a cover, and funded the project using a grant that Keerbrock had funneled through a cutout. Because she was working alone and because she had to maintain utter secrecy, the main problem was logistics. She needed to get the material from one lab to another, stored safely and in the proper conditions, yet transportable by one 120-pound female (albeit a strong one). Similarly, the elephant egg collected for enucleation needed to be transported and stored safely. Worst of all, they were betting the ranch on there being sufficiently well-preserved DNA in one tooth to find an intact strand of DNA that hadn't been degraded over millions of years.

Through sheer luck—or the genius of the race of ancient elephants—the elephant, whose tooth Camilla ground up to extract the DNA, had died in perfect meteorological conditions for the long-term preservation of DNA, and the tooth itself was the perfect vessel for preservation. The Messinian Salinity Crisis that killed off Bart and his ancient species saw temperatures soar to levels that would kill off microbes and desiccate material, with further protection afforded by the salt that encrusted the tooth, and the enamel and dental material that formed a protective barrier around the interior of the tooth.

With a full strand of DNA, Camilla was able to use well-developed somatic cell nuclear transfer (SCNT) techniques to fuse the ancient DNA with the modern elephant's enucleated egg. Then it became a matter of safely transferring the egg to Boisbeaux and implanting it in Flo.

This was the part of the process that Claire worried about the most. In session after session the team discussed the trade-offs. Implantations could be done either by surgery or through the insertion of a catheter. Because this had to be done by an exceedingly small team and with a minimum of disruption, they, reluctantly, opted for the catheter.

There were other complications, of course. And during one particular brainstorming session, the three women had decided it might be best to make the procedure seem like a normal in vitro pregnancy. But, as one of the groups pointed out, they also had to bind or convince the vet to confidentiality, which would make it seem anything but normal. Worse, they had to do the implantation when the staff and volunteers were away, which dictated a holiday like Christmas, New Year's Day, or July Fourth, and Flo either had to be in estrus or estrus had to be induced. Zoe and Katie knew scores of veterinarians, but the biggest pool of those with in vitro fertilization expertise typically dealt with thoroughbred horses, not elephants.

As the conversation continued and the pros and cons of each suggestion were discussed ad nauseam, the mention of thoroughbred horses made Claire pause and recall something from the past.

The original goal of the Kazakhstan dig that Claire had taken over was to find evidence of the domestication of ancient horses. She remembered a free-wheeling conversation one evening where one of the topics was the astonishing stud fees champion stallions commanded, and how this had created an illegal market for thoroughbred horse semen. Given the money involved, and the high powered, not always nice players involved in this fraud, any vet performing the in vitro fertilization would be known for both superb skills and complete discretion.

The others noticed that Claire had dropped out of the conversation.

"Claire has an idea," said Katie.

"Not so much an idea, but I think I know where to look for our vet." She looked at Katie. "Do any of the wild animal traders you've busted owe you a favor?"

Katie looked at her quizzically. "Where is this going?"

Zoe chimed in, "Yeah, where is this going?"

It was then that Katie laid out her idea.

# 9 DEV SINJIN

DEVEREAUX SINJIN HAD GROWN UP IN THE HORSE COUNTRY
where Pennsylvania and Delaware meet. He was the scion of an old
family whose fortunes had been diminished by generations of wastrels.
Growing up amid the landed gentry, Dev (as he was called) naturally
acquired the coloration of his social milieu, a milieu where understate-
ment is de rigueur, discretion is noted and prized, and where the ability
to converse with elegant ambiguity and efficient wit was both admired
and required (though the wit evident at cocktail parties in horse
country was no threat to the reputations of Oscar Wilde or Benjamin
Disraeli).

Needing to make a living, and more serious than his siblings (not
to mention several preceding generations of Sinjins), Dev had gone to
veterinary school at the University of Pennsylvania, after graduating
from Princeton. He then moved to Lexington, Kentucky and quickly
established a practice performing in vitro fertilization of thoroughbreds. His manners and good humor, and, perhaps, most of all, his
looks, enabled him to blend effortlessly with the aristocratic owners
who came to him from all over the world to breed their hopes for a
triple crown. The other class of owners, self-made men and women just
getting into horse racing, also appreciated Dev for his self-deprecation
and welcoming manner. Despite his pedigree, there was not a snobbish
bone in his body.

Dev had successfully avoided almost all of the very long list of vices
that had made his family history such a train wreck. He never did

drugs, he drank socially and only in moderation, and his cellar and bar had a global reputation. If he was first meeting a potential client and it was after six o'clock in the afternoon, he would offer them a snifter of Pappy Van Winkle's 23-year-old Reserve Bourbon.

There was one Sinjin vice, however, that no generation had successfully escaped. Dev had begun gambling on horses as a teenager, and then broadened his wagering ambit into anything where he thought he might have an edge in handicapping; polo, golf, even professional croquet. He started gambling with his eyes open—he had grown up on stories of the spectacular failures of his forebears. Indeed, the family fortunes took a turn for the worse from which they never recovered when, in 1845, Manice Sinjin, was forced to sell his prized whaling ship, the *Sea Leopard*, at distress prices to settle gambling debts he had incurred during a debauched month in London.

Still, despite his more measured approach, Dev had his own epic losses. Once, during a phone call with his sister, when he told her of his financial straits, she suggested downsizing his lifestyle (she didn't have to ask how he got into his straitened circumstances). Given his usual breezy manner, his reply was relatively harsh, "Lexi, you of all people should understand that I cannot be seen to have a lesser lifestyle than my peers."

Lexi laughed. "That's pure Sinjin," she said, "Exactly what Poppy would have said—and probably did say at some point." She chuckled, ". . . and for precisely the same reasons you're saying it now!" She adopted a more serious tone. "I'm sure you'll find a way out, Dev. That's what you do."

And he did. His way out involved taking on a new, rougher class of client. These were the people who trafficked in the underground economy of thoroughbred sire semen. Given that the seed of Triple Crown winners might sell for several million dollars, even getting a fraction of that price on the illegal market proved to be an irresistible temptation for some with access to the horses. Papers would subsequently be fabricated to note the origin being from a more ordinary sire, and the foal would be off to the races, with a decided advantage over what might otherwise be predicted from its humble pedigree. This type of client valued Dev's discretion over his social skills, and Dev was well aware that the cost of indiscretion would be vastly more severe than being ghosted at the country club.

He was also conflicted. He had tried to escape the family history, which was littered with not quite up-and-up dealings and more than a few of his forebears had crossed the line. On the other hand, he considered what he was doing close to being a victimless crime, since the crime was to deprive some small increment of income to the billionaire owners, many of whose fortunes had involved some line crossing of their own. Similarly, Dev knew that many of his impeccably mannered neighbors had their own uncomfortable secrets. If his sideline condemned him to one of the shallower circles of Hell, he knew that he would be greeted by plenty of familiar faces.

Given this dual-track career, Dev was used to getting messages delivered in unusual ways, with communicants wanting to set up meetings away from prying eyes. Even so, this latest request took the cake. Had it not come initially from one of his trusted intermediaries he would have thought it was a joke. But it wasn't a joke. Moreover, the promised fee was four times what he would be paid for a thoroughbred insemination, with an additional bonus to be paid if the insemination never became public. The extraordinary thing was that the job would be to impregnate an elephant, not a horse.

The offer came to Dev via an encrypted call to a burner phone that arrived in his mailbox. A woman who didn't identify herself told him about the job, but gave no reason for the extraordinary measures taken to maintain secrecy—Dev was to be picked up in a windowless van and taken to the elephant in an unidentified location where all the equipment he needed would already be in place. If he agreed to the terms, Dev was to get half the fee in gold coins up front as a good faith gesture, with the other half coming after completion of the procedure, and then bonuses that would together match the original fee, which would be distributed in successive years should the implantation be successful, and the pregnancy come to term.

Dev felt he had to ask. "Is this illegal?"

There was a pause. "No."

"Then why the secrecy?"

"All I can say is that a major donation for elephant welfare in Africa is contingent on this effort and also on secrecy being maintained."

"OK, when are we talking about?" Dev didn't believe the explanation for a second, but he needed the money.

# 10 DEV, MEET KATIE

CLAIRE OPENED THE SLIDING DOOR AND DEV SINJIN CLIMBED out of the back of the windowless van, stiff from the two-hour journey from the Biloxi, Mississippi airport. A barrier had separated him from the front seat so he couldn't talk to the driver, and Claire hadn't introduced herself when she had picked him up. His departure from the van marked their arrival in Boisbeaux, although Dev didn't know that fact. Zoe had taken down any signage relating to Boisbeaux before Dev's arrival, and he had no concept of direction while seated inside the van. So, he had zero idea where Claire had taken him.

"Sorry about all the cloak and dagger, and also for pulling you away on Christmas. You can call me Anna," said Claire, finally extending her hand to Dev as Zoe and Katie walked over to greet the two new arrivals.

Dev shook her offered hand. "No worries, I had the time to solve Blaise Pascal's challenge."

Claire and Anna looked confused at the remark, while Katie looked amused; she was clearly entranced by Dev's louche good looks and manner, and she also noted that he didn't stare at her as most men did. As Katie's interest piqued, Claire took the bait, "Pascal's challenge?"

"Yes, I discovered that I can sit quietly while alone in a dark room. So now I'm prepared to solve all humanity's problems," Dev responded.

Katie suppressed a laugh.

Claire smiled, but then returned to business. "Right. Well before you save the world, let's take a detour and get about the process of making our favorite elephant pregnant. Rachel," Claire nodded toward Zoe, "has assisted at a lot of elephant births, and Alice (Katie) has also worked with elephants. Our elephant, Marie (Flo), is in estrus, and Rachel sedated her once we heard you were on your way. The straps supporting her are in place. We can sit down and go over all the steps and then get started."

Dev bowed. "At your service."

As they walked toward the veterinary barn, Claire noticed that Katie kept stealing glances at Dev. She also thought she heard Katie mutter to herself, "Too cute for words." Katie saw Claire looking at her and, busted, actually blushed. *Now that was a first*, thought Claire. She smiled, thinking that the two of them would make one good-looking couple—were it not for the downer fact that no such relationship was going to happen until security could be relaxed, and that might be a long time.

Dev looked around and was impressed with the setup. It wasn't the gleaming multimillion-dollar facility where he performed legitimate inseminations, but it was far above the makeshift operating rooms where he performed his underground operations.

Dev had spent a good deal of time in the weeks since the call familiarizing himself with elephant anatomy and the ins and outs of insemination of an animal that weighed ten times as much as the thoroughbreds he typically treated. He'd called up a friend from veterinary school who now treated mammals at the Bronx Zoo and deftly steered the conversation toward the tricks of elephant insemination. His friend, a woman, was quite voluble and colorful. "We don't do them anymore, but I talked to an old hand who did a couple back in the day. Imagine inseminating an orca," she said, "and you can get a feel for the logistical problems. The implantation is quite routine, but the prep work, getting the animal into position, monitoring the anesthesia and heartbeat is ninety percent of the effort."

Dev examined "Marie." Her heart rate was steady at about thirty beats per minute. He turned to Claire. "How old is she?"

"About twenty-five."

"No history of health problems?"

"Nope, she's in fine fettle."

"What sedative did you use?

"Ketamine?"

"Yes, and we'll use yohimbine for recovery."

"How much longer will she be under?"

Rachel answered. "We've got another three hours, and we can always give her a boost, though I'd rather not have to."

Dev nodded. "Of course, and agreed." He paused. "Just curious, but how did you get her into position?"

Claire fielded this question. "Marie was trained as a youngster to get veterinary exams, including gynecological ones. She's a pro. Rachel and Alice worked the straps."

Dev looked at the elephant and nodded approval. "OK then, let's get to it. Rachel will assist. Alice, can you monitor Marie's vitals?"

"You betcha!" said Katie with a bit more enthusiasm than the question warranted, earning herself another bemused stare from Claire.

Dev turned to Claire. "Anna, please be ready to get stuff to Rachel as needed. Rachel, take a couple of minutes to familiarize Anna with what you might need. There are moments when we might have to act fast."

All of them sanitized their hands and then donned surgical masks and gloves. The next ninety minutes were a blur as Dev talked them through how to help him with the procedure of transferring the egg from its sealed container to the flexible tube catheter and then laparoscopically implanting the egg in the uterine wall. Even though it was December, it was hot as hell in the barn, and, more than once, Dev asked Alice (Katie) to mop his brow, while Zoe handed him implements as needed. In the middle of it all, while Dev was fully occupied with the insertion, Zoe turned to Claire and mouthed, "This guy is good!" Claire smiled happily. Katie witnessed this and added her own thumbs up.

Even as she efficiently backed up Zoe, Claire had noticed the deft move Dev had made in asking Katie (Alice) to mop his brow. *Maybe the laws of attraction worked in two directions. A smooth one, this guy.*

After they finished, Dev stripped off his gloves and turned to the three women. "Now we let nature take its course." He turned to Rachel (Zoe). "Shall I administer the yohimbe?"

"Please, you're the pro."

Flo came back slowly. As she stirred, Zoe and Katie loosened and then released the straps. Claire had brought to the barn all of Flo's favorite treats, and as she was released into her enclosure, she was treated to a feast.

Dev looked at Claire. "She seems fine. My work is done here."

Katie spoke up for the first time. "It's Christmas. Maybe Dr. Sinjin has time for a drink to celebrate before he goes."

Claire gave Katie a look that could freeze the Mediterranean. Then she softened. "You're absolutely right." She turned to Dev. "Can you stay another hour?"

Dev smiled wryly, "You are my ride, and it's your plane so I'm your happy hostage." He reached into his briefcase. "Actually, I was hoping you would ask, and brought something just for such a contingency." He brought out a bottle of Pappy Van Winkle.

Zoe gasped. "That's like a Yeti, I've heard rumors but never seen one." This brought quizzical looks from Claire and Katie. Zoe jerked her head toward the bottle. "Legendary bourbon."

Zoe brought out glasses and they all took a seat on her porch. Dev gave each a generous pour of bourbon and then raised his glass to make a toast. "Here's hoping you have a bouncing baby elephant in twenty-two months."

They all clicked glasses, and sipped in silence. Dev knew better than to ask questions, but he liked these women (one in particular), and they seemed legitimate and serious for all the secrecy. If he couldn't ask questions, he could still make an offer. "I don't know what you're doing, and I won't ask. But if you need a vet down the road, please call on me. I'll do it without fee. You—or someone—has paid me plenty."

Katie perked up and seemed about to speak, but Claire stopped her with a small hand gesture. "That's very kind, Dr. Sinjin," Claire said in measured tones, "and we'll consider that offer quite seriously. But I'm sure you understand that we have to give it some thought."

"Of course. Just let me know if you need me." He smiled, "And someday maybe you'll tell me your real names."

Claire laughed. "Let me assure you that what you helped happen, fingers crossed, will be very good for all elephants." She stood up. "Now let's get you back to the plane. I'm afraid you're going to get another chance to rise to Pascal's challenge."

Before he stepped into the back of the van, Dev turned and gave Katie the bottle of Pappy Van Winkle. "Save some for Anna when she gets back." Katie snapped to attention and gave him a salute, following it up with a wink.

Observing this interchange, Claire shook her head and smiled. Most men would be reduced to a puddle at this point. Some women were just born with it.

Later, after Claire returned from dropping Dev at the airport, she found Zoe and Katie sitting on Zoe's porch. Zoe handed Claire a shot glass of the fancy bourbon. "Per Dev's instructions."

Claire raised her glass. "To a happy pregnancy!" They all clinked and sipped.

Zoe, ordinarily taciturn and gruff, raised her glass again. "And to Dev. He's quite something."

*That's the elephant in the room*, thought Claire with a chuckle. Then out loud, "We might as well address it now. What do you think?" She looked at Katie. "I already know what you think."

Katie astonished Claire by blushing again. She was always so cool and in control, Claire hadn't thought Katie was capable of blushing.

"I do think he's trustworthy."

Claire looked closely at Katie. Her key word. "Trustworthy? He does off the books thoroughbred inseminations for the illegal market!"

"Exactly, to survive in that world, he has to be trustworthy."

Claire thought about that. "Maybe . . . Let's sum up. We've already brought one more person into the circle—Camilla—and everyone additional we bring in exponentially increases the risk of discovery—a slip to a relative or friend, an awkward explanation of an absence . . . any number of things."

"True that," said Zoe. "But down the road we're going to need a vet."

Claire nodded. She glanced at Katie again. Claire had been intrigued by Katie from their first meeting. She was jealous of Katie's effortless beauty—the woman was a veritable thesaurus of synonyms for winsome—but quickly discovered that beneath that allure there was an austere, complex soul, driven by an almost messianic fervor. With looks like Katie's, Claire assumed she must have had some flings since she first got involved with the project, but she also knew that since they launched the effort to get Flo pregnant, Katie had kept a very low profile. Claire had Sergei and Sofia (with Sergei holding the fort back at Rushmere for the few days Claire was away). On the one hand, Claire thought that Katie deserved some romance in her life, while on the other she realized that if that's what Katie wanted, she could get it without Claire's help.

"You're right, down the road we do need a vet. Katie, keep in touch with Dev; maybe do a little more digging beforehand."

Back to being Miss Cool, Katie looked at Claire levelly. "I can handle that, boss girl."

# 11 OTHERS TAKE INTEREST

IT WAS BROILING HOT IN ASTANA, THE CAPITAL OF KAZAKH-stan, but, thanks to a hyperactive air conditioner which roared in his apartment window, the young man might have been in Greenland—or at least the Greenland that pre-dated global warming. Unshaven and wearing a ragged sweater and T-shirt, the man took a deep drag on his cigarette and absently crushed it in a dish on his desk. He stared intently at his computer screen. Then he typed a quick message.

A moment later a well-groomed man in a crisply pressed officer's uniform popped up on his screen. "So, the great Dimitri Medvedev decides to check in," said the soldier in Russian. He offered a wintry smile. "The betting in the office was over whether you were dead or in love. Dead had a commanding lead, but it may have been the men voting with their hearts."

"I'm not dead," said Dimitri, "and I think I have something that will make you glad I'm alive."

"That will definitely be a first."

Dimitri was tempted to give a smart retort, but held his tongue. He believed that he had the best job in Russia's vast network of hacking efforts—hacking into and investigating yet-to-be-published research in the world's great laboratories and institutes—and he intended to keep it. "Here's the thing," he said, "Some years ago an American researcher working in Kazakhstan found the petrified remains of an ancient elephant that seemed to imply an intelligence, far in advance of any other animal living at that time . . ."

The soldier interrupted, "Yes, yes, we all read about it. *This* is why you got in touch?"

Dimitri wasn't fazed. "Actually, it is. You remember the huge stir caused by the discovery?"

"Of course . . ."

This time Dimitri cut him off. "Good, so what have you heard about it since?"

"Nothing, but that means nothing. It takes time for research."

"In this case nothing may mean something big."

There was silence on the other side of the line.

Dimitri continued. "What caught my attention was that while there were ongoing publications from the discoverers about the flora and fauna of the era and the physical aspects of the bones unearthed, they've published nothing about the nature of this supposed elephant intelligence—the most interesting aspect of the discovery."

"Again, so what?"

"All the publications on the nature of this ancient intelligence have been speculations offered by outsiders. Given the extraordinary nature of the find, that's odd."

Hearing no response, Dimitri plunged on. "So, I looked a bit deeper into the story of the woman who made the discovery, Claire Knowland. Her obsession with these bones almost ruined her career. She risked everything to bring this to light, and yet, since then nothing. It's as if she's hiding something."

"Maybe she had a kid and is just being a good mom. Also, why would she be hiding something?"

"Exactly! Oh, and she did have a kid. But I don't believe she wasn't publishing because she had to change diapers." Dimitri paused, enjoying himself. "Why would a woman who found herself virtually expelled from academia and ridiculed by eminent scientists, go completely dark on the finding that vindicated her? Why would the rest of the team go silent about the animal's intelligence as well? A team that included a Nobel Prize–winning geophysicist? Were they all raising her kid?" Dimitri instantly regretted the sarcasm.

"I suppose you have answers to all of these questions."

Dimitri quickly went on. "Could it be that they had discovered much more than just the cranial bones; something that said something about the animal's intelligence that was so extraordinary that they felt the need to go completely dark? Oh, and there's this: one crucial member of the team, a woman, has dropped out of sight."

After a moment of pondering, the soldier, a Colonel in the cyber-corps, spoke. "You think the US government classified their work?"

"That was my first thought, but I've not been able to find any indications that any US agency has stepped in. Quite the contrary. I hacked into a few conversations suggesting that they're quite interested—and frustrated."

"Why would they be any more interested than I am?"

Having set the hook, Dimitri realized that he'd better start reeling in. "I'm just speculating, but elephants use ultra-low frequency waves to communicate over long distances. What if these abilities hyper-developed in this ancient species? I can think of all sorts of agencies that would want a piece of that. I would."

"First, we don't know that she's hiding anything. Second, how do you get from finding a long-dead elephant with a big head to new communications and weapons?"

"Before they shut things down—if that's what happened—a lot of people knew something about the discovery, or knew someone who knew about the discovery. Other students were on the dig, and these students had friends, boyfriends, girlfriends, and not all were as invested in secrecy as the core team. Not everything on the dig was sweetness and light from what I've seen. I did a one-man show version of what you and the NSA do—hacking into email and chats, and applying big data analysis tools to search for key words relating to the discovery—it was doable because there weren't that many people to cover."

"And?"

*This is it*, Dimitri thought. Time to really set the hook. "One of the things recovered with the bones was a stone that looked like it had been shaped to resemble an elephant yam."

"I get it now," the Colonel said, "This yam stone was Fred Flintstone's cell phone!"

Dimitri chuckled, "That's not bad, but right now that's just surmise. What's interesting is that the whole team saw the discovery of the stone, and there was tremendous resulting excitement. Some emailed friends about it and what it might mean. A young woman named Katie was supposed to lead the investigation into the stone. But after that initial flurry there's nothing—no mention of the stone, which turned out to be jadeite, and no subsequent publication on this particular discovery. Indeed, subsequent chatter suggests that no one knows where this jadeite is. Oh, and Katie's the woman who has disappeared."

"That's it?"

Dimitri was expecting this response. "Not quite. I did an intensive search trying to track this woman, Katie. After returning to the States, she showed up at an elephant refuge in Louisiana. Some of the volunteers and staff there commented on weird goings-on in which they were all suddenly given time off. One of them had forgotten something and went back to fetch it. In the distance, this woman recognized the Nobel Prize–winning physicist, Willem Keerbrock."

Once again, there was silence at the other end of the line.

"So, Colonel, why would a Nobel Prize–winning physicist, who'd co-authored a scientific paper on the discovery, be at an elephant sanctuary at the same time as a young woman who was given responsibility for investigating this stone, but who never published anything then or since?"

"Good question," said the Colonel, "That's why we hired you. Keep digging."

Dimitri could have been content to take yes for an answer and left things there. But he wanted full-throated support, and he thought he knew how to get it. "There's one more thing," he said.

The Colonel had been about to hang up. "What's that?" he said irritably.

"There's a Russian angle."

The Colonel was instantly on his guard. "Go on."

"Remember that *volneniye*, when the oligarch Bezamov fomented an uprising in northern Kazakhstan in an attempt to grab Transteppe, the mining concession?"

The Colonel remembered it well. Some dustup; it almost brought about World War III. Years later, it was still unclear who at or near the top had blessed that disaster. Bezamov, the oligarch, wouldn't be telling anything as he was dead—which was all well and good.

"What does *that* have to do with this yam cell phone?" There was a warning in his tone.

This was decidedly not the response that Dimitri expected. He decided to proceed cautiously. "Well, it turns out that Knowland's husband is a Russian, Sergei Anachev, and he and Bezamov had a history—not a friendly one at all."

The Colonel's mind was racing, trying to integrate this new element. "And this is relevant how?"

Dimitri realized that he'd entered dangerous waters. "Well, it's more your department, but if this turns out to be something you want to act on, at some point you'll be looking for leverage."

The Colonel relaxed. Clearly his contract hacker had only limited knowledge of what actually happened in Kazakhstan.

The story of Bezamov's downfall had become legend in Russian intelligence circles, though it was never discussed openly. The oligarch had launched an audacious plot to foment an uprising in the area of Kazakhstan surrounding Transteppe, and thereby scare the foreign partners in the venture to sell their interest to Bezamov for pennies on the dollar. Fletcher Hayden, a board member representing Canadian mining interests, stood in the way, but died when his helicopter was hit by a rocket as he left Transteppe during the uprising. Not long afterward, Bezamov was brought down by an article in a local Kazakh paper linking a hired assassin to the death of Hayden, and then by a voice recording linking Bezamov to the assassin. The voice recording looked as though it was an insurance policy and that it had been sent by "dead man's switch" (the hitman had disappeared and was presumed dead). The source of the article, however, remained a mystery, although rumors had it that Sergei Anachev had somehow played a role. Anyone who could bring down an oligarch as powerful as Bezamov was not to be trifled with. Moreover, the last thing the Colonel wanted was for higher-ups to wonder why he had authorized an investigation that might reopen an issue that every member of the *nomenklatura* wanted forgotten.

After a long pause, the Colonel closed the conversation. "You're absolutely right, Dimitri, that's my department. Keep digging, but don't do any digging regarding Anachev that might be traced. Am I clear?"

"Understood." Dimitri knew he had to regain the upper hand, and he had one more tidbit, he'd been holding in reserve, but had only planned to use it if the Colonel's interest or attention faded. "Actually, there is one more thing."

The Colonel was irritated. "I thought we were done."

"Remember how I said that nothing has come out in the years since the discovery?"

"Yes, you said that while I was still a young man—thirty minutes ago."

"Well, it turns out that one of the scientists at the original dig will be presenting a paper on his analysis of what a skull of that creature would look like. It will be at a conference at the Dinosaur National Monument in the state of Utah, and I would expect that all the conferees will be there. I'm planning to go."

There was a brief silence on the other end of the line. Then the Colonel spoke. "You're a hacker, not a spy . . ."

Dimitri cut him off, "I've an advanced degree in anthropology and have published on echolocation. It's perfectly natural that I would attend this . . . and nobody knows I'm a hacker, or of my connection to you."

"I'm not paying for this."

"I didn't expect you to."

"I don't like it."

"Please don't rush to judgment. I'll report after the conference."

After the call, a flood of emotions passed over Dimitri: exultancy over getting the green light, but guilt over the world of hurt this might bring down on the woman scientist and her colleagues.

Dimitri did have the best job in Russian hacking. While other groups spread disinformation or penetrated government, critical infrastructure, finance, and entertainment targets, Dimitri scoured computer systems for pioneering research that might have future military or advanced technology uses. He thought of himself as the Russian version of GoogleX, the arm of the search giant that explored ultra–long shot ideas that might prove transformative, albeit that in this case he was stealing other people's ideas.

In fact, Dimitri had long harbored dreams of working for GoogleX, but he had yet to figure out how to finesse the nettlesome issue of how to describe his previous work experience in some other way than what it was—hacking into and stealing America's most advanced research. Nor would it help his GoogleX job prospects to explain that the reason he was working with the SVR (Russia's foreign intelligence services) in the first place was that he was caught hacking into and stealing a billion rubles from Sberbank, whereupon he was given the choice of going to jail or working in cyber espionage.

Were it not for his career in criminal hacking, and cybercrime, Dimitri would have been a catch for any research institution simply because, in the world of computers, he was a unicorn. With advanced degrees in mathematics, physics, and anthropology, and with training in cryptography, he had world-class quantitative skills, while his side interests covered an extraordinarily broad range, encompassing artificial intelligence and robotics, as well as music and literature; Benjamin Franklin meets Meyer Lansky.

The son of a bookie and jazz singer, Dimitri began hacking at thirteen. The family computer was too slow for video games, so Dimitri first started exploring ways to speed it up, and then began using his newly acquired knowledge of software and hardware to hack into his classmates' computers, mischievously altering their home pages and playing other practical jokes. Naturally competitive, at fifteen he joined *Antichat*, a Russian hacking forum, which allowed various levels of access depending on demonstrated hacking skills. Dimitri quickly rose to the inner sanctum, though he assiduously avoided the "Kilroy was here" end-zone dances of some other rock star hackers. Dimitri's particular skill was finding "zero day" opportunities—vulnerabilities in software systems that were unknown to their users or developers—which allowed him to do his prowling unnoticed.

It was a zero-day opportunity that enabled him to rob Sberbank at age twenty-six, and it was another zero-day opportunity that at age twenty-eight gained him access to the Rushmere University computer systems and security cameras. He'd targeted Rushmere because he'd been fascinated by the initial reports of the discovery of what appeared to be an ancient intelligence. One of his interests was the evolution of wave-based echolocation and communication systems in animals ranging from bats to whales and elephants, and, reading about the enhanced cranial capacity of the ancient elephant, he had wondered whether that represented runaway natural selection enhancing that creature's ability to generate, interpret, and use sound waves. He'd been frustrated when the few follow-on publications from the discovery had focused on gross morphology and the flora and climate of the elephant's environment at the time of the discovery. The absence of research on Bart's cognitive capacities was so striking that it occurred to him that the absence of publications was not because there was too little to publish, but the opposite—that the researchers had come upon something so extraordinary that Knowland and her colleagues decided to continue in secrecy.

Now, invigorated by the Colonel's green light, he started making plans to travel to Utah. He had moved to Kazakhstan after going to work for Russian intelligence to have a geographical buffer in case his employer had a bout of buyer's remorse in allowing him to keep the Sberbank money. The move turned out to have an added benefit after the Russian invasion of Ukraine because, living in Kazakhstan, it was easier to dodge the restrictions on Russians travelling abroad.

If he had any qualms that his investigation might ruin people's lives and endanger something near miraculous, those feelings faded quickly.

# 12 THINGS GET REAL

THE IDEA OF PRESENTING AT A CONFERENCE WAS THE RESULT of Claire having the same chain of thought as the hacker, Dimitri. Given the brouhaha that followed the discovery of the bones, the utter silence Claire had enforced in the subsequent years was having the perverse effect of prompting speculation about why nothing had been published since. The last thing Claire wanted was for people to speculate that she might be hiding something.

Claire contacted Francisco Farnese, an Italian computer scientist, another veteran of the dig in Kazakhstan. Francisco had done some of the first critical analysis of the ancient bones and skull that Claire had discovered. Beneath his casual, aristocratic demeaner, Francisco was a serious scientist and a whiz at three-dimensional reconstructions. Equally important, Claire knew that he could keep his cool in the hot seat. She also knew that Francisco had completed his analysis of the skull months ago, but, out of respect for Claire's concerns about publicity, he had held off presenting his findings. So, she arranged a meeting at Rushmere, the New Hampshire university that, nominally, sponsored her research.

Francisco was delighted to get the green light from Claire. They went over what he was planning to say about the skull, and the best forum for unveiling his findings. They settled on a meeting of The Society of Vertebrate Paleontology that was to take place in May at the National Dinosaur Monument in Utah. Claire had little doubt that they could get his presentation into the section on imaging. After discussing some details, Claire gave him a level look. "Francisco, this is going to be the first paper presented since our initial paper. You're the sole author. Are you sure you're prepared for the shitstorm that's going to come down on you?"

"Can't be as terrifying as an inquisition by Keerbrock, when he tries to probe whether you've gone beyond the data."

Claire nodded, remembering the dismemberment Keerbrock had inflicted on her thesis defense many years back. "You're right about that. Nothing is."

Francisco didn't know that Claire had guided him to choose a conference that would take place exactly as Flo and three other elephants from the compound were due to embark for Mbembe. Francisco's paper was sure to attract wide attention, and would serve as a perfect distraction for a departure that might otherwise attract a lot of attention. Claire wasn't worried about Francisco inadvertently alerting people about the effort to get Flo pregnant since he knew nothing of that project.

Flo's egg implantation had established a clock. Katie had enthusiastically, but, discreetly, thrown herself into the vetting of Dev (Claire had kicked herself for giving that job to Katie, as asking her to vet Dev was akin to asking Cleopatra to vet Mark Antony). To no one's surprise, Katie came back with a glowing endorsement. Through a cutout Katie had learned that Dev was well-respected as a vet, with an impeccable reputation in the close-knit community of horse country. He paid his bills, and he was a generous donor at benefits. Claire accepted the verdict, in part for practical reasons—they needed a vet for a follow-up exam of Flo—but mostly because Claire liked Dev too. Katie's inquiries did not, however, turn up Dev's predilection for gambling.

Dev had his own surprise for Claire, Katie, and Zoe, when they brought him back two months after the implantation. Stepping out of the van and having his hood removed, he smiled and said, "Ah, it's great to be back at Boisbeaux." Then, seeing the alarm on Claire's face, he quickly continued, "Not to worry, I did my search on the library computer, and haven't told a soul. Nor will I." With the merest glance at Katie, he finished, "I was *very* glad to get your invitation to come back."

Claire sighed, "OK, I guess we can dispense with the rest of the pretense, I'm Claire."

Dev, gave a slight bow, "I know." He turned to the other two. "And you must be Zoe, and you're Katie."

Though the three women were planning to reveal what they were doing, once they had brought Dev on, they were still shocked at how easily he had put two and two together.

Dev smiled. "And since I figured out who you are, I also figured out what you're trying to do. It's truly extraordinary and I agree, it's vital to keep it under wraps."

Claire shook her head, but relaxed a bit. "Thanks, let's go check on Marie, er, Flo." They all laughed.

Later, after Dev had determined that Flo was indeed pregnant (Dev used progesterone metabolites in Flo's feces as a measure), he turned to Claire and Zoe, saying, "Someone's smiling on you and Flo." Later, when the group was celebrating with more of Dev's bourbon, rough-around-the-edges and straight-to-the-point Zoe turned to Dev and bluntly asked, "How is it that a guy like you is single?"

Claire and Katie were secretly pleased Zoe had come right out and asked. Claire was interested out of concern for leaks. Whereas Katie, who knew Dev was single, was interested for entirely different reasons.

Dev actually blushed. "I take it this is a question relating to security concerns?"

Zoe smiled, an unusual event, and shyly looked down. "Yes, and also because . . . you know . . . single guys who look like you are about as abundant today as aurochs."

Dev chuckled but looked uncomfortable, "Well, if you're worried about pillow talk, don't be concerned, not sharing a pillow with anyone these days." He wasn't about to address part two of her question.

Given an opening, Katie followed up, "Don't you want children?"

To everyone's surprise, Dev snorted with laughter. "If you knew my family, and my family history, you would be dancing in the streets on the news that I don't plan to bring another Sinjin into the world."

*He's perfect!* thought both Claire and Katie simultaneously, again, for entirely different reasons.

"Welcome aboard," said Claire, and she proceeded to lay out the plan to get Flo to Africa and the role she hoped Dev would play.

As the sun was setting, Claire looked at her watch. "We'd better get Dev to the airport. Katie, will you drive him? No need for anymore cloak and dagger."

"Sure boss," Katie said this with only a hint of a smile, and then frowned at Zoe who was suppressing a laugh. Facing Dev, she adopted a stern expression, "If you're naughty, that hood goes right back on."

Observing the scene, Claire shook her head. *Jesus!* she thought. *What have I done?*

As he was getting in the van—front seat this time—Dev turned to Claire and said, "Please tell whoever is paying for my services to redirect my future bonuses and fees to this project. I'm all in."

Claire clasped her hands over her heart, "That was not necessary, but thank you!"

# 13 OPERATION BUZZKILL

THE LAND AROUND DINOSAUR NATIONAL MONUMENT REMINDED Claire of Kazakhstan. Steppes and cliffs with sharply defined stratum set amid a vast, arid high desert. In late May, before the furnace-like heat of the summer, the weather was quite pleasant, with warm days and cool evenings. Francisco, Claire, and her seven-year-old daughter Sofia first went to see the "Wall of Bones," an extraordinary rock face with thousands of dinosaur bones partially exposed. As they walked through the exhibit hall, they were trailed by a mob of journalists, paleontologists, and students.

As Claire had both hoped and feared, the conference organizers had accepted Francisco's submission with enthusiasm, and had asked Claire whether she would hold a press conference. She had declined, saying, "This is Francisco's show." That did not stop the mob following Claire from peppering her with questions. After waving off a few, she decided she had to say something. Stopping by a strikingly preserved skull of an *apatosaurus,* one of the giants of the Jurassic era, Claire turned to the group and said, "It sure would be nice if we had a skull like this to work with, but we don't, and that's why we need Francisco to fill in the blanks." Claire smiled and waved off a dozen follow-up questions as they continued their tour.

Before coming to the conference, Claire had carefully looked over the list of registered attendants. She also sent the list to Rob for help in determining whether any of the attendees had any noteworthy associations. Rob got back to her the day before the conference. "Nothing obvious that's scary, but keep in mind people can register the day of the conference. Oh, and there's one Russian, Dimitri Medvedev. The guy's got more degrees than a thermometer, but I can't find anything on what he's doing now. Maybe Sergei can turn something up."

Sergei probably could turn something up, but Claire didn't want him doing anything that piqued the interest of Russian authorities who might well be keeping an eye on Sergei. The smart thing would be to steer well clear of Dimitri Medvedev.

Claire needn't have worried about doing so though, as Dimitri was planning to steer well clear of Claire. He was interested in what Francisco had to say, to be sure, but he was also interested in who else was interested in Claire and these ancient bones. To this end, he planned to work the social events and bars and pay attention to the chatter at Francisco's session. And he too was interested to learn who showed up at the last minute. The Dinosaur National Monument was in an isolated part of the American West, and it was unlikely that last-minute attendees had decided to attend on a whim. So, after checking in, Dimitri stationed himself near the signup station with a book, explaining to the staff that he was waiting for a friend he was supposed to meet.

As expected, there were very few last-minute sign ups. Of the dozen or so people that drifted in over the course of the morning, most looked like graduate students and were of little interest to Dimitri. But a few were. A man and a woman came in. They were dressed like typical young scientists—jeans, plaid shirts, and safari vests—but everything was just a bit too neat. It was though aliens came to earth and went to L.L. Bean to buy clothes in the hopes of fitting in. Dimitri noticed the two's quick eyes. They were scanning the room, and Dimitri quickly returned to reading before they noticed him.

One other man caught Dimitri's eye. Definitely, not a scientist, this guy was wearing a sports jacket. His hair was long, but neatly combed. And he too had quick eyes. Dimitri was Russian, but he knew law enforcement when he saw it, and this guy screamed enforcement. He was definitely not a spy. *Why would a cop be here?* wondered Dimitri. *An amateur fossil hunter in his spare time?* Maybe. Ordinarily, striking up a conversation with a cop would be the last thing on Dimitri's to-do list, but Dimitri's scientific credentials made him a natural fit for this conference, and he had a business card with a legitimate email address (thanks to the Colonel) that identified him as a consultant to the Mammoth Museum in Yakutsk, in the Russian Far East. He definitely was going to have a casual chat with the cop, and he was going to have to walk a tightrope in the conversation—Dimitri had never been to Yakutsk.

Before entering the conference, Dimitri went outside to walk around the grounds. He'd never been to the US either, and he was excited to see the country. He took a deep breath of the fresh desert air. He liked the landscape, and he liked the aura of excitement and intellectual curiosity that bubbled up from the conference attendees. For a moment, he wished he had taken a path that would have made working for GoogleX a possibility. But he hadn't, and now he had a job to do. He went inside and took a seat toward the back of the auditorium.

The organizers had decided that Francisco's presentation had real news value. They shifted the schedule so that he would lead off, and they moved his presentation from one of the meeting rooms to the main auditorium. Seated on the stage, Francisco looked around the packed house as he was introduced for his presentation. Introducing him was a professor of paleontology from the University of Colorado.

"We're going to kick off this conference with news from the relatively recent past—5.3 million years ago," the professor began, bringing a chuckle from the many Jurassic-era specialists in the audience. He reminded the attendees of the sensation created by the publication of the discovery of the ancient elephant bones that seemed to have been arrayed in parallel by some ancient intelligence. "And sitting in the audience with her daughter is the woman who brought the bones to the world's attention," he continued, beckoning Claire to rise. The crowd of paleontologists spontaneously rose to give her a standing ovation. Overcome, Claire smiled and gave an abashed wave, and then, as the applause continued, she rose briefly and waved again. It was a deeply satisfying moment given that seven years earlier this same community had mocked and ostracized her in the months before the distinguished scientific journal *Science* published the findings of her and her team. Sofia beamed at the attention her mom was getting. The professor then reminded the audience that this was the first presentation of any analysis of the bones since that initial publication, and with that stepped back to let Francisco take the podium.

As planned, Francisco gave a just-the-facts ma'am presentation. He first went through the techniques and assumptions he used in creating his reconstruction and then put his model up on the screen. There were audible gasps from the audience when they saw the pronounced forehead of the skull. The most dramatic moment of the presentation came when Francisco matter-of-factly went through the possible explanations for this morphology. "Of course, I considered the possibility that this might be the result of selection for secondary sexual characteristics. If, for instance, competition for mates included head-butting, we would expect a pronounced thickening of the bones in the forehead. Based on the evidence we have, however, I don't believe that this was the case. The bone remnants we have suggest that this part of the skull has not noticeably thickened." Francisco paused. "Another possibility is that the forehead is the result of selective pressures for an extraordinarily enhanced frontal lobe related to selective pressures for enhanced interpretation of auditory information amassed in the temporal lobe." Again, there were gasps, and Francisco paused before deflating the balloon. "Efforts to find more fossil remains continue, though the political situation in Kazakhstan makes that difficult. Until we have a more complete picture of this creature and its life and times, any hypothesis about the phylogeny of that pronounced forehead will, alas, remain speculation. Thank you."

Francisco received a thunderous round of applause, and a forest of hands went up with questions: "Do you think you've uncovered an ancient elephant civilization? Why would these elephants need special abilities to process auditory input? What selective pressures might justify the metabolic tradeoff of directing more blood flow to the brain?" Again and again, Francisco deflected speculation. After a few moments of this the professor stepped forward, saying, "I'm sure Dr. Farnese would be happy to take a few more questions over cocktails, and I invite those attending to the main hall to continue any discussions." Claire looked around at the many disappointed faces with satisfaction. She caught Francisco's eye, and nodded her head toward him in gratitude. She owed him . . . big time.

As she walked over to the cocktail reception, Claire was intercepted by Adam Constantine, a reporter for the *New York Times* who had first broken the story about the discovery of the bones for the mainstream press.

"Hi Claire, the years have been kind to you."

Constantine's presence was a surprise. He was one of the people she had hoped to avoid. "Good to see you too, Adam. Still at the *Times*?"

"Guilty. Look, I'll cut right to the chase. This presentation is it? Thought you'd be further down the road after seven years."

Claire looked him straight in the eye. "I've learned not to venture beyond the data. You of all people should appreciate that."

"Of course, and I'm glad to see some publications coming out. You'll give me a heads up if more detail is coming, yes?"

Claire put a hand on his shoulder. "I haven't forgotten what you did seven years ago. You'll be my first call."

Adam looked at her curiously. Then nodded and melted into the crowd.

Still in his seat, Pete Roznik puzzled over the situation. Neither Keerbrock, nor the woman Keerbrock had met with in the café in Dobbs Ferry were in attendance, even though this was a big moment with regard to the discovery of the bones. He dismissed the idea that the project Keerbrock had discussed with the woman was a rogue operation—everything he had read about the man suggested that he was a complete straight arrow. More to the point, earlier Keerbrock had put his reputation on the line in support of that woman, Claire Knowland. Also, there was a yawning gulf between the extraordinary project of bringing back a long dead species and the rather pedestrian presentation he had just heard. That raised the possibility that this whole presentation was a kabuki dance, a smokescreen to deflect attention from something else going on at the same time, perhaps something relating to the resurrection of the long dead elephant. He resolved to do some digging.

Then, Roznik turned his attention to the attendees, and whether there might be potential buyers of his info about the plan to resurrect the elephant among them (he too had paid special attention to who was attending the conference). That's why he had come. He, like Dimitri, had immediately picked out the government spooks who were not on the original list. *What did they know?* he wondered. *Probably not much, or they wouldn't be here.* And, in any event, approaching them would get him arrested. Then, there was that Russian from the Mammoth Museum in Yakutsk. Obviously, a mammoth expert would have legitimate reasons to be here, but still it was a long way to travel for a relatively anodyne presentation. Before he got up to join the cocktail social, he did some quick searches for Dimitri Medvedev. Almost nothing came up beyond the fact that the man had multiple advanced degrees.

Roznik got up to walk to the reception in the main hall. Then it hit him. If this presentation was a deflection, then some important part of their plan to bring back the elephant was happening right now! Since no one else seemed aware of the project, this meant that his information was at or near its peak value.

Even before the applause had died down, Dimitri had left for the cocktail hour. Dimitri felt that the presentation was anything but anodyne. He was exhilarated. He felt all the questions that Francisco deflected were right to the point—why would that ancient elephant need brain power, and yes, there was a trade-off with redirecting blood to feed a big brain. The elephants must have gotten some extraordinary benefit to adding that brain power to justify the costs. He was sure both Francisco and Claire knew far more than Francisco was revealing in this presentation. *What are they hiding and why?*

There was a bar set up in the main exhibit hall. Surrounded by reconstructed predators and other giants, Dimitri felt glad that he hadn't been born one hundred million years ago. He picked a glass of sauvignon blanc off a tray as a waiter walked by and scanned the room. Twenty feet away, Roznik was also scanning the room. When he saw Dimitri looking at him, he nodded, and then casually walked over.

Looking at Dimitri's badge, he said, "Mammoth Museum. Very cool. I'm Pete Roznik. I assume you speak English since you're here."

Dimitri laughed. "Yes, I speak English." He looked at Roznik's badge which only had his name on it. "Dimitri Medvedev, nice to meet you."

Roznik took a sip of his Seven and Seven and said, "Well, what did you think of the presentation?"

Dimitri was a bit nonplussed to be directly approached by Roznik. For one thing, it suggested that some part of US law enforcement had a direct interest in him. He needed to keep his cool. "Oh, I thought it was terrific. I've been waiting to hear more about those bones since they were first announced."

Roznik looked at him. "Really? I was a bit disappointed. After seven years I would think they would know more . . . a lot more."

Dimitri decided the best way to project innocence would be to be direct. He smiled, "If I can ask, Mr. Roznik, why would US law enforcement be interested in five-million-year-old bones?"

Roznik looked at Dimitri with true amazement. "Law enforcement! How'd you make me for that?"

Dimitri laughed, "Oh, in Russia, recognizing the various authorities is like high-stakes bird watching—life and death high stakes. Your well-being sometimes depends on being able to recognize all the varied species." He smiled at Roznik, "You might as well have had a large arrow following you around reading, 'This guy is a cop.'"

Roznik laughed and took another sip of his drink. Then he smiled, "OK, you got me. I used to be an FBI agent." He looked directly at Dimitri, but there was no discernable reaction. "I retired a bit more than a year ago. Now I just pursue hobbies. This," he waved around the room, "is one of them." *This is it*, thought Roznik. *This is where we begin a pas de deux of ambiguity.*

Dimitri thought for a moment. "Again—if I can ask—what was your specialty? Are you allowed to talk about it?"

Roznik chuckled. "I can talk about what I did, but, obviously, not specific cases. I spent most of my career in surveillance." He caught the alarm that briefly ran across Dimitri's face.

Dimitri collected himself quickly. "Surveillance! Ah, I can see why you might be interested in an ancient creature with astonishing auditory capacity."

"Bingo."

"Bingo?"

Roznik laughed again. "An American game. Means you hit it on the head." He decided to dive in. "So, I've read that a Russian team is trying to bring back the mammoth. Are you involved in that?"

"No, I've been following that too. I'm not sure where that stands."

Here goes, thought Roznik. "Do you think it might be possible to bring back this 5.3-million-year-old elephant?"

Dimitri paused a long moment, his mind churning. Something was going on here. "If you have a complete strand of DNA, you can bring back anything. But all they've got is a few petrified bones, right?"

"Of course, but wouldn't it be extraordinary to bring back that animal with those near supernatural abilities to collect, interpret, and maybe project sounds? Imagine the technologies that might come from understanding that?"

Dimitri's heart was racing. "Again, you'd need DNA."

"Are we sure that all they've got are petrified bones?" Roznik looked around the room. No one was close, or paying attention to them. He turned and directly faced Medvedev. "You know, one of the strange things about surveillance is that during an operation you often hear things unrelated to the case you're working on, things that have nothing to do with illegality, and sometimes these are extraordinary things."

Dimitri also took a glance around the room. He got the message. Roznik was saying he'd done nothing illegal and the information, whatever it was, couldn't be extorted. "This is not my expertise, but my colleagues at the museum would love to hear your thoughts on this. Would you like to come to the museum? Yakutsk is the coldest city in the world in the winter, but it's quite livable before the midges, gadflies, and mosquitoes descend in the summer."

Roznik looked him directly in the eye. "I'd love to see the frozen mammoths, but I'm a retired cop, living on a pension."

Dimitri nodded. "Of course, I'm sure we can work something out." He thought for a minute. He needed to talk to the Colonel. "Would you like to join me for a hike on the Fossil Discovery Trail tomorrow afternoon?"

Roznik pulled out the schedule for the conference, and pretended to look for what he might be missing. He looked up. "That works, say 4:00 p.m.?"

"Four o'clock it is." Dimitri put down his drink. "I'm going to circulate. See you tomorrow."

At the far end of the room, Claire and Francisco were in conversation with the man and woman who had registered at the last minute. They had introduced themselves as working for the Defense Advanced Research Projects Agency (DARPA). The woman, who introduced herself as Gwyneth Sawyer, said that she had studied paleontology at

Williams, while the man merely gave his name as George and let the woman do the talking.

"This seems pretty far afield for DARPA," said Claire amiably.

"Actually, not at all," said Gwyneth. "Nature has billions of years to work out solutions, and we realize that natural selection optimizes for efficiency. We've been funding efforts to build a robotic octopus for decades, and we still haven't come close to what nature worked out over the course of six hundred million years."

"Glad you recognize that," said Francisco.

Claire decided it was best to pour icy water early. "Well, as you can see from Francisco's presentation, we're still a long way from knowing what this elephant used its brain for, or even if it had any special abilities at all." As she spoke, out of the corner of her eye she saw the Russian scientist speaking to someone. Both looked out of place at the conference, and the man the Russian was speaking to had the body language of a cop.

She returned her attention to Gwyneth who wasn't to be put off that easily. "The wave spectrum is an area of special importance for us, and it would be remarkably interesting to know what these elephants did with auditory information. If more money would speed up your research, we're here to let you know that any application from you and your colleagues will get special attention."

"That's certainly a generous offer. Let me confer with the group and we'll get back to you."

After they exchanged cards and shook hands, Francisco looked at Claire. "I take it you're not considering taking them up on this offer?" Francisco didn't know about the project with Flo, but he was wary of what might happen once the government had their hooks into the research.

"Not for a minute, but it's better to string them out rather than give a flat-out no. Anyway, I'm fairly sure this was just an opening salvo."

Claire looked around the room. Dimitri and Roznik had already gone their separate ways. She noticed now that a group of scientists had been waiting to talk to her and Francisco. "Time for your curtain call," she said to Francisco. "I'm going to peel off and get a drink." As she walked over to the bar, she thought that overall, Operation Buzzkill (as she thought of the two-step presentation/embarkation) was a thorough success.

# 14 GRIGORY



AFTER CONSULTING WITH THE COLONEL, DIMITRI BEGAN NEGO-tiations with Roznik during their walk on the Fossil Trail the next afternoon. They stopped near a massive thigh bone partially jutting from a rock face. Roznik waited for Dimitri to make the first move. He knew that he had to give them something as a teaser, but could not give any names or the Russians could run down the information themselves. Dimitri gazed at the remnant of some Jurassic giant. "They don't make 'em like that anymore, do they?" He turned to Roznik, "OK, I've talked to my colleagues. They are interested to hear what we're talking about."

Roznik thought a second. "I'd like to know who I'm negotiating with. Scientists?"

"Yes and no," Dimitri said smiling. "My colleagues—scientists and technologists—are curious about what Dr. Knowland and her team know about the abilities of this ancient elephant that they haven't published."

Roznik digested this. "What I can tell you before we discuss terms is that there is a truly massive gap between what we heard in the presentation yesterday, and what they are investigating."

"Really?" Dimitri said, arching an eyebrow.

"Here's the deal. In the course of an investigation into organized crime, my surveillance picked up a conversation between two scientists. They were being quite secretive, but the project they were discussing was similar to what Russian scientists are trying to do with the mammoth."

Wow! Dimitri thought, as he felt his pulse race. This was far more than what he'd hoped to find when he began his hacking of Rushmere. "Then they must have DNA. Do you have names? Backup."

"Yes, I have names, and I have a transcript."

Dimitri thought about this. "OK, here's what we're prepared to offer." Dimitri then laid out a payment schedule with payment in bitcoin. He offered a substantial sum for an initial conference call with his colleagues, and then subsequent payments so long as they had exclusivity (and Dimitri assured Roznik that they would be closely monitoring to see if others—government or private entities—got wind of Claire's project). There was some back and forth over the amounts, but they eventually settled on a $1 million guarantee, with the possibility of another million if word didn't get out.

A week later, after the encrypted conference call took place (the Colonel set up the call), Dimitri had an immediate follow-up conversation with the Colonel and someone who only identified himself as Grigory. "Well," asked Dimitri, "what do you think?"

"It proves my point," said the Colonel.

"What point?" Dimitri was irritated that the Colonel baited him so easily.

"That hacking only gets you so far; often the most valuable information isn't written down."

That the Colonel described the information as valuable somewhat softened his denigration of hacking. "What next?"

Grigory stepped in. "Nothing."

Dimitri felt deflated. "Nothing?"

"Continue to monitor and gather more details, but cover your tracks. This information is useless unless there is a baby elephant, and it will be a few years before anyone will know whether that baby has special abilities. Anything we do now might wreck the project or let others know what this woman Claire is up to. If anything, we and Claire have a common interest in helping her maintain secrecy. And keep an eye on

Roznik. He might get greedy. Maybe we send him a message that greed comes with a heavy price tag . . ." Grigory paused, apparently bemused by something. "You know," he said, "in the old days we had sleeper agents who wouldn't surface for decades. Now—maybe—we're going to have a sleeper elephant."

# 15 FLYING ELEPHANTS



THE EMBARKATION PORTION OF THE TWO-STEP PROCESS unfolded in late May, simultaneous to the conference in Utah. In Baton Rouge, Louisiana, Zoe and her staff supervised loading the elephant cages onto the chartered 747-8, extended range, air freighter. The elephants chosen for the move had all previously experienced transport by air, and habituating them to the travel crates went smoothly. Zoe put out an anodyne press release on the PR wire, with the realistic hope that it would be lost in the continual flood of releases that went out on that site each day. Claire wanted the departure to attract as little attention as possible, and she succeeded with only one local paper running a snippet about the move.

Zoe accompanied the elephants on the chartered plane. Dev joined them at a refueling stop in the Canary Islands, and then the group flew on to Bangui in the Central African Republic (CAR), where they were met on the tarmac by Rob Rebolet, along with a fixer and a small group of mercenaries. Rob had handpicked former members of the French Foreign Legion who knew the region and also spoke Lingala. The fixer, a local expatriate and former missionary, generously paid off the customs and airport officials to ensure a smooth entry, and the presence of the mercenaries served as a tacit message to the officials not to try to re-trade the deal. Zoe and Dev gave the elephants a feast of their favorite foods and then they loaded the giant crates onto two waiting trucks that would be their transportation for the arduous 400-mile drive on logging roads along the Bomu River that marked the boundary between CAR and the northern Congo. The fixer had hired trusted local drivers, and each had a former legionnaire riding shotgun. Zoe and Dev rode with the elephants, one to each truck. Rob, the fixer and the third legionnaire led the convoy in a land cruiser that had been rigged with especially high clearance to deal with the deeply rutted tracks. The Land Cruiser towed a large trailer, which held bales of hay, grain fruits, and water tanks, as well as provisions and tents for the crew. It was the dry season, so they didn't have to worry about flooding or washouts.

They did, however, have to worry about extortion. There were no rebels operating in the area—the various factions focused on areas with mineral or other riches. But they did encounter a succession of local scammers as they drove through villages. The locals would set up impromptu roadblocks of trees across the road and demand payment for road repairs, or some local "official" would demand to see papers. The fixer would genially banter, and grease a few palms here and there, and if someone tried to escalate demands, the armed mercs would step out of the cab, and their mere presence calmed things down.

As they drove east from Bangui, the countryside turned from relatively dry brushland to rainforest. Dirt roads connected a patchwork of small villages. Palm plantations gave way to tiny farm plots that might house a plantain plant, a mango tree, and small plots of maize. Children would run alongside the convoy as it slowed through villages. After 150 miles, there were fewer villages, and they became progressively more rudimentary. The dirt roads gave way to logging roads, which petered out as well.

Zoe found her mind wandering a bit and she soon made a unique observation. As the convoy grew farther from their starting point, and closer to their eventual destination, Zoe noted that it was essentially driving back in time. With each mile traveled, the air became purer, the trees larger, and the sounds of animals and insects more present and insistent.

Six days after leaving Baton Rouge, the crew and trucks reached the edge of the swamps that separated, and protected Mbembe. Encamped and waiting were three people: a tall Bantu woman dressed in safari gear, and two Bangombe Pygmy guides dressed in ragged shorts. The tall woman stepped forward and introduced herself to Zoe, "I'm Salina," she said, in English and waved the two guides forward. The two were quite short but looked extraordinarily strong. Both smiled. "This is Ndokanda," she said, gesturing toward the stockier of the two, "and this is Seraphime. Both know more about the rainforest than any tropical biologist living or dead. We'll take care of the elephants—from a distance. Zoe will accompany us, so the elephants know we're taking them to a good place. Rob, as we talked about, it might be best for the rest of the team to encamp here until Zoe returns. This is the only place a logging road reaches the swamp. If any bad actors followed you, they have to come through here."

Rob nodded, "Got it."

Salina continued, "We'll take the dugout and lead the elephants across the swamp, and after two days, I'll bring Zoe back. We've set up camp on the other side of the swamp. I've got a sat phone and will send a short burst to Rob if trouble arises, though I don't expect any. All anyone knows is that this is a private elephant sanctuary."

"Agreed," said Rob, "But it's a private sanctuary on the border of two of the most corrupt failed states on the planet. We've set up hidden monitoring on the logging road seventy miles out, so we have a bit of time to mobilize if uninvited visitors head your way. I'll be back in Kazakhstan, but I can coordinate any response required from there."

Salina smiled, "We've also got the swamp and the quicksand to slow anyone down."

Zoe looked up, "Quicksand?"

Salina smiled, "Don't worry, Ndokanda made a secret path through it—it's safe as long as you don't trip."

"That's reassuring," said Zoe grimly.

"We should get going; it's going to take a few hours to cross the swamp and get to the bai where we'll spend the first night."

"Bai?" Zoe asked.

"It's the Ba'Aka word for clearing," Salina answered. "So, what do you say we introduce the elephants to their new world?"

"On it," said Zoe. "First we prepare a banquet."

Zoe took charge, asking Rob and the mercenaries to set up the sturdy ramps on the trucks, and then drop out of sight. Then she laid out a sumptuous feast of elephant treats on the shore of the swamp—hay, melons, apples, all the foods they liked. Then she got up on the first truck, which held Flo. She unbolted the door, but had difficulty pulling the heavy metal door open. "Flo, give me a hand," she said stepping back. Flo, the old pro, lowered her head and gave the door a gentle shove, easily opening it. But Flo stayed in the giant crate.

"Come on out and look at your new home. You're gonna like it—I think."

Zoe held out an apple and Flo took it in her trunk, but she had already seen the array of treats laid out on the ground, and tentatively walked down the ramp. Once the other three female elephants saw Flo digging through the food, they trumpeted, and required no coaxing by Zoe to get them to come out.

As the elephants enjoyed the treats, the crew strapped supplies in waterproof bags into one dugout, and Salina and the two guides climbed into a longer dugout. Zoe walked up to Flo. "Hey Flo, can I ride with you?" Flo turned her massive head toward Zoe, in what she took for a yes. At one point in her years of captivity, Flo had given rides to kids at a roadside zoo. She seemed to enjoy it, and so, after the staff had left for the day at Boisbeaux, Zoe had occasionally ridden Flo on walks around the sanctuary.

Dev gave Zoe a boost and she was on Flo's back. "OK, Flo, we follow them." Zoe accompanied her words with a sweeping hand gesture forward, and Flo seemed to sense that she was to follow the dugouts.

Ndokanda and Seraphime watched Zoe settle herself with bemused amazement. Sitting in the longboat, they both gave Zoe a thumbs up, which Zoe returned with a salute. Flo was the matriarch and, as she started walking into the swamp the other three elephants dutifully followed. Ndokanda set a deliberately slow pace, and Zoe kept up a continuous soothing chatter, while praying that nothing would spook the elephants before they got to the far shore. Throughout it all, Dev photographed the strange procession from shore.

The elephants were tentative at first, taking a few careful steps and then looking around, but they soon gained confidence. The water was never more than four feet deep, and while the bottom was muck, after sinking a foot or so with each step the elephants hit more solid ground. All four were African elephants and Flo and one other had been captured as babies in the wild. Flo must have sensed something familiar in the warm, moist African air because she started rumbling contentedly.

Zoe had never been to Africa, and she was pleasantly surprised by the air. Yes, it was hot, but the only word she could think of to describe it was "delicious." The swamp was several miles wide at this point, and as they walked toward the center, it became profoundly quiet. In the pure water she could see the reflection of cotton candy clouds that lightly floated across a bluebird-colored sky. Zoe patted Flo, as she felt tears flowing down her cheeks. Surprised, she realized that this was pure happiness. "Flo," she said quietly, "you're home, you're free, and you're going to have a baby."

# 16 MANNA FROM HEAVEN

It was mid-August, and at 6:00 p.m., as the insufferable heat of the day mellowed to the barely tolerable, Zoe walked down Boisbeaux's driveway to retrieve the mail. She picked up a pile of Penny Savers, solicitations, and a few envelopes. Nothing unusual. Every week, Boisbeaux would receive small donations, from elephant lovers, a fifth-grade class, elderly shut-ins, etc., most of whom were local. Back at her farmhouse, Zoe dumped the solicitations in the trash, and began opening this week's crop of mailed-in donations. A couple were addressed to particular elephants, and one had a $20 bill and note in a child's scrawl saying that the donation was to buy Flo a special treat on her birthday.

The last envelope had no return address, and Zoe was tempted to toss it without opening it since such envelopes usually contained offers to consolidate her debts. The envelope was pale blue, and it was not standard business size. *Fancy*, she thought turning it over. She slit the top with a steak knife. Inside was an unsigned, typed note and a folded check. The note simply read, "Please use this money as you decide, for operating expenses." Zoe unfolded the check; and gasped. It was a cashier's check for five million dollars.

Zoe collected herself and examined the check more closely. It was drawn on the Alhambra Bank and Trust. Putting the check down she opened her computer to learn more about the bank. It was an offshore bank in the Cayman Islands serving ultra-high net worth individuals. Next, she looked at the envelope. The postmark was from the Cayman Islands, and the stamps depicted flowers. Zoe went to the stove, put on the kettle, and when it whistled that it was ready, she proceeded to steam open the flap of the envelope. On the upper left side, a part of the envelope previously concealed by the flap, she saw the word Pineider. Zoe went back to her computer. Pineider was a high-end purveyor of stationery, founded in Florence, Italy in 1774. She was briefly excited, but then saw that such envelopes could be bought at high-end stationers around the world.

She looked at the note again. No requests for progress reports or audits, no stipulations about how the money would be spent—unrestricted funds being the most valuable kind of contribution, and no way to make a report (or send a thank-you note) in any case. No strings whatsoever. It was too good to be true. Just weeks ago, Claire had confided to Zoe her worries that the combined expenses of Boisbeaux and Mbembe might become too much of a burden for Helen Hayden and Keerbrock. Five million would buy several years of salaries and food. But . . . the Caymans?

She sent a coded, encrypted message to Rob, saying that something urgent had come up, all hands needed.

Two hours later, Claire, Sergei, Katie, Rob, and Keerbrock were on a secure video chat. Rob was in Kazakhstan, Keerbrock in his office at the geochemistry laboratory. Claire was in her office at Rushmere, Sergei was in his office in their house, and Katie was in her rented cabin in the mountains of New Hampshire. Zoe walked them through what she knew, and held up the check. "Well," said Keerbrock, "We now know that someone saw the Mbembe press release."

"That's what troubles me," said Claire, "They had to be looking for it."

"Which means they probably had a prior interest in Boisbeaux, or those connected to Boisbeaux, most likely you or Keerbrock," said Rob.

"G-men?" asked Zoe.

"No strings," said Keerbrock, "If it was government, or any other institution, there'd be more strings than a harp quartet. No requests for any rights, not even any info."

"Maybe some really rich person just really likes elephants?" Katie offered.

"Sergei? We can't see you."

Sergei turned on his video. "Sorry."

"Any thoughts?"

Sergei looked uncomfortable. "Lot of oligarchs parked money in the Caymans." He shook his head. "But the sanctions mean they don't have free access…" He now looked confused. "…and Andrei Besamov is dead … not to mention that if it was someone connected to Besamov who somehow knew about the discovery, they wouldn't give the money anonymously and with no conditions . . ." Sergei looked like he was about to say something more, but then stopped.

There was a momentary silence and then Keerbrock spoke up. "Maybe Rob can dig a little more, but in the meantime, let's take it for what it is."

Again, there was silence. Claire also seemed lost in thought.

"OK, then," said Zoe, "Should I deposit the check?"

Claire looked up. "Do we need to consult a lawyer?"

"I don't see why," said Keerbrock, "people make anonymous donations all the time."

"Go ahead and deposit it, Zoe," said Claire, "but maybe set up a separate account for it while we try to figure this out."

Once Sergei exited the meeting, he sat back and thought. A single word had come into his head after Zoe described the check. He had become used to thinking in English, but the word had appeared in his mind, unbidden, in Russian: *iskupleniye*. Then it came back in English: *atonement*. But who? There was one person who had the motivation and the means, but he really didn't want to open that door.

# LIVING THE DREAM IN THE PLEISTOCENE

# 17 BART

ACCOMPANIED BY HER PRE-ADOLESCENT SON A FEMALE FOREST elephant walked through the moist rainforest air on a well-trodden trail. The trail has been maintained over the centuries, not by humans, but by an elephant civilization that has survived unmolested for thousands of years in the most inaccessible part of the Congo. The region is called Mbembe—which means monster in Lingala—a name bestowed by the neighboring Pygmies, who believe the forest houses an ancient dinosaur-like creature. It is one of the last places on the planet where life proceeds much as it has since the Pleistocene. Here the elephants are in charge, and they have created a grid of trails linking favorite waterholes and mudbaths with trees that are sources of natural medicines and tasty fruits.

For elephants, life in Mbembe was a succession of halcyon days. On one such day, a female and her young son were walking along an elephant boulevard. Coming upon a *Myrianthus arboreus* tree, the big female sampled the fruit with its juicy kernels. She playfully tossed another fruit at her son, who casually snatched the fruit out of the air with his trunk and popped it in his mouth. They next came upon a giant Afrormosia with its technicolor and mottled bark. The presence of this prized giant was yet another sign that this part of the Congo rainforest has been undisturbed by humans. Nearby a red colobus monkey glanced at the scene and then continued feeding, while deeper in the forest a yellow-backed duiker briefly looked up from its grazing and regarded the group with mild interest. After their snack, the two elephants continued on their way. The big female started briefly when the two heard sounds of chimpanzee hoots and vocalizations in the distance. They continued walking until once again, the female stopped, agitated. The little male looked around calmly, and listened. Then, he lowered his head, touched his mother's shoulder with his trunk and emitted a soft rumble. At this, the big female relaxed, and they resumed their walk.

About a half mile ahead of them, coming in their direction, a small group of humans could be seen walking along the trail. This was an exceedingly rare intrusion in this part of Mbembe. The group consisted of a white woman, a Bantu African woman, and two male porters, carrying gear strapped to their backs with strips of cane. The white woman's lightweight safari gear was completely sweated through from the equatorial swelter. In the shade, the air was dank but bearable; not so when the sun broke through. The group stopped as another man, who had been scouting up ahead, came back toward them. He said a few words in Lingala to the African woman, who then turned to the white woman with an excited smile. "This is Ndokanda. He found them. They're up ahead about a kilometer and walking this way."

Hearing this, the white woman gasped and then gave a timid hug to her female companion—she had hurt her shoulder, having slipped and fallen on the trek into the forest. "Five years!" she said, "I can't believe it's finally going to happen." The blonde woman turned serious. "Is it OK if I go ahead alone, just for the initial meeting? Salina, please ask Ndokanda and Seraphime to hang back with you out of sight, maybe a couple of hundred yards."

Salina said, "Of course," and then fired off a few rapid-fire sentences in Lingala. The porters shook their heads, and looked down. Salina turned back to her companion. "They don't think that's safe—these are forest elephants, very dangerous."

The blonde woman smiled at them, but directed her words to Salina. "Please tell them that I really appreciate their concern, but that these elephants are my friends." She paused a minute as though considering whether to say something more, but apparently thought the better of it and simply nodded to Salina.

After Salina passed this on, Ndokanda and Seraphime both arched an eyebrow and looked at the blonde woman with real interest. The scout rattled off a few words to Salina, who nodded in turn. "Ndokanda says that there's a bend in the trail about half a kilometer ahead and that you should wait there, about fifty meters back so that you don't surprise them."

"Thanks, makes sense." The blonde woman checked her small backpack and then headed off, turning back to say, "Remember, out of sight." And then, "Wish me luck!"

"Don't worry," said Salina, "We'll wait back here."

Once Claire was in position, there was nothing more to do but stand in the middle of the trail and wait. She didn't have long.

In their natural habitat, large as they are, elephants can walk almost silently. And so it is that the big female and her son seemed to materialize out of the air as they came around the bend. Elephants can identify which humans are threats by gender, clothes, and even language—Kenyan elephants are known to distinguish between tribes that hunt elephants and those that don't solely by hearing them speak—and they also have extraordinary retentive memory of those humans they have met in the past. At first, the big female trumpeted alarm when she rounded the bend and saw a person on the trail, but then she immediately followed with a trumpet of joy as she recognized the woman. The big elephant followed this with a soft rumble, almost like a cat's purr as she started to walk toward the woman, followed by her son, who looked at the woman with great curiosity.

Knowing that she was recognized, the woman started trembling and crying. But there was a smile on her face as she wiped away her tears. She shrugged off her backpack and reached in to fetch two apples. "Hi Flo," she said, though she was so choked up that she could barely get the words out, "It's me, Claire."

At the word *Claire*, the young male immediately looked up, staring intently. He cocked his head to the side. Claire also stared. The juvenile looked like an elephant, but had a very pronounced forehead, and his bone structure was more gracile than other elephants. Even more striking was his demeanor. The little elephant projected an aura of preternatural calm even as his eyes blazed with intensity and intelligence. Before giving her full attention to the young elephant, Claire turned to Flo offering her an apple, saying, "I'm sorry Flo, I don't have much in the way of treats—I had to travel light." Flo munched happily, still emitting soft rumbles, and Claire turned back to the young elephant.

Before speaking, she again reached into her backpack and pulled out a device the size of a laptop and switched it on. She held an apple, and the little elephant took it with his trunk, but instead of putting it in his mouth he placed it carefully on the ground beside him and resumed looking intently at Claire. She started to speak, but once again she was overcome and struggled to get the words out. "And you must be Bart," she said with tears in her eyes, then laughed. "I'm Claire, your godmother."

Bart looked at her calmly with his head slightly cocked. He emitted an almost imperceptible rumble and, almost immediately, words came out of the device Claire was holding, "I know," the words were clear and resonant.

Claire started. She knew that the device worked—Bart had been taught to create his own sounds for human words which were then converted to English by the device—but it was still disorienting to hear an elephant speak. She had a million questions for Bart, but knew she needed to go slowly. "How?" she asked with a smile.

More rumbles, "Salina showed me pictures."

"Of course," said Claire beaming. She thought back to the day six years earlier when she had shown up at the Transvaal Elephant Sanctuary in South Africa. Claire had approached the confident young woman, who was then working with a newly orphaned baby. That conversation had been preceded by a long and thorough background check, and even then, Claire had first approached Salina in utter secrecy and under an assumed name.

The precautions were necessary, and the project proceeded entirely in analogue, with no technology (save the synthesizer) more sophisticated than what would have been available in the 1960s. Claire and Salina had sent Ndokanda forward to locate Flo and Bart because the elephants did not wear transponders—signals might be intercepted.

Salina was there because, apart from being indispensable, she could keep a secret, and it was a big secret that she was being asked to keep. Claire had first heard about Salina from Zoe, who was very well connected with the global network of people who sought to help rescued elephants.

Salina turned out to be a perfect fit. She had a degree in cryptography, and was familiar with maintaining absolute discretion as a result of several years spent working with the National Security Agency in the US. A South African native, Salina had decided that the spy life was not for her, and chose to follow her heart's desire, which was to work with orphaned elephants in her native land. It was Salina who had invented the device Claire now carried which turned Bart's ultra-low frequency utterances into words through a CPU and a synthesizer.

Until now, Salina had been the only person who visited Bart and Flo in Mbembe. Her cover was that she was doing research on elephant use of tree barks and herbs as natural medicines. In reality, she was using the device to create a mutual, translatable language for Bart so that humans could gain some insight into his otherworldly abilities.

And even the narrow view offered by the language instruction suggested awesome capabilities. Physically, elephants mature at roughly the same rate as humans, but Bart's intellectual development surpassed any human child of equivalent age. By two, Bart clearly understood what Salina was trying to do, and took control of instruction. He would bring her a fruit or flower from the rainforest and make a distinct sound, often too low for Salina to hear, but still recorded on the synthesizer. Claire would give the item its English name, or scientific name if there was no English word, and Bart would make the sound again. By three, Bart was using the synthesizer to talk in complete sentences, and also to barrage Salina with questions, some of which she could answer, and some of which she couldn't, or wouldn't.

So much more could have been done to explore Bart's abilities if he was being raised in the US, but the very nature of these abilities and the scramble to get access to Bart that news of his existence would inspire, made that impossible (later, they would discover another reason that made life in a developed country out of the question).

With a spotlight on her, Claire had pursued a low-key life—her daughter providing the perfect excuse. She had devoted much of the six years since bringing Flo to Africa to being a mom, while her professional work focused on the description and analysis of the physical evidence she and her colleagues had uncovered in Kazakhstan. Once Bart was born, however, Claire was determined to meet him, but this also took several years to organize. Claire had prepared the way for this trip by taking several trips to parks and elephant sanctuaries around the world to establish a pattern of vacations to remote jungles.

Bart brought Claire back to the present with a question. "I've been hoping you would come, because Salina won't answer my question."

Again, unnerved to have an elephant speak to her in complete sentences, Claire was taken aback. She also had a strong suspicion of what that question would be, and she knew it would open up extremely uncomfortable avenues she didn't really want to explore. For one thing, if she was right, she had no adequate answer, and also because what answers she did have still left her anguished with the moral compromises entailed in her actions. Still, she knew she owed it to Bart to answer.

"I'll try sweetie. What do you want to know?"

"Why am I here?"

She turned away so that Bart wouldn't see the shocked look that passed over her face. This was the ontological issue Claire desperately wanted to avoid. She chose to interpret the question literally. "You're here because it's one of the few places on Earth that is safe for elephants."

Bart wasn't buying it. He began a series of sounds that were immediately uttered by the device. "Yes, I know that, but who am I? I'm not like Mom. I'm not like any of the other elephants here. I've looked at my reflection in the bais and I know I don't look like them. They're smart, but they think differently than I do. They talk differently than I do. People think differently than I do too, but I can ask Salina things I can't ask Mom or other elephants."

Claire stared at Bart, she knew he needed an answer, but she was fascinated by the implications of what he had just said.

"I'll try to answer your question, but can you tell me just a bit about how you think differently than both elephants and Salina?"

"When Mom wants me to know something, she makes sounds, but what I receive is like a living painting of a scene—me and her in a mud-bath, a leopard hunting a gorilla, a tree heavy with fruit. With Salina, each word refers to an object, and she is teaching me both the objects, and the rules that connect them. When I look around, it's different; I see the things around me as separate but also in a web of connections and possible connections that aren't in the rules Salina tells me."

Bart gave this account in a series of short rumbles, and waited patiently while the synthesizer translated each phrase before continuing. While he waited, Bart thought about what he was not telling Claire—yet. The troubling and mounting feeling that the way learning about the human way of thinking and communicating interfered with his own way of thinking. He had yet to make a decision, his abilities had not fully matured, so for the moment he felt comfortable trying to describe his world.

"Once at night, when we were looking up at the sky, Salina told me about lights that appear in the sky far away from here where it's cold.

They're called the Northern Lights, and she said they were like a shimmering curtain of assorted colors. That's how I see everything. When I look at you, I see you but also waves of colors, purple, pink, and yellow.

"But it's more than that. When I use words—like we're doing now—I feel detached from the world. That's your world. In my world, I'm part of . . ." Bart stopped, searching for a word the synthesizer had learned so that he could describe how he experienced the world around him. He realized that he couldn't, it was something beyond human vocabulary, much less the synthesizer's. "Like I'm a part of an ocean that includes land, water, animals, plants, everything. There is no separation . . ." Bart stopped in frustration.

After the synthesizer finished translating his words, Bart looked at Claire. She felt dizzy at the possibility that Bart might be her guide to all the worlds he had access to. One world came to mind immediately. Bart might help translate the images Bart's ancestors had encoded in the jadeite that Claire's team had uncovered in Kazakhstan. But Claire knew that enormous logistical problems impeded getting Bart together with that stone. She came back to the present; this opportunity was precious.

"Please go on. I know it's hard—the synthesizer can't say words it hasn't learned."

The little elephant thought for a minute. "If I can't tell you, I can show you what it's like. I'm connected to everything, but I can also influence things around me."

"Influence?"

"I think that's the right word. I know your shoulder is hurt."

Claire looked at him in astonishment. *How?* She wondered.

Bart said nothing, but after a few seconds, Claire felt a pleasant, electrical-like current flowing toward her shoulder. The energy built and her shoulder felt warm. Then it popped, and it was like a release, as the tension flowed out of it. Claire felt an enormous sense of well-being, almost euphoria.

They stood there in silence for a few seconds. "Bart," Claire said with a smile, "I very much like your world."

Bart was not giving up on his question. "So, you see—I'm different. But why?"

Claire knew she couldn't lie to him, but, even with his manifest wisdom beyond his years, she wasn't sure it would be fair to burden him with the full drama of his origins. So, she chose an answer that was honest but incomplete.

"You are the last of a beautiful and noble race of elephants," she said as she gave him a hug. She decided not to tell Bart about the stone and its record of his past, at least not just yet, as that knowledge also was dangerous. She patted Bart affectionately. "Someday, hopefully soon, I know that you will learn more about your kind and where you came from. In the meantime, I will devote everything to making sure you have the most fulfilling life possible."

"I come from the past."

*He knows! But how?* wondered Claire. There was no way he could know how old he really was. Yes, Bart was five years old, but it was equally true that he was 5.3 million years old.

Claire looked at the battery level on the device. It was getting low. "Bart, there's so much I want to talk about, but this machine is about to die. Tell me where I can meet you and your mom tomorrow, and we can talk some more." She gave Bart another big hug (or as big a hug as a 120-pound woman could give to a 1,000-pound juvenile elephant), and Bart reciprocated by squeezing her with his trunk. Bart turned to Flo who had been watching their interaction with interest and made a series of low rumbles. She responded, and Bart turned back to Claire. "There's a mudbath down this path—Mom's worried about ticks."

Then Bart did something that brought a new flood of tears to Claire's eyes. "I'm so happy you found me. Can I call you Mom too?"

"Oh yes, Bart," said Claire. "Please do call me Mom."

# CHILDHOOD'S END

# 18 FOUR YEARS LATER

BART WAS AWARE OF THE MEN APPROACHING EVEN THOUGH ten miles of rainforest separated them. The men appeared as perturbations of the wave field, which is one way he perceived the surrounding rainforest. The metal of their guns stood out sharply against the endless expanse of flora. He knew they had come for him.

In this extremely remote part of the Congo rainforest, there were no cell towers or any other microwave transmitters. Thus, the emissions of the groups' heat-imaging equipment stood out as a plangent intrusion. He didn't know what type of equipment was generating those emissions, but he knew that if it was thermal imaging, his large heat signature was sure to be noticed. He immediately neutralized the equipment by cloaking himself with wave cancelling emissions on the exact frequency of the imaging equipment. Instantly, the largest creature in the rainforest became invisible to the most sophisticated thermal detection equipment. Then, as he moved deeper into the forest, he pondered possible responses.

A series of scenarios presented themselves to him, the more probable possibilities being more vivid, with more positive outcomes having an aura shading toward the lightest green as they became more positive, while negative outcomes became more intensely red as the scenarios became darker. The highest probability negative scenario involved the men capturing him. He didn't think they were here to kill him; he knew that he was too valuable alive.

He was not defenseless, but revealing his powers would only increase interest among the groups that seemed to be pursuing him. *What to do?* A scenario presented itself, and he felt relieved.

Ten miles away, a group of men armed with both weapons and tranquilizer guns puzzled over the screen of their heat-imaging equipment. The heat signature that had briefly flashed on the screen had disappeared. In the midst of this confab, the leader of the group sat down, leaning against a tree. Waves of sleepiness came over him. The four other men in the group also sat down. "Let's take a break . . ." he started to say in Russian, but never finished the sentence. It didn't matter as the others in the group were already asleep.

When they awoke, several hours later, the men discovered that their weapons and equipment were gone. In their place were a multitude of ticks, mosquitos, flies, and other rainforest insects that had flocked with alacrity to any patches of exposed skin on the sleeping men. These were tough men, but they were aware that the forest was rife with pathogens, and they all began wondering how many were already proliferating in their bloodstreams.

At least one member of the group saw a warning being delivered by the rainforest. "I think these bugs are saying we're not wanted. I agree. Let's get out of here."

Their leader looked resigned. Without weapons, he was hardly in a position to disagree. He sighed, now regretting that they had not enlisted the help of guides. How was he going to explain this to Grigory, who did not seem like the forgiving type? The situation was more than embarrassing, it was dangerous. Compared to Grigory, the Wagner Group's head, Arkady Petsov (who had taken over after Prigozhim met his end), was a clumsy oaf. Wagner recruited special forces; Grigory had a select group of former intelligence operatives on contract. The leader, a Cossack named Petro Denisov, envisioned the conversation: "So tell me again, you were outwitted by an elephant?"

With a hand he gestured for his men to get up. He looked around noting that whoever or whatever had taken their weapons and satellite communications gear had not taken their canteens. He shook his head, confused by this act of consideration. "We'd better get started. It's thirty miles to the river—if we can find it."

Ten miles away, not even half grown, an elephant summoned all the herd. An observer would have been astounded by the subsequent scene as the rainforest giants obeyed the summons, even the magnificent bulls. They formed a circle around their diminutive peer, nodding deferentially as he conveyed his request, and then they melted away, this time in all different directions.

After they had gone, Bart pondered the events that had just transpired. Although the animal didn't think in English, or any language for that matter, sometimes he found language useful to capture a moment. So, it was now as his thoughts would have translated to the phrase, "and so it begins." At nine, he was no longer a child, but not yet an adult.

# 19 THE JADEITE

KATIE SEGAL HAD BEEN ANTICIPATING THIS CALL FOR SEVERAL years. She was grateful that the call hadn't come sooner because the plan that had just been triggered required an intricate series of operational details and contingencies. On its surface, the operation sounded simple: Katie had to arrange to get the yam-shaped piece of jadeite from the United States to Mbembe. The jadeite only weighed about a pound and could be carried in a purse or a briefcase. The problem was that she had to get the stone to Mbembe without anyone knowing where it was going.

Katie had pursued studies of the effect of the stone on the elephants at Boisbeaux, taking pains to schedule her rare sessions with the elephants when no other workers at the refuge were around. The elephants were getting some sort of message—a message about what life was like for an extinct, five-million-year-old elephant species—but even after many sessions Katie was no closer to deciphering the message the ancient elephants had encrypted in the jadeite.

But Bart might.

Once Bart touched the stone, he might open a window on the world of his ancient forebears. Keerbrock, though stunned by the properties of the stone, had been adamant that the scientific world was not ready for any publication on the properties of the jadeite until it was better understood. Worse, he warned that should news that an ancient intelligence had managed to create a stable field from a collection of five-million-year-old messages, the team would be besieged by corporations, intelligence agencies, and governments who would not necessarily have the goal of scientific advancement on their minds.

Claire and the tiny group that knew about Bart and the jadeite, had both dreamed of and dreaded the day when Bart would be asked to translate the messages of the jadeite. They dreaded the moment because they knew that even as it was important to keep secret the properties of the jadeite, it was orders of magnitude more important that Bart remain hidden from the world; and bringing the jadeite to Bart potentially opened up a world of risk.

Thus, Katie's apprehension and excitement when she received a message that simply read, "Hoping you can get to Boisbeaux for lightning bug season." The message came from a computer in Louisiana, but it had been prompted by another anodyne email from the Congo. Something had happened in Mbembe, something which convinced Claire that she couldn't delay any longer the moment when Bart would see his past.

"I'll make a point of it," Katie typed. She took a deep breath and hit send. She had an unsettling sense that her life was about to change.

# 20 QUANTUM ENTANGLEMENT

FOR CLAIRE, KATIE WAS SOMETHING OF A BLACK BOX. FROM their first meeting in Kazakhstan years ago, Claire had been intrigued by the young woman. She seemed completely unconcerned with the impact her looks had on other people. She was also perfectly comfortable with silence, which led many who encountered her to underestimate her. Over the years, however, Claire had noticed that when the stakes were high, or a problem knotty, most often it was Katie who cut through the confusion. She had a gift for seeing the obvious.

Nine years earlier, when Katie, Keerbrock, and Claire were puzzling over the properties of the jadeite, it was Katie who suggested an elegant series of steps to untangle the mystery. Katie suggested that the uncomfortable energy encountered when someone held the jadeite for too long was because the animals that created or manipulated that field had done so with the assumption that it would be touched by creatures twenty times human size. Keerbrock had suggested creating a virtual elephant, and Katie had countered that it wasn't necessary to create a virtual elephant when they could take the stone to a real elephant.

Katie was a woman of action, and often played things close to the edge. She had almost fractured her relationship with Claire when she had gone rogue and driven to Boisbeaux with the stone without seeking permission. Since they had reconciled, however, Claire had learned that it was always worthwhile to listen when Katie had an idea. Now, meeting in Rushmere, she and Katie were discussing the ins and outs of bringing the jadeite to Mbembe to see whether Bart, now nine, could understand and communicate to them what messages or images the ancient elephants had encoded within it.

The problem was deceptively complex. Once they got the stone to Mbembe (no mean feat in itself since they could not risk having it examined by customs inspectors or bringing it through a metal detector), Bart might well connect with what his ancient forebears had intended. But how would he communicate that message to humans?

Although Bart's access to English through the voice synthesizer had increased by several orders of magnitude since he and Salina first started using the device, both Salina and Claire were aware that Bart had misgivings about the device, as well as a desire to limit its use. At various times, he had told them that while using English and thinking in English allowed him to communicate with and understand humans, it came at a price. The way that people thought, communicated, and analyzed was alien to the way Bart thought about things. Worse, he said, human thought was corrosive to his abilities.

People factored communication and science into symbols and rules; Bart told them that his inner world was a continuum of waves and fields. Where humans manipulated the environment by trying to understand the properties of materials and the laws of physics, chemistry, and biology that govern them, Bart described his world as a multi-dimensional, seamless field of interconnections. He seemed to have inherited from his long-dead antecedents an ability to influence those fields to achieve specific results, such as the healing he performed on Claire's shoulder during her first visit to Mbembe.

Long before Claire told Katie of Bart's healing her from a distance, Katie had become interested in how Bart's ancestors' hyperdeveloped ability to sense waves up and down the wave spectrum might have been used, and how differently they might see the world. In the years since the original discovery, Katie had tried to understand some basic ideas of quantum mechanics, specifically the notion of quantum entanglement and action at a distance, a phenomenon first posited by Einstein and colleagues in a thought experiment published in 1935. Ironically, Einstein had hoped the thought experiment would prove the absurdity of quantum mechanics (a field he had helped lay the groundwork for) because if it was true, quantum mechanics violated the fundamental limit of the universe which was the speed of light. Subsequently, an Irish mathematician named John Stewart Bell came up with a way to experiment with this, and he paved the way for a number of physicists to actually test quantum entanglement. In every credible test, quantum mechanics won, and conventional reality lost.

Briefly, this idea posited that if two subatomic entities—e.g., photons—became correlated by a common event, they would remain correlated, even if the particles were split apart and sent to the opposite ends of the universe. Then, if one of these photons passed through another field, once again changing its orientation, its partner at the other end of the universe would simultaneously change its orientation too. Despite the fact that this violated Einstein's posited speed limit for the universe, this aspect of quantum mechanics has since become fundamental to the development of quantum computing. Reduced to its simplest form, in their wave incarnation the photons remained connected, or entangled. *Perhaps these ancient elephants—and Bart—were able to influence wave function,* Katie thought. *And perhaps their thinking was better explained by quantum mechanics than any measurable interaction of neurons.*

Over the years, Katie had entered innumerable reveries, trying to let her brain sort out what this might mean. In one such reverie, Katie realized that this model for thinking would be a dead end using our traditional modes of understanding that involved thinking about problems in terms of objects and the laws governing them. Indeed, in quantum mechanics the act of measurement "collapses" the wave function so that those amorphous connections binding photons across time and space would instantly disappear. *This is why neuroscience, or any other modern science, can't explain the boundless examples of ESP that pop up around the world,* Katie thought. *Maybe this property of action at a distance might explain Bart's mysterious ability to both read minds far out of sight, and also heal Claire's shoulder without touching her.*

The weird implications of quantum mechanics were only intended to apply to the subatomic world, but since this predictive tool's invention, many thinkers have wondered whether quantum laws also applied to the visible world. This was exactly what Katie had been wondering about Bart since she first encountered the powerful properties of the jadeite. Perhaps he lived and thought in quantum reality terms.

Early on, Keerbrock had recognized that Katie's mind took her in original directions. Even though he was punctilious about adhering to scientific rigor in studies, Keerbrock's creativity came from a career-long openness to ideas that came from outside the high walls of academe. To colleagues who asked him about this contradiction, he simply replied that if he only read material coming from the credentialed, he would be ignoring the most imaginative literature. So, while he cautioned Katie about the risks of publishing results beyond the data, he also encouraged her to follow her thoughts where they took her because if an idea had validity, someday the data might catch up. Bringing together her thoughts about ESP and Bart, Katie wondered if it represented a relic ability that had been crowded out by language and the scientific method. If that was true, she thought, and there were still examples of it out there in the world, then perhaps that ability was not entirely extinct in humans. Where would those abilities most likely be found?

One of the pioneers of artificial intelligence once remarked that solving a problem is a matter of formulating the question in such a way that the answer becomes obvious. Katie's formulation of the question led her to Buddhism, particularly the Buddhism practiced by a scattered group of monks in Tibet.

Katie's cabin was only a thirty-minute drive from Rushmere. The cabin had a wood-burning stove, a long desk, and a rudimentary kitchen. The neighbors had horses and were delighted when Katie asked if she could help exercise them. On those occasions when Dev came up (they were now a long-distance couple), they would take long rides through the hills. In fact, once Katie decided that Dev was the one, he didn't stand a chance. After their first such ride, they'd returned to the cabin. They sat down next to the stove to warm up. Giving Dev a soulful look, Katie said, "You know the best thing about riding clothes?" Dev shook his head, not knowing where this was going. Without waiting for an answer, she said, "They come off." She pulled off her top and turned toward Dev.

Happily startled, he started to say, "Katie . . ."

He never got to finish the sentence as she pulled him to her saying, "You silver-tongued Devil. Who could resist?"

The occasional pastoral notwithstanding, most of the time, Katie was alone. That gave her the space to fully flesh out her idea.

After Claire had laid out all the pitfalls they had to navigate, she looked up at Katie. "Any thoughts?"

They were sitting in Claire's office at Rushmere. Katie drummed her fingers on the desk for a few seconds. "I've been thinking about this for years, so yes."

Claire looked up, "Care to share them?"

Katie laughed. "You have to promise not to laugh until I'm finished."

"I'll do my best."

"OK, it turns out that the best way to maintain secrecy may also be the best way to really understand what is encoded in the stone." Katie reiterated the limitations of the speech synthesizer, particularly Bart's growing aversion to that form of communication. She then ticked off the security risks of Claire and Katie going to Mbembe with the stone. "So, maybe we could send Dev on a veterinary mission to Mbembe with the stone. He gives it to Salina. She records Bart's reactions as best she can on the spot, while we get a more fleshed out picture remotely."

"Katie," Claire looked mildly miffed. "We can't risk anything involving satellite communications."

Katie looked triumphant. "Exactly."

Now Claire looked confused. "Smoke signals? Where would we be?"

"Tibet!" Seeing Claire's expression, Katie hastily continued. "Bear with me." She took Katie through her thought experiment that led her to conclude that, based upon several researched stories, certain Tibetan monks had already achieved remote viewing through the eyes of eagles and hawks, and that they might be the ideal receptors of whatever images or visions Bart accessed through the jadeite. She reminded Claire that Bart had already demonstrated his ability to affect people at a distance. "If the right monk agreed to cooperate, he might be able to share what he experienced—and we'd be in Tibet, far away from Mbembe."

Claire digested this. "I take it, you've identified a monk."

Claire nodded, and described a revered lama named Rencho who meditated in solitude at a remote monastery in Tibet.

"How do we find out whether this Rencho is interested?"

"First, we've got to tell Bart what we want to do. While we're there, we'll ask Bart to reach out to Rencho. I think Bart will know whether he'll be receptive."

Katie paused a minute, uncertain, "Bart needs to agree too. Do you think he will?"

Still absorbing what Katie was proposing, Claire waved a hand, "I'm fairly sure he will. The jadeite offers him a way to learn about his own kind." Claire thought a minute more. "What if Bart can't make a connection with this Rencho monk?"

"Dunno, plan B—the voice synthesizer. But that would be like trying to pick out Saturn's rings in the night sky with a magnifying glass."

"Should we run this by Keerbrock."

Katie gave Claire a piercing look. "Think about his likely reaction—it'll only take a second."

Claire considered this and sighed. "OK. We tell him after the fact—if we get something."

As she was getting up to leave, Katie turned to Claire. It was a question that she could only ask in person. "What triggered the need to get the jadeite to Bart?"

Claire shook her head. "We knew that day would come. A group of men—Russian mercenaries it seems—were intercepted in the Mbembe concession."

"Intercepted?"

"Yup, by Bart?"

"What the Fuck?!"

Claire gave a rueful chuckle. "Bart sensed their presence. Then he knocked their drone out of the air and he put them to sleep."

Katie looked at Claire, bug-eyed.

Claire gave her a wistful look. "Yeah, we're just beginning to see the extent of his powers. Who knows what else he can do. Anyway, once they were asleep, he somehow got his herd to pick up their weapons and deposit them near Ndokanda's campsite. He and Seraphime brought them to the legionnaires."

"Weapons?!"

"Yes, weapons, but most interesting was that they had tranquilizer guns."

"They were going after Bart."

"It gets worse. The legionnaires gave Ndokanda a couple of miniature tracking devices to place on the sleeping mercenaries. When they awoke, the Russians re-crossed the swamp and headed up a trail toward a clearing. The legionnaire sent up a drone to follow them at a distance. They boarded a Russian Mi-26 helicopter and took off. Rob told me that helicopter could easily lift an elephant."

"How on Earth did they find out about Bart?"

"We don't know, nor do we know whether they even know Bart exists. They never got within ten miles of him—but they do know something. We've been wracking our brains to figure out how they got on to this. In the meantime, it's our worst nightmare, but it's also one reason I like your idea. If they're somehow following you and me, I'd rather that both of us are in Tibet when Bart meets the jadeite."

# 21 CHANGE OF PLANS

DIMITRI DREADED THE CONFERENCE CALL, AND HE WASN'T
disappointed. The Colonel set the tone, starting with sarcasm. "Just so
I get this straight: Our crack team of mercenaries was outwitted by a
herd of elephants?"

"Maybe just one elephant," said Grigory.

"Or maybe American agents, using some new psychotropic
weapon."

Grigory, who was clearly senior, batted this away. "We've seen no
traffic suggesting that the Americans know anything about what's
going on in that part of Africa. We want to keep it that way."

"Maybe nothing's going on," ventured the Colonel. "Maybe it's just
what they say it is, an elephant sanctuary."

"You know the old saying, 'it's quiet, maybe too quiet,'" said Dimitri, "That applies here. My monitoring shows nothing but the most
ordinary communications over the past several months. My guess is
that they're going to extraordinary lengths to protect something in
Mbembe. Moreover, what happened to our men suggests that this
young elephant has extraordinary powers. From what they told us, they
all felt this irresistible wave of sleepiness. Then, while they were asleep
someone, or something stripped them of their weapons and communications gear. Bottom line: what happened to them is proof that there's
something in Mbembe that we need to have."

The Colonel started to object, but Grigory cut him off. "He's right.
What we should be talking about are next steps. I don't think another

snatch attempt is the way to go. Too big a chance that we will wake up the Americans. What do you suggest Dimitri?"

Put on the spot, Dimitri was glad they couldn't see the anguished look on his face. He knew exactly what to do next, but he wasn't going to say it. He saw himself as a hacker; distinct from a criminal.

"Offer them cash?"

The Colonel snorted with contempt, to which Grigory wheeled around. "Do you have a suggestion?"

"We don't have to snatch the elephant to get access to the elephant."

"Go on," said Grigory who had taken control of the conversation.

"Say we snatch a member of their core team—that Katie woman would be my choice. Claire Knowland is so fanatical she probably wouldn't trade the elephant, but she might let us observe it."

Dimitri panicked. This was getting out of hand. "Why wouldn't that cause her to go running to the Americans?"

Grigory had a ready answer. "She knows that the Americans will be no more subtle in investigating the elephant's powers than we would be. That's why." He paused a minute. "Why Katie?"

"Because she keeps such a low profile that only her colleagues would ever know she was missing, and they won't report it."

"OK, so Katie," said Grigory. "Let me think a bit about how we do this. When it happens, it absolutely cannot be traced back to us."

Dimitri said nothing, which was noticed by the Colonel.

"Having an attack of scruples, Dimitri?" he said with some sarcasm. "What do you think that show trial was with the American basketball player, Brittney Griner?" Answering his own question, the Colonel went on, getting angrier. "Strip away the stupid pretext—a couple of vials of cannabis oil, and it was nothing but a state-sponsored kidnapping. They do it to us too. Happens all the time."

"That's enough," Grigory interrupted, for a number of reasons, he didn't like the direction the conversation was taking. "Let's focus on the plan."

Dimitri still said nothing. In the years since he first brought the Colonel's attention to the ancient elephant bones and then functioned as go-between with Roznik, Dimitri had pulled back from hacking. He still had much of his ill-gotten wealth from his youthful forays into cybertheft, and, with the successful transaction completed with Roznik, the Colonel had left Dimitri alone to pursue his interests, which, at that point in his life included travel, scuba diving in the Maldives, gambling in Malta, dating, and pursuing his varied intellectual interests. Always though, there was the understanding that Dimitri was on call for the project 24/7 if needed. Before being summoned by the Colonel, Dimitri had begun to hope that the project had been forgotten.

The Colonel had given Dimitri a longer leash under orders from Grigory. Grigory had known going in that this was a very long-term project, and wanted Dimitri to be available should the need arise, and not rotting in some prison because of a hacking job gone south, or, worse, spilling the beans to cut a deal. Grigory had other reasons for keeping the circle around the project as small as possible, reasons that he did not tell the Colonel.

Off the phone, Dimitri took stock of his life. He was now in his mid-thirties, and thinking of settling down and starting a family, preferably in the West. He acknowledged his past criminal acts, but he rationalized his past thefts as analogous to what banks did in the ordinary course of business. His transaction with Roznik was defensible, and he had made the deal to further Russian interests. With his mind and skills, Dimitri knew that he could thrive in the legitimate world—if he could get free of the Colonel. Now, in one casual phrase, Grigory had killed that dream. Kidnapping was not a victimless crime, and he was shaken by the blasé way Grigory had greenlighted the plan, particularly since Katie seemed like the kind of woman Dimitri would like to have in his life. Far from going legit, he was settling in with a nest of vipers.

# 22 TEMPS PERDU AVEC LUDMILLA



NO ONE WAS MORE ALARMED BY THE NEWS OF THE FAILED Russian attempt to snatch Bart than Sergei. He'd left Russia behind more than a decade ago, but he couldn't help feeling that his past had morphed into some teasing, malevolent, and vaporous presence, periodically reminding him that though he might be done with Russia, Russia was not done with him. There was the threat that some associates of Andrei Bezamov might come after him or Claire if they figured out his role in the Oligarch's downfall. But then there was a different kind of threat from Ludmilla, Bezamov's widow and Sergei's first great love.

After meeting at a chess match, (in which Sergei had humiliated Bezamov and earned his undying enmity), Sergei and Ludmilla had dived into an intense, two-year relationship that ended as abruptly as it had begun. Sergei later learned that Bezamov had launched a sophisticated smear campaign against him that caused Ludmilla's wealthy and influential father to threaten to cut her off completely if she did not break off the relationship. She then married Bezamov, only to bitterly regret that decision, particularly after learning of Bezamov's role in smearing Sergei's reputation. Years later, she reached out to Sergei to warn him of Bezamov's continuing hatred. In that note, Ludmilla also wrote that her biggest regret was caving to her father's ultimatum and that the two years with Sergei were the happiest years of her life.

Sergei considered himself happily married. He loved Claire, but remembered an incandescent intensity that imbued every moment with Ludmilla. Because their relationship had ended at its height, it never had a chance to transition into a more mature love. When Ludmilla had contacted him, he remembered their lost magic, but made his choice. Now with Sofia, who delighted him every day, he knew where his commitments lay. Still, it wasn't easy. His memories of those halcyon days with Ludmilla glowed dangerously at the edge of consciousness like one of those radioactive elements with a long half-life.

As soon as he had heard about the anonymous check to Boisbeaux and Mbembe, that word *atonement* had come into his head. And it didn't take long for him to figure out why. Ludmilla was the most likely candidate. She'd told him they were getting divorced, but Sergei guessed that Bezamov had died before anything was finalized and that Ludmilla had ended up with at least some parts of what remained of his fortune.

After some soul searching, the group decided to use the money. It took some burden off Helen and Keerbrock.

Sergei hadn't told Claire about his suspicion that Ludmilla was behind the gift, and now, several years later, he couldn't without raising the question of why he hadn't told her earlier. As he thought about it, Sergei realized that he didn't know why he hadn't told Claire or the others that Ludmilla was the likely donor, but he decided in this case that ambiguity was for the best. A straightforward interpretation was that the donor wanted the gift to be anonymous, but Sergei was Russian and almost instinctively rejected straightforward answers. What if it was a test to see if it would prompt Sergei to find Ludmilla, and thereby reveal that he still carried a torch? And what would he do if he did find her? Some deep instinct warned Sergei that some doors best remain closed.

# 23 MOVING A HOT ROCK

FOUR YEARS AFTER HER FIRST TRIP TO MBEMBE, CLAIRE returned, this time with Katie. They came separately, using two wildly different routes which eventually brought them together in Cameroon. They had left their phones and all electronic equipment behind. At a small town on the Sangha River in Cameroon, they were met by Rob, who brought them by chartered twin-engine plane to an abandoned logging landing strip in the Central African Republic, where they were met by two of the three legionnaires. The ordinarily louche mercenaries almost snapped to attention when they saw Katie. Observing their reaction, Claire sighed inwardly; all these years and she still wasn't used to playing the role of chopped liver to Katie's Venus de Milo. Sitting in the backseat, Claire leaned forward and whispered to the two mercenaries, "*C'est une honte, mais elle est avec quelqu'un.*" Katie suppressed a chuckle, and they both settled in for the sixty-mile drive over deeply rutted tracks to the shore of the swamps bordering Mbembe.

The first time she had crossed the swamp to Mbembe, Claire had felt exhilarated. Now, she was filled with angst. Memories of the attempt to capture Bart were fresh, and the effort to see his reaction to the jadeite involved an entirely new suite of dangers; that is, if he even agreed to see the stone. She also felt honor bound to warn him that what he experienced through the stone might leave him the saddest, loneliest elephant on earth.

Katie had her own angst to deal with. Since her first trip with the jadeite, she and the stone had never been separated. Now—if Bart agreed to the plan—she would be giving what was probably the most precious relic ever recovered to Dev to bring to Bart accompanied only by Salina. Katie's one source of solace was that once the stone was safely in Mbembe there was no better place to hide it on the planet.

At the edge of the swamp, they were met by the third mercenary, Salina and the guides. Salina had arrived ahead of Claire and Katie in order to make contact with Bart and arrange a place to meet. As they were loading their backpacks and food in one of the dugouts, the two legionnaires who had driven Claire and Katie had a short conversation with the third who had remained at their small camp. The leader, a sun-burned Frenchman named Andre, walked over to Claire.

"French OK," he asked with a smile.

"*Bien sur.*"

Andre spoke slowly in French, telling her that the drone had found no activity of any sort in the previous weeks, but that he suggested that one guide remain with the legionnaires in case something came up and they needed to get her a message.

"How will he find us?" Claire asked.

The mercenary laughed. In English, he said, "For a Pygmy, your trail will be as obvious as a lighted runway."

While they were talking, Katie wandered around, taking in the sights, aromas, and sounds of the rainforest and swamp. She was absolutely beaming. She turned to Salina who had finished helping load the dugout. "I've never been to Africa. I don't know how to describe it, but you can almost taste the air."

Salina nodded and smiled as well. "Wait 'til you taste the water. Wait 'til you hear the sound of the bai when the frogs get hotted up in the evening."

Claire joined the two women, and told them about the security arrangements. "Anyway, she is our security," she said, nodding at Katie, "I'm expendable but they aren't going to let anything happen to her." Salina laughed and Katie shook *her* head.

Claire and Katie took Salina aside. As soon as they were out of ear-shot, Claire turned to Salina. "What's he like now?"

Salina shook her head. "It's too much to explain it all now—we've got to get across and set up—but I find it increasingly difficult to do our simple lessons, because . . ." Salina seemed at a loss for words.

"Is he being difficult?"

Salina laughed and shook her head again. "Just the opposite, "His presence . . . it's like an immense wellspring of awareness . . . and good-ness . . . it's so far beyond what we can capture with the synthesizer . . . it's just humbling, like being in the presence of a god . . . Even though he's still an adolescent, all the elephants defer to him, even the big males . . ." Salina paused again and then looked directly into Claire's eyes. "I have to tell you this—the more I learn about what a miracle Bart is, the more I'm scared about what might happen. What will happen if word gets out? He'll be besieged. Here he is, virtually unprotected in one of the most lawless places on earth. I can't sleep worrying about it."

Claire placed a soothing hand on Salina's shoulder. "I've been worrying about this since Bart was conceived. We've tried to make Mbembe seem to the outside world like the most boring, do-good proj-ect on the planet—a privately owned animal sanctuary, protected by swamps, quicksand, and nearly impassable roads that stop miles from the edge of the concession. And ticks! But you're right—those Russian mercenaries show that we've got to have a plan B ready. You and I can brainstorm about it while I'm here, but let's get across the swamp and talk more later."

After crossing the swamp, they camped in a clearing near the Mbembe edge of the swamp. The women set up tents, while the guides fashioned their own out of broad leaves and bent over saplings. They made bed mats out of bark, and cups out of leaves. Vines had supplied the cords, which they had tied expertly to perfectly distribute impossi-bly heavy loads on their diminutive frames. No supply chain issues for the Bangombe Pygmies.

Claire wanted to get up bright and early the next day so that they had as much daylight as possible for their time with Bart. That evening, sitting on logs next to a fire, Salina briefed Claire and Katie on what to expect.

"He's grown up a nice guy, actually a real gentleman, but he knows his own mind and what he needs to protect it, and he treats the synthesizer as a necessary evil."

Claire was concerned. "Still?"

"It's what you told me after your previous meeting with him. Frankly, I'm torn about this because what I want to know is what he sees that we don't, and the last thing I want to do is interfere in a way that obscures his abilities." Salina had a rueful expression. "Truth is that the tables have turned. Mostly, he directs our conversation, asking me for information on assorted topics."

"Such as?"

Salina thought a minute. "Evolutionary biology, the placebo effect, neural networks. Lately he's been asking about various religions. Oh, and he loves music, particularly Bach—I bring an MP3 player . . . I do the best I can."

Again, she looked Claire directly in the eye. "I'm perfectly happy with this role reversal. He knows best what's good for him."

Katie had been listening intently. Now she smiled and put a hand on Salina's shoulder. "I know exactly what you're saying, and if that is the case, he's going to love what we're going to try to do tomorrow."

Now Salina was confused. "What do you mean?"

Claire jumped in. "We're going to ask him if he wants to connect to someone who might think more like he does."

"How?"

"By asking him to reach out to this man."

"Again, how?"

"By using the powers we already know he possesses."

"And this man knows that Bart is going to try to reach out to him?"

Claire laughed, "Not yet." Realizing that she was being a tease, she went on. "Look, this is a completely benign experiment, if it doesn't work, no harm, no foul, but if it does . . ." Claire and Katie went on to explain what they were asking Bart to do. At the end, Claire cocked her head at Salina. "Well?"

Noting Salina's hesitancy, Claire made a decision. "I haven't told you what we're planning because the only way to keep a secret is not tell anybody." Seeing Salina's expression, Claire hurried on. "Of course, I'm completely confident you'd never slip up, but I'm thinking about other circumstances.

A veteran of the National Security Agency, Salina understood. "You mean duress?"

"Unfortunately, yes, that's a non-zero possibility. Think about those Russian mercenaries." Claire took a deep breath. "That said, I've never felt right keeping you in the dark. So, here's the deal . . ." and Claire laid out the plan.

After she finished, Salina relaxed and smiled. "Definitely worth a shot."

Ndokanda, Seraphime, and Salina accompanied Claire and Katie until they were about half a kilometer shy of the bai where the two women were to meet Bart. Claire was carrying the backpack with the voice synthesizer. Ndokanda handed Katie a flare gun. Salina motioned toward the gun. "That's for you to use if there's an emergency—very unlikely here, the animals here are all sweethearts. Even the leopards are chill—at least about humans."

Claire looked at Salina. "Are you OK with the plan? You reintroduce me to Bart and introduce Katie, and then drop back."

Claire glanced at Katie. "Ready?"

Katie was almost trembling with anticipation. She stretched. "Haven't felt this way since I ate some Peyote buttons back at Berkeley."

Salina got up. "Best if I lead the way."

# 24 REACHING IN, REACHING OUT

THE THREE WOMEN WALKED SLOWLY ALONG THE ELEPHANT trail. They walked in silence, but their progress was marked by noisy chatter of a group of *Cercopithecus* monkeys, as well as rustles in the brush as curious animals came forward to see these strange bipeds. "See that," said Salina pointing to a red river hog that had stopped walking across the trail to stare at them, "that's one of the most hunted animals in Africa. That it's not running away tells you that no one comes into this forest."

"That's reassuring," said Claire absently. She and Katie were in a different place than Salina. Both were pumped with adrenaline, hyperaware of their surroundings and contemplating whether what they were about to try was sublime or ridiculous.

As they walked, Salina kept up the chatter pointing out different trees, and what animals eat their fruits—"That's *Myrianthus arboreus*, gorillas eat the kernels of the fruit; they're delicious. Oh, and there's *Autranella congoensis*, also tasty." She looked concerned when she saw a copse of fallen trees. "Bad sign. They're *Gilbertiodendron dewevrei*, a tree extremely sensitive to drought. Might be a sign that the northern edge of the rainforest is drying out."

Katie pointed to a large black-and-yellow bird sitting on a branch with an almost comically disproportionate beak. "What's that?"

The bird saw them and made a high-pitched alarm call that sounded like an ack-ack gun played at 78 rpms. Salina looked at the bird. "Don't worry silly, we're not going to hurt you." Then she turned to Katie.

"That's a Pied Hornbill. Once pretty common in this part of Africa."

The trail turned sharply to the left, and Salina held up a hand for them to stop. "There he is." They were standing on the edge of a large bai, and Salina was pointing about one hundred yards to the left, where a half-grown male elephant stood, serenely swaying his trunk, and watching them approach. Various storks, cranes, and smaller wading birds were scattered throughout the bai, and at the far end, where the bai and forest met, a herd of elephants were gathered. Bart raised his trunk in greeting as the three picked their way across the mud and ground cover to meet him.

Bart waited patiently while Salina set up the synthesizer. Once Salina gave a thumbs up, Bart looked at Claire, "Hi Mom, I'm glad you're back." Claire was so choked up she couldn't talk, so she came forward to give him a hug, problematic since he was now seven feet tall at the shoulder. Bart wrapped his trunk around her and gave her a gentle squeeze.

After a moment, Salina gestured toward Katie. "And this is Katie. Remember I told you she was coming with Claire?"

Bart emitted a series of low rumbles, and the synthesizer came to life. "Yes, welcome to my world." Bart bowed his head briefly.

Katie beamed. "Hi Bart, I'm so glad to finally meet you."

Computer assisted pleasantries over, Salina patted Bart and took her leave. Claire cleared her throat. "OK Bart, first I want to apologize for not coming more often, but I hope you understand it's because my number one concern is your safety."

Bart rumbled and the synthesizer spoke. "I knew that. The armed men made that clear."

Katie watched these exchanges, fascinated. Even with the limitations of the synthesizer, something of Bart's personality was getting through. *Quite the charmer*, Katie thought.

Claire went on. "We never have enough time, so please forgive me if I go fast, but I want to tell you about something that will answer your question about where you come from."

Bart's giant ears flapped forward in anticipation. Claire continued. "But, before getting into that, Salina told me that you would like to limit using the synthesizer or using words."

Bart cocked his head. "That's correct."

"Could you tell me why?"

Bart rumbled slowly pausing now and then, so that the synthesizer could keep up. "The synthesizer enables us to talk to each other, which is wonderful, but the more I use it, and think in words, the more it interferes with the way I was born to think. I've learned to isolate that way of thinking. Still, there are ways I like to use the synthesizer."

Katie and Claire both looked confused. "Use differently?"

"Yes, all it does is translate the sounds I can make into sounds people can hear that are like your words, correct? So, it can also generate other sounds. If you let me use the synthesizer, I can show you."

"Of course," Claire gestured toward the instrument.

Bart gently used the tip of his trunk to hit record, and made an extended series of rumbles. Then he hit play, and out of the synthesizer came the sounds of a piano playing what Claire instantly recognized as one of Bach's Goldberg Variations.

Katie clapped her hands excitedly. "How did you do that?"

Bart tapped the machine again to resume translate mode. "Sounds and waves are my world. Music is a bridge between our worlds. Listen." He again tapped record, and then proceeded to make another, longer, series of rumbles. He then tapped play, and their part of the bai and surrounding rainforest were filled with a variation on what they had just heard, only this variation was so intricate, complex, and rich, that neither Katie nor Claire could imagine the dexterity and control needed to play those phrases on a piano, or even if they could be played on a piano. It was also deeply satisfying at a level beyond words.

Thrilled, Claire just stared in silence for a few seconds after it finished. When she could talk, she asked simply. "I don't know that piece, is it Bach?"

"It's Bart's version of Bach."

Claire was puzzled. "Has Salina heard this?"

"I don't know. I did it when she left the synthesizer one day. I think she was not feeling well."

Claire looked at the synthesizer. "I can't believe you got those sounds out of that machine."

"There was more, but the synthesizer does have its limitations."

Almost reverently, Katie said, "That was a wonderful bridge between our worlds."

Bart looked at her with interest. "When Mom was last here, I knew I faced a choice. I could grow up in your world, or grow into the world I inherited. I can't do both."

Claire had no hesitation. "Bart, we would much rather have you see the full flowering of your abilities rather than try to squeeze you into ours. That's why we are here today. Katie why don't you explain what we hope to do."

Speaking slowly and clearly, Katie told Bart about the jadeite, about the reactions of Flo and the other elephants, and how Claire and she thought the jadeite contained a message from Bart's ancestors. Then she told Bart that there were people who devoted their lives to trying to think in ways more similar to his world than the world of objects and rules. She mentioned one holy man in particular who might be receptive if Bart used his mysterious powers to reach out to him through whatever through-waves or fields accessible to Bart might connect them. As she spoke, Bart stirred; his eyes becoming more intent. Katie brought out pictures of the weathered, old monk and described his monastery, high up in the Himalayas nearly 6,000 miles to the north and east.

When she finished, Bart turned and faced northeast. He was silent, though the two women sensed a thrumming. Without being told they turned and faced in the direction Bart was facing, and then, again without being told, they bowed their heads in unison, putting their fingers together in the universal gesture of respect. They held this position for what seemed an eternity, slowing and deepening their breathing. The noises of the rainforest receded, replaced by their own pulse, which seemed to synchronize with the pulse of the universe. Neither had studied meditation, but, accepting Bart's all-encompassing psychic embrace, they felt tension ebb from their bodies. Nor did they have Rencho's decades of preparation and discipline to receive the full richness of whatever subtle perturbations of the universe's connective waves Bart was emitting, but colors flooded their minds, and a flush of euphoria swept over them. Then, the colors gently faded, and their surroundings and the sounds of the rainforest came back into focus, even as the euphoria stayed with them.

Both women looked at Bart in awe. Bart didn't need to tell them. His message had gotten through.

# 25 NIGHT VISION IN DAYTIME

RENCHO, A VERY OLD AND WEATHERED BUDDHIST MONK, SAT
on a rock high on the slopes above the Pho Chhu River in Tibet and
watched the two Europeans walking toward his home, the Chuku
Monastery. They were still several miles away. The two women
were laboring in the thin air at nearly 16,000 feet above sea level.
"Watched," was probably not the right word as Rencho was observing the approaching strangers through the eyes of a Tibetan Golden
Eagle that was surfing the updrafts along the sides of the river valley. Rencho had spent decades meditating and communing with this
eagle, but it was only late in life that he had attained the inner calm
that allowed the monk access to the panoramas that were the eagle's
daily purview.

Nor were the approaching women really strangers, although they
had never met the monk. Their visit had been presaged by a vision,
more like a waking dream, that the monk had experienced weeks earlier. Deep in meditation, he had been surprised by a series of profound
waves that seemed to wash through his body and brain, producing a
deep exaltation. Rencho was unsettled at first because the waves were
as powerful as a seizure, and alien to anything the monk had experienced even after weeks of intense meditation and prayer. He pulled
back from his meditation and made himself a pot of butter tea. After
a few sips, he put down his cup, and waited to see what might happen
next. The waves gently subsided and for a moment there was only quiet.
Rencho calmed his pulse, and, surrendering to the extraordinary disci-

pline he had developed over a long life of prayer and meditation, he let his senses quiet and his mind open.

Imperceptibly, he entered what seemed to be a lucid dream state although he was still awake. Whatever it was, it was infinitely more vibrant than the dreams released by the Vajrayana techniques of yoga. He found himself in a place far away. In exquisite detail he felt himself in a rainforest clearing. He could hear African grey parrots and hornbills chattering in the surrounding giant trees. Staring at him (or whatever avatar had placed him in the scene) was an elephant, an elephant unlike any that Rencho had seen during his one trip to India in his youth. This elephant, which looked half-grown, had a pronounced forehead, and radiated an awareness beyond intelligence. The elephant nodded and the vista broadened. In the dream state, he could see the two women that he would later see on the trail. They were with the elephant in the clearing. They turned to him and smiled as though they could see him. Then, bowing their heads, they put their fingertips together in the universal gesture of prayer and respect. Their eyes were asking for something, though as yet he did not know what.

The scene slowly dissolved into a kaleidoscope of colors that resolved into a slowly pulsing and shimmering mandala that, too, gently faded. As his surroundings came back into focus, he felt a profoundly moving sense of euphoria and well-being. At eighty-eight years of age, he finally felt what it was to be whole. He had no words to adequately describe what he had just experienced, nor did he need them. He knew it was good, and that it was momentous. Moreover, even though Rencho did not know what this visit portended, it somehow felt destined, and in some sense the purpose of his many decades of meditation and prayer. Rencho, who had not received a visitor from the outside world in over fifty years, decided that he would be open to whatever resulted from this visitation. Then he laughed, a deep resonant, throaty, multi-dimensional laugh that seemed to bubble up from the center of the cosmos.

Each day that followed, at the same time of day, Rencho received a message from that elephant, though these waking dreams were far less intense. He knew that they were from the elephant because that first vision had dissolved into an intense blue dot, as did these. He recognized that he was being asked to be patient—and prepared.

# 26 DEV MEETS A GOD

ONCE AGAIN, DEV FLEW TO BANGUI, THE CAPITAL OF THE Central African Republic. He was met on the tarmac by a fixer and the two mercenaries as he stepped out into the sweltering heat at Bangui airport. It was nine in the morning, and, already, the heat and humidity were suffocating. As his second trip, he knew that being met by mercenaries was not a courtesy but an absolute necessity. Without them, his chances of getting through customs without being robbed or detained were slim to none. Arrayed around the periphery of the airport were rough looking white soldiers. They had shoulder patch insignias featuring a skull in the center.

He jerked his head, "Who are they?"

Andre had a half smile on his face. "Wagner Group. Keep going, and don't look at them. The last thing we want is to attract their attention."

Dev looked away and glanced toward a mass of shanties and tents beyond the fence that were home to thousands of internally displaced refugees. Several times over the past few years, mobs had overrun the airport, shutting it down. As soon as Dev debarked, the Transteppe plane fired up its engines and headed back for the runway to *didi mau* it out of Dodge.

For several decades, the Central African Republic has set the standard for failed states: religious wars, tribal violence, rebellions, crippling strikes, coups, corruption, and sheer chaos, CAR had it all, often several crises at once, and periods of peace were as rare as a black rhinoceros. The French pulled its Legion out in the 1990s, but had been forced to return several times as a rotating cast of tin pot dictators assumed control, looted what they could, and then hightailed it to neighboring countries before rallying for their next go round. Now, the foreign legion had been replaced by the Wagner Group mercenaries. The cycle continued, the difference being that the Wagner mercenaries reveled in brutality and brazenly looted the country's mineral riches.

The three former legionnaires Rob hired to protect Mbembe were veterans of several of the earlier French interventions and knew the ropes, and, more importantly, the names of the local airport officials whose palms needed greasing to spirit Dev from the airport to Mbembe. Flanked by the mercenaries and led by a local fixer (ironically a former missionary), they marched through the empty customs hall, waved through by the agents. Dev was travelling light, one bag and a backpack that contained a priceless cargo.

As they were going through the dilapidated arrivals hall, they passed a group of lean, sullen-looking men wearing torn T-shirts, probably waiting to prey on the unlucky visitor who didn't have a fixer and guards. One stepped belligerently toward Andre, the mercenary to Dev's left, and challenged in French, "Why do you carry weapons in my country?"

Andre smiled, "J'ai peur des rats." He looked relaxed, but he slipped his hand toward the trigger. At first, the challenger looked like he was going to escalate things, but then cocked his head with a toothy smile and said, "Moi aussi." Andre tipped his beret, and they walked briskly to the SUV where the third mercenary waited with the car idling.

It was a simple matter to set up a plausible pretext for Dev to visit Mbembe as Zoe would naturally want a trusted vet to make sure Flo and the other rescued elephants were doing OK. It was not a simple matter to get Dev there with the jadeite without going through a metal detector. Sergei, as usual, thought of a simple, elegant solution. As he put it, "If the problem is that a small rock will stand out going through a screening device at an airport, the solution is to put the rock among many, much bigger rocks, that don't go through airport screening." He explained that rock samples are regularly shipped between Transteppe and the sophisticated labs at its Canadian headquarters. Dev could go along because Helen Hayden was a supporter of Boisbeaux, and making a stop in Africa to drop off Dev could be written off as a contribution in kind to the sanctuary.

Sergei's idea required that they bring Helen into the loop on what Claire and Katie were planning to do. She was still a major Transteppe shareholder. She was skeptical at first, saying, "You do realize that if this goes awry and gets out, you'll be exposed to a whole new level of ridicule." (Helen knew about the lambasting Claire had endured when the ancient elephant bones first became known.) After Claire explained Bart's aversion to relying on words, and his uncanny ability to affect things at a distance, Helen warmed to the idea.

"What about Will?" Helen asked, referring to Keerbrock.

"At the get-go, he told Katie that he wouldn't support publishing anything on the stone, just because it would invite ridicule. Katie took that as a green light to use whatever might be the most productive way to understand its messages—regardless of whether it fits the empirical method."

Helen chuckled. "Keeping him out of this until you have results makes perfect sense—but for health reasons. He'd have a stroke somewhere between the words ESP and Buddhist monk."

With Helen's agreement, they didn't waste any time putting the plan into action.

Once past the outskirts of the city and on the road to Mbembe, the two mercenaries relaxed. The one riding shotgun pulled up a cooler and offered Dev a Castel beer. Dev accepted gratefully. Fluent in French, Dev struck up a conversation. When they learned he was a veterinarian, they peppered him with questions about their dogs and cats They didn't know about the jadeite, and Dev was not about to tell them.

It was 3:00 p.m. by the time they arrived at the embarkation point at the edge of the swamp. Salina and Ndokanda were there to meet them. Needing to set up camp in Mbembe before sunset, they introduced themselves, and then they quickly loaded the dugout and were underway. As they were pushing off, Andre gave them a cooler with three cold beers. Ndokanda waved off his beer—he'd seen what alcohol had done to Pygmy villages where residents had little ability to metabolize alcohol. He pulled out a joint and, smiling, showed it to Andre, who laughed and told Salina and Dev to battle it out for the third beer.

As they paddled slowly across the swamp in their wobbly dugout, the delicious air, the delicious water ("sure you can drink it," Salina had said, handing him a cup), and the sounds and smells of Africa at its most natural, saturated Dev's senses, and tensions ebbed away. With a wide grin, he spread his arms. "This," he said to Salina, "is better than any five-star safari." Salina translated what he had just said into Lingala for Ndokanda who broke into a wide smile and gave Dev a thumb's up.

As they paddled, a large crocodile surfaced nearby and eyed them curiously as it swam lazily, parallel to the dugout. Ndokanda kept paddling steadily and made a sharp whistling noise. The croc turned away. Salina pointed to the animal. "That's a slender-snouted crocodile. That it's so big tells you how little hunting there is in these parts. There're only a few of those bad boys left."

Dev had brought with him several boxes of long-lasting canned provisions for Salina, as well as eggs (which keep for a surprisingly long time in the rainforest heat), sausage, jerkies of various sorts, and a whole bunch of chilis and other spices. He also brought two cartons of Marlboros for Salia should she need them as bribes at the impromptu roadblocks that often sprang up going and coming to Mbembe.

Seraphime met them at the far shore and he and Ndokanda cut vines to make straps as they expertly distributed the weight of the packages on their backs. Dev was in awe at how much these diminutive men could carry. He insisted on carrying the knapsack that held the stone. As they walked to the campsite Dev wheeled at every sound, peppering Salina with questions. Seraphime had already started a fire before he met them, and, as he brought it back to life, Salina prepared their standard camp meal of rice and piquant sauce. After the meal, the two guides went off to smoke, and Salina and Dev settled around the fire to talk about the stone and what would happen the next day.

Katie and Claire had thoroughly briefed Dev on Bart and what they hoped to learn by giving him the stone. They told Dev about the extraordinary reaction the stone has elicited in the Boisbeaux elephants, and about their hope that Bart might be able to convey what was causing such strong reactions, if not directly through the synthesizer, then through his mysterious powers of projection. Dev, a born skeptic, thought it a long shot, but then acknowledged to himself that Bart himself was something of a miracle, and decided that he wasn't going to prejudge what Bart could and couldn't do. He asked Salina for her thoughts on the project.

She looked down, "Do you believe in magic?"

"Not really."

She looked Dev squarely in the eye, not challenging, but direct. "I'm going to ask you that question again after you meet Bart."

Salina and Dev left at first light for the bai where they would meet Bart. They needed to get there early because Tibet was seven hours ahead, and Claire and Katie had said that mid-afternoon would be the best time to try to reach out to Rencho.

It was 6:30 a.m., and the forest was just waking up, when the two entered the clearing. Dev sensed Bart before he saw him, sensed in that he felt a subtle tingling wash over him. Salina was watching him closely. He gave her a quizzical look.

"I told Bart you were coming today. I think he's just taking a reading on who you are."

Dev felt his louche, cavalier facade falling away as he realized that he was about to encounter a being who could literally see right through him.

"I also told Bart that without you he wouldn't be here, so don't be nervous."

Dev gave a quick smile. "Nervous is definitely on the table . . . what's the etiquette for meeting a god?"

Salina was relieved, this was going to go OK. "I know you're kidding, but he might just be that."

"I wasn't kidding."

"Just let me introduce you. Then I'll set up the synthesizer and you take it from there."

In the distance they could see Bart. He wasn't alone. A leopard was sitting calmly near Bart, and he was allowing her two cubs to chase his trunk. Salina stared open mouthed. "This is new," she said. Dev dumbstruck, just stared, any doubts that this could be a normal interaction erased.

After a few more moments, Bart made a soft rumble, and the leopard mom got up and started trotting toward the forest edge with the cubs tumbling and racing to follow her. Far to the left, at the edge of the forest, Dev and Salina could see Flo and the other elephants. Bart turned toward Salina and Dev and briefly bowed his head, a signal for them to approach.

Salina led the way. Bart waited calmly while Salina set up the voice synthesizer. Having switched it on, she gave Bart a thumbs up. She gestured to Dev. "Hi Bart, this is Dev, the veterinarian I told you about."

Bart looked at Dev for a few seconds and then made a series of rumbles. "Hello Dev. Welcome to Mbembe. I know I'm in your debt."

Dev waved a hand, embarrassed. "Not at all. I'm so happy to finally meet you." He looked at Salina confused.

She shook her head, "Don't worry, Bart can understand English. He needs the machine to generate words."

Salina turned to Bart. "When we were approaching, we saw that you have new friends." Saline gestured with her head in the direction of where the leopards had gone.

Bart rumbled. "She is my friend, also my eyes. And I love all babies." "Does she have a name?"

Bart tapped the synthesizer with his trunk. "She doesn't use words."

Dev was fascinated and wanted to know more, but he also knew why he was here, and that time was precious. He pulled off the knapsack, and retrieved the padded pouch that held the stone. He put on a pair of gloves and pulled the stone from the pouch. Approaching Bart deferentially, he held out the jadeite. "I believe this belongs to you."

Several things happened at once. Bart gently took the jadeite with his trunk. Once he made contact, the air virtually sizzled. Salina and Dev felt a strong wave pulse through them, something like a shock wave, and a few seconds later they heard trumpeting from the edge of the forest where Bart's herd waited. Bart went rigid. He gently put the stone down. "Mom and the others know what you gave me. They want to come."

Dev, still in the thrall of the pulse that went through him could barely speak. "Can you ask them to wait for a while?"

Bart turned to the herd and, after a few seconds, turned back to Dev. Whatever he had done, it was on a part of the wave continuum that was inaccessible to humans. "They will wait. We can begin."

# 27 THEY ARE EXPECTED

CLAIRE AND KATIE WERE AWAKENED BY A TIMID TAP ON THEIR door just after dawn. "It's time," said a voice through the door, "should I restart your fire?"

"Yes, thank you!" said Claire. She was freezing in the dawn chill. A Tibetan woman came in with a pan full of hot coals. She put some twigs and branches on top of the coals and soon there was a brightly blazing fire in the small wood stove.

"Breakfast ready now," the woman said bowing, before she left the room.

Katie, wearing long johns from head to foot, sat up, stretched, and began rummaging in her backpack. "What do we wear when meeting a holy man?"

"Long sleeves, long pants, nothing flashy. At least that's what the guidebook says."

The guesthouse was primitive, but neat, and their room was simple in the extreme. "I'll be ready in a jiff," said Katie disappearing into the bathroom.

After Claire dressed, they went to the small breakfast room where they were joined by their translator, Chodrak. In preparing for this trip, Claire and Katie had devoted considerable time to thinking about how they would find a translator. They were stymied because anyone reachable via the internet was immediately off-limits. They decided to trust fate, and try to find someone once in Tibet. On arriving at the guesthouse, they told the owner that Rencho was expecting their visit and asked if he could recommend a translator. The owner's eyes widened at the mention of Rencho. He looked at the two women long and hard for a moment.

"His holiness has never accepted visitors, but if you are expected, the monks will let you see him." He paused a minute and then recommended Chodrak as translator. A devout village layperson, Chodrak delivered firewood to the monastery, and spoke English, German, and French. Claire asked the owner to invite Chodrak for breakfast.

When the two women entered, Chodrak rose, smiled, and placed his two hands together in greeting. Because they were going to the monastery, the young man had dressed in a traditional Tibetan robe, closed by a cloth sash that went over his left shoulder and under his right arm. Claire and Katie responded to Chodrak's greeting with gestures in kind and introduced themselves. "Why don't we talk over breakfast," Chodrak said in mildly accented English, and they sat down. "I'd suggest you fill up as we have a 10k hike to the monastery." Breakfast is a big meal in Tibet, and before them was a feast of barley porridge, several types of bread, and tea.

Over breakfast they talked about logistics and etiquette. Chodrak listened intently, and spoke carefully. Claire had been waiting for the right moment to bring up a sensitive and critical part of their introductory conversation. Listening to Chodrak, she thought she saw a way in.

"How did you learn so many languages—the internet?"

Chodrak looked embarrassed. "Actually, no. I don't have a computer. Very few foreigners come here, but a few that did were kind enough to give me language books."

Claire and Katie exchanged a look. This was good. Katie gave Chodrak a wide smile. "Clearly you have a gift."

Taking day packs, they left for their trek to the monastery. The path was little more than a trail, and over the six miles they would gain fifteen hundred feet. That sounded easy enough, but they were starting at 14,700 feet, higher than either of them had been in their lives. Katie and Claire had spent a week in Thimphu, Bhutan before travelling to Tibet in order to acclimate, but there still was a significant difference between 7,600 feet and the 16,200-foot altitude of the monastery.

The landscape possessed a geometric grandeur. It was starkly beautiful, but it was the scale that was mesmerizing. They were surrounded by bare rock with intermittent patches of grass on the flatter areas. In the distance they could see the snow wind blowing off the peak of Mount Kailash, perhaps the holiest mountain in all of Asia. A four-sided mountain, it rose from a high plain apart from the Himalayas, with its faces looking out in the cardinal directions of the compass. Its foothills are the source of four of Asia's greatest rivers, including the Indus and the Brahmaputra. In part because of the regard in which it has been held, the mountain had never been climbed.

As they walked, Chodrak chatted softly about the pilgrims and adventurous tourists that came to visit the five monasteries arrayed around the mountain, and the rigors of the three-day trek around the base of the mountain. Then he went quiet. He seemed to be gathering courage to ask something. Claire glanced at him. "Something you want to ask Chodrak?"

Chodrak looked flustered. "Yes, if you don't think a question is impertinent."

Claire had no idea where this was going, but she smiled, "Please, go ahead."

"Thank you. It's just that when Dache [the owner of the guesthouse] approached me, he said that Rencho was 'expecting you to arrive.'"

"That's right."

"That confused me."

Claire was interested. "Why is that?"

"Because Rencho is among the holiest monks in all of Tibet. He has no computer, and, has no communication with the outside world. How did you contact him?"

Claire thought a moment as she weighed how to answer this simple question. "I can't really explain it, but I think you will see, when we get to the monastery. You will see that Rencho is expecting us."

There was then silence, and Chodrak looked troubled.

"Is there something else?" Claire asked.

Chodrak looked down. "I don't want to pry," he said, "but Rencho has not received a visitor in my lifetime. Are you sure he will see you?"

Claire smiled. "I'm not certain, but I believe so. In any case, we will find out when we get there, yes?"

That seemed to reassure Chodrak. "Of course."

Having lived entirely in this remote, high-altitude redoubt where the spiritual is omnipresent and miracles discussed over yak-butter tea, Chodrak readily accepted this explanation.

A bit further up the trail, Katie pointed excitedly to the sky, "Look—an eagle."

The great bird looked down at them as it serenely rode the updrafts along a ridge line to their left. Chodrak looked up and his eyes widened. To their surprise, Claire and Katie saw tears form at the edges of his eyes. Chodrak beamed. "Yes," he said, "You are expected."

# 28 BLIND MEN (AND WOMEN) FEELING AN ELEPHANT

AT THE ENTRANCE TO THE MONASTERY, THEY WERE MET BY A layperson. Chodrak spoke briefly with the man in Tibetan. They were ushered into a spare, stone-walled antechamber. The layperson pointed to simple benches and invited them to sit while he sought a monk. A few moments later, a young monk appeared. He smiled and bowed at Claire and Katie and then had a brief conversation with Chodrak. His brow furrowed in consternation at something Chodrak said. He looked over at Claire and Katie, gave a slight bow, and then disappeared through a door. Chodrak seemed quickened with anticipation, but didn't say anything to Claire and Katie about his conversation. The women sat in silence. Claire looked at her watch and then at Katie. "I think we've got an hour. This is getting tight."

Katie shrugged. "Not sure there is anything we can do to speed things up."

A few minutes later, the young monk reappeared and spoke to Chodrak, who turned to the women. "It's appropriate to leave your shoes here. Please, let's follow this monk."

As austere as the antechamber was, the opposite awaited them on the other side of the door. As they walked through a corridor, everywhere there was an extravagance of color and design. Benign Buddhas arrayed along the walls looked down on them, murals depicting scenes from long past events and miracles were painted on the wooden walls, sculptures and bronzes lay on tables, and every doorway they went through had intricate geometric designs painted on the framing. The saturation of color and image was almost too much to take in, an accumulation of meticulous artistic ingenuity dating back eight hundred years. They climbed stairs and, as the monk led them upward, the decorations became more elemental and sparser. They climbed a final set of stairs, and the monk gently bade them to wait while he entered a courtyard on the roof of the monastery. He reappeared after a moment, and then stepped to the side and invited them to enter the courtyard. He then bowed and retreated.

Chodrak ushered the two women through the stone entryway to the courtyard. Sitting cross-legged on the far side of the courtyard sat an old monk. His eyes blazed with merriment. On either side of him, incense burned in silver censers. Claire detected scents of sandalwood and cedar, but there were clearly other woods and herbs in the mixture. Chodrak bowed and, with his eyes lowered, said a few words in Tibetan. Claire and Katie bowed modestly as well. Rencho beckoned them to approach, and then to sit in front of him. His eyes radiating kindness, he looked at the two women for a long moment and then said a few words in Tibetan, and laughed, a bubbling, resonant laugh that seemed to come from everywhere within the old man. Chodrak looked confused, but then turned to the women. "He said it's nice to see you again."

Claire and Katie broke out into smiles. Still smiling, Claire said, "I'm so happy our message got through to you."

They were all silent for a moment, then Rencho raised an eyebrow. Claire looked briefly at her watch and then turned to Chodrak. "Please listen carefully. Please tell his holiness that the same messenger will reach out to him in a few minutes." She waited while Chodrak translated. Rencho's eyes brightened, and he nodded. Claire continued, "Please ask his holiness if he will describe what he sees as he experiences it, and please ask him if it is permissible for my colleague," she nodded at Katie, "to take notes."

After Chodrak translated, Rencho looked thoughtfully at Claire and Katie. Then he spoke and Chodrak translated. "I agree. It is only right; this would not be happening but for you. But please be aware, speaking may take me away from the experience, and if I fear that is happening, I suggest that I stop describing and speak afterward so as not to interrupt."

Claire had expected something like this. "Of course, your holiness. Whatever you think best."

After hearing the translation, Rencho smiled in gratitude and said a few short words. Chodrak turned to the women. "He said, 'and now I must prepare.'"

Katie discreetly took out a note pad and pen. She and Claire had agreed not to use any recording devices—the last thing they wanted to do was risk interfering in what might happen.

Claire whispered to Chodrak. "We wait."

Rencho, attuned to the intangible flows of the universe by years of training, sensed it first. His eyelids, half-closed, fluttered briefly. Claire, Katie, and Chodrak had all slowed their breathing and tried to empty their minds.

Claire experienced a subtle, almost imperceptible tingling that washed pleasantly through her body. The tingling became a slow pulsing, and a shimmering curtain of colors filled her mind, her very own aurora borealis. Beyond the curtain lay something amorphous, something she could not grasp or see, but she sensed that something momentous was going on behind that diaphanous, ever-shifting veil. She dared not move or look up for fear of breaking the spell. There were sounds too, a fuzzy thumping, and one distinct, brief, and quickly fading note that sounded like a distant, anguished elephant trumpet. Gripped by the spell—for that is what it felt like—she felt a series of emotions wash through her: awe, pure elation, but then pure devastation and loss. It was as though she was an instrument being played by some alien being, a being that knew how to orchestrate her entire repertoire of senses and feelings, and she also knew that whatever images and messages were being conveyed, she was not completely receiving—her brain and being were not sufficiently developed and organized to receive them. As the curtain of color dissolved and the pulsing returned to subtle tremors, she prayed that Rencho's years of meditation had prepared him to receive what she could not.

Once the spell was broken, Claire looked around. Katie had a half smile on her face. Chodrak looked awestruck and nervous. Rencho looked completely at peace. He was breathing slowly, and his eyes were closed. Claire thought about what had just transpired. She turned to Katie, "We're," she gestured with her head toward Chodrak and Katie, "the blind people trying to describe an elephant. Maybe Rencho," she nodded toward the monk, "has the training to actually see what we couldn't."

Katie was still smiling, "Maybe I couldn't see everything, but I was in a different place, and it was wonderful."

Claire turned to Chodrak, "When his holiness opens his eyes, please ask him whether he can describe what he just experienced."

Chodrak nodded, and then asked Claire, "What just happened?"

"A god tried to show us his world."

Chodrak looked at Claire, trying to determine whether she was kidding. His ruminations were cut short as Rencho breathed a deep sigh and opened his eyes. He was smiling. He started speaking in Tibetan, pausing to let Chodrak translate and catch up,

"In Buddhism we strive all our lives to free ourselves from wanting more. I just discovered I'm a bad Buddhist. I want more."

# 29 THE AWAKENING

RENCHO LOOKED TOWARD ONE OF THE ARCHES THAT surrounded the roof courtyard. Immediately, a young monk appeared, bowing as he approached the revered lama. Rencho said a few soft words. The monk bowed and retreated, and Rencho waited in silence for a few moments until the young monk returned. First, he brought Rencho some rice paper and drawing implements. Then he fetched some cups of butter tea which he placed in front of the guests. Rencho gestured for them to drink and took a sip of the tea himself.

He held up a finger, a universal gesture to wait. Then he picked up a fine brush and began to paint on the rice paper. Having finished sketching on one page, he picked up another piece of paper and began anew. Eventually he put the brush down, but did not show them what he had painted. He spoke a few words to Chodrak, and then nodded to the two women.

"His holiness expresses his gratitude for being chosen for this experience."

Rencho spoke some more.

"It was . . ." Chodrak seemed to be struggling to find the English word for what Rencho was saying. He drew a large circle with his hands.

"Encompassing?" ventured Claire.

"Yes, encompassing, thank you."

Claire's heart began to sink. If they were going to have to play charades, they were never going to get a full picture of what Rencho had experienced. It had been a gamble hoping that there wouldn't be too much signal lost in the daisy chain from the stone to Bart to Rencho to Chodrak to them, but it was beginning to look like that gamble was a losing bet. She smiled at Chodrak. "Take time to translate. It's important that we understand everything that his holiness says."

Rencho too seemed to understand Claire's consternation. He said a few words to Chodrak. "His holiness apologizes because there are things we experience that cannot be put in words and shouldn't be reduced to words."

Claire started. "He used the word 'reduced?'"

Chodrak said something to Rencho, who nodded. "Yes, reduced," said Chodrak.

This is what Bart had said in describing his reluctance to use the synthesizer. "Please tell his holiness that we understand that we are not equipped to share what he experienced. We just hope to learn about what we cannot experience ourselves."

Once Chodrak had translated, Rencho seemed pleased and nodded. He spoke briefly and Chodrak translated. "His holiness asks what you experienced?"

Though eager to hear Rencho, Claire had also been wanting to ask Katie about her experience, so she was happy for the question.

"Katie?"

Katie had a distant look in her eyes. She took two slow breaths and then answered pausing every now and then to let Chodrak catch up. "It was as though parts of my brain I didn't know existed had been awakened, but I was still half asleep. I felt as though I was in the grip of a seizure, and felt completely energized. And, in this state, I was transported . . ." she looked at Chodrak, "carried, somewhere strange. I felt that I was in the midst of momentous events that were around me but undefined as though I was embedded in some three-dimensional gauze." She looked frustrated—there was no way Chodrak knew the Tibetan word for gauze. "Maybe I passed through the veil of Maya." At the word Maya, Rencho looked up. "Colors became sounds and sounds became colors, shapes partially resolved, came together, and then dissolved. I was in the middle of all of it."

Claire watched Rencho carefully as Chodrak translated, wondering how much of what Katie had said had been accurately conveyed. To her surprise, Rencho smiled.

Chodrak turned to the women, looking down shyly. "I did the best translation I could. I was helped because I think I experienced exactly what Miss Katie did."

"Thank you, Chodrak," said Claire, "As did I. Please tell that to his holiness, and add that I did hear an elephant trumpet at one point."

Hearing that, Rencho looked at Claire with interest. He said something to Chodrak.

"That was their last cry."

"Their last cry?"

Chodrak and Rencho had some quick back and forth.

"Before their world ended."

Claire felt her pulse quicken. Rencho had seen what they couldn't! "Please ask his holiness to tell us about their world."

In response to Chodrak's translation, Rencho handed the first of his pages of sketches to Chodrak and gestured that he should pass it on to the women.

Claire and Katie bowed their appreciation, and then looked at the rice paper. Rencho had drawn a number of animals, using only black. Their eyes were immediately drawn to an elephant that looked like Bart. It had a pronounced forehead, a relatively small trunk, and very large ears. Rencho was an efficient and accomplished artist, and had, with relatively few strokes, created a tableau of the elephant with a number of very strange creatures arrayed around it. On one side of the elephant loomed a gigantic bird. It looked like an ostrich, but was clearly much larger. He'd also drawn what looked like a giant hare, and a diminutive goat. Rencho had also drawn an exceedingly strange animal. With short hind legs, long muscular forelegs ending in clawed toes, and a long-wide head, it looked like a cross between a giant sloth and a horse. Claire pointed to it and said softly to Katie, "Chalicotherium." Claire had become something of a student of ancient steppe fauna. Katie nodded.

What sent Claire and Katie reeling, however, was a small figure that looked human, but also had ape-like features such as an elongated jaw.

Claire and Katie looked at each other. Claire held the paper up. "Please ask his holiness if this is what he saw?"

After some back and forth, Chodrak said, "Yes, but his holiness says that he didn't see them, he was with them."

"With them?"

"Yes, for brief moments he was in their world. The animals were moving, they were doing things."

"Doing things?

This precipitated more back and forth between the men and Rencho gestured at Chodrak to retrieve his sketches. The two women couldn't see what Rencho was pointing to, but he seemed to be explaining something to Chodrak. Then he handed the drawing to Chodrak to return it to Katie and Claire. After returning the sketch, Chodrak spoke. "His holiness says that one scene was of perfect harmony. It was amid endless grasslands. Hanuman-like creatures," he pointed to the standing early human in Rencho's drawing, "were working with the giant birds. That monster," he pointed to the horse-sloth-like creature," used its claws to clear the grassland and open the soil. The monkey-men planted large seeds. Ganesh," he pointed to the elephant, "seemed to be the leader."

"Please ask his holiness if they used tools?"

More back and forth. Rencho handed Chodrak another sheet of his drawings which he looked at, and then passed on to the women.

Claire looked at the simple line drawing and gasped. Katie's eyes widened. They looked at each other. Sketched on the rice paper was a scene. The hominid-like creature that Rencho had sketched in the previous drawing was forcing what looked like a large bone into the bottom of a hole dug into the steppe. Rencho had drawn an emaciated elephant watching over the scene. He'd also drawn water coming out of the hollow center of the bone. The bone drawn by Rencho was an elephant ulna, identical to the bones that she, Sergei, and Rob had uncovered in a remote corner of the Transteppe concession in Kazakhstan over a decade earlier. She now knew why Bart's ancient ancestors had arrayed those elephant ulnas 5.3 million years ago. Keerbrock had earlier guessed this was the case after observing the reactions of the Boisbeaux elephants, and now his intuition was confirmed.

Rencho spoke briefly with a sorrowful expression. Chodrak translated, "His holiness says that this was the end of their world. He was there."

Rencho handed another drawing to Chodrak. It depicted a ritual of some sort. The ancient elephants were in a circle around an array of ulnas. At the periphery of the circle were a group of hominid-like creatures, standing upright, their heads bowed with respect. The landscape was desolate.

Claire looked at the drawing and sighed. She was almost overcome with dizziness. The array of bones looked exactly like the array Sergei had uncovered on the Transteppe concession. It was clear now; the jadeite was delivering a message as to the meaning of the array, a message that was finally received more than five million years later, and which started a chain of events that had ultimately led to the resurrection of their kind.

Katie looked up with a sad smile. "They knew the end was near and left a record that only a highly intelligent species could understand."

Chodrak translated and Rencho held up a hand. He said a few sentences and nodded to Chodrak. "His holiness says that perhaps he experienced this more fully than others, but he had the sense that there was so much more that he wasn't getting. His holiness says that being in each scene awakened all his senses. It was overwhelming and that he would be . . ." Chodrak searched for the English words, ". . . transported into their midst, but that there were periods between the scenes where he felt something was going on that was beyond his ability to feel or understand."

Claire looked at Katie who nodded; it was time to go. "Please tell his holiness that we are deeply appreciative of his willingness to participate in this…" Claire searched for the right word, "…this experience. There is much good that can come from this. And please ask him if there is anything else about the experience that he could tell us before we go."

After Chodrak spoke, Rencho smiled at the two women and bowed his head, and then spoke a few more words. "His holiness says that he is in your debt for opening those gates to their world. He blesses you and wishes you a safe journey." After Chodrak finished, Rencho said a few more words. "His holiness says that there was one final, strange scene. The elephants were gathered in a circle around a stone that shined. The elephants faded from that scene until only the shining stone remained. It was more than shining; it seemed to be smoldering. His holiness wonders whether you can tell him what the importance of that stone is?"

Katie gave Claire a blazing look. She felt her heart would burst. "Please tell his holiness that the shining stone *is* the gateway to their world."

Hearing this, Rencho nodded and smiled. The two women got up and bowed toward Rencho. He bowed in return, and they slowly backed out of the courtyard. Just as they were leaving, Chodrak gasped. Claire and Katie turned and saw that an eagle had wheeled into the courtyard and landed in the spot they had just vacated. Rencho seemed deep in meditation.

They retrieved their shoes and began the walk back to the village; both were too overwhelmed by the experience to discuss what they had just been through. Chodrak knew enough not to break the spell. Katie saw an eagle, perhaps that same eagle, perhaps not, riding the evening updraft along the ridge line. With tears of happiness streaming down her face, she smiled and pointed the great bird out to Claire. "I think Rencho has sent a protector."

# 30 WORLDS BEYOND WORDS

AS KATIE AND CLAIRE WERE WALKING BACK TO THE guesthouse, Dev and Salina were sitting quietly in the clearing in Mbembe, patiently waiting to see whether Bart would communicate what he had experienced. They had felt the overwhelming energy field that enveloped them when Bart picked up the jadeite, but their experience had been entirely different than that of those in the monastery in Tibet. After Bart put down the stone, he simply stood there. Even though Salina had become an expert in reading Bart's moods, she was perplexed by what she was seeing in the aftermath of his encounter with his phylogeny. He seemed both exhilarated and exhausted, but then she also thought she saw a wave of sadness pass through him. Dev was not expert in elephant moods and decided to take his cues from Salina.

After several minutes, Bart turned to face his herd, gathered at the far edge of the clearing. He emitted a soft rumble, which precipitated a round of trumpeting from the herd. Led by Flo, the elephants started walking toward him. Stopping about fifty yards from him, they formed a circle. Bart gently picked up the jadeite, once again shuddering as though a jolt of energy had gone through him, and carried the stone toward the circle of elephants. He set it down in the middle of the herd, emitting another soft rumble as he did so. Then he walked back to Salina and Dev. Bart gestured with his trunk toward the speech synthesizer and Salina turned it on.

Pausing to let the machine keep up, Bart started talking. "The story in that stone was probably created for Mom and the others."

Salina took this as a cue that Bart was ready to talk. "Is that what you saw?"

Bart paused, apparently framing his answer. "Yes." Bart paused again. "It was the end of the world. It was the world as it was. It was the world as it should be." He paused. "It was the world I should be in."

As long as he was willing to use the synthesizer, Salina was going to keep going. Dev took out a notebook and started writing down what Bart was saying.

"Why was it as it should be?"

"Other animals were cooperating with the elephants, helping each other to survive. As it got hotter and drier."

"What kind of animals?"

"I don't know. They were different than the animals here. The land was dry. There were giant birds with tiny wings, a large animal with long forelegs and claws for digging."

"Were there people?"

"Not people, but something like both people and chimpanzees. They walked upright and helped the elephants use bones as pipes to find water under the ground."

"These apes used tools?"

"Yes, the elephants made the tools, out of elephant bones, out of trees, and the ape-people used the tools to help the elephants find water, and plant seeds." Bart paused for a long moment. "Now they are gone, and I am back."

Salina felt tears welling up. "Oh Bart, Claire and Katie thought you had a right to know about your people."

Bart rumbled quietly, "I thank you and I thank them. I've been wanting to know since I discovered that I'm different from Mom." He paused again and shifted his weight. Something was making him uncertain. "How long ago did my ancestors die?"

Salina froze. By rights Claire should tell him, as the answer would only underscore how alone Bart truly was. "I think that's a question that Claire should answer."

"You know the answer and you're here."

Salina was taken aback. Never before had Bart so directly challenged her. She thought furiously. Their relationship was precious, and it was built on honesty and trust. She had no choice.

Bart seemed to realize that he had put Salina in a bind. "The answer will help me understand what happened to my ancestors."

"A bit more than five million years ago."

Bart thought about this for a long time. "What happened back then?"

*In for a dime,* thought Salina. "Again, Claire can tell you more, but here's what I've learned. Sometime before that, the entrance that connected the oceans to an exceptionally large sea called the Mediterranean became blocked and over a long time, the sea dried up. This led to heating and drying throughout the surrounding lands, including the grasslands where your ancestors lived. It was so hot and dry that the surrounding grasslands became a desert, trapping your ancestors and those other animals on an ever-smaller island in a giant desert. Eventually, all food and water disappeared." Salina felt helpless. "That's all I know."

Bart was silent.

Dev had been watching and listening. He stood up. "Bart, may I say something?"

Bart turned to Dev. "Yes."

Dev spoke slowly. "I've listened to Katie and Claire talk about whether it was right to bring you back, and Katie said something that stuck with me. She said that when your ancestors created that record that's in the stone, they knew that only an extremely intelligent species could receive its message, and most likely they realized that such a species would have to be something very like themselves. In other words, they created that record in the hopes that it would be received, and some future noble species would be there to understand it. I know it's presumptuous, but I think your ancestors would be overjoyed to know that the future species receiving that message was actually one of them." He paused and then continued quietly, "And now, through you, they live again."

Bart thought about that, seemingly for a long time. "All I know is this, my home." Bart waved his trunk at the surrounding rainforest. "But the efforts you all have been forced to take to protect me make me wonder whether there's a place for my kind in this world."

Neither Dev nor Salina had a ready answer for this question, but Salina felt obligated to offer reassurance. "Our world is troubled, stressed, crowded, and often violent, but Bart, there are a group of people who will do anything to make sure you are safe and fulfilled. I'm one of them."

"I know."

There was an awkward silence, broken by Dev, who stood up. "Bart, one of our concerns is your health. I'm also here as your doctor. Is it OK if I take a blood sample for analysis later?" Bart cocked his head. "Yes, you're the expert."

Dev retrieved a butterfly needle and sample bottle from his briefcase and then asked Bart if he could take the sample from the inside of his hind leg, where the skin was thinner. Bart patiently waited while Dev collected the sample.

"You look healthy as a horse," he said, adding, "That was a joke—horses are my specialty. This is just to make sure."

After Salina and Dev had packed up and made their goodbyes, Bart turned his attention to his herd, still gathered around the stone. Bart made a series of rumbles and Flo, and the others stepped back.

After more rumbles between Bart and the herd, Bart picked up the stone and started walking toward the forest, followed by the other elephants.

As Salina and Dev retraced their path back to the campsite, Salina looked lost in thought. "I don't think Bart told us everything that he experienced."

Dev looked at her closely. "I had that same sense, but I don't know Bart, or elephants, as you do. Could it be simply the limitations of the synthesizer and his vocabulary?"

"Yes, but if that was the case, he would have said that." She thought a bit more. "Maybe he experienced something that he felt only elephants should have the privilege of knowing."

They walked in silence a bit more. Just before they regrouped, Salina turned to Dev. "I hope we did the right thing."

As they picked up their gear at the campsite, Salina watched as Dev took out the blood sample bottle. He poured tiny amounts into two small, opaque plastic bottles, smaller than the hotel shampoo bottles. In fact, they were labelled as shampoo. Then he mixed in silk fibroin, saying to Salina, "the silk preserves the blood when refrigeration isn't available." Then he poured tiny amounts on two pieces of cardboard which he put out to dry in the intense sun. He gave one of the small bottles to Salina. "Keep this somewhere safe with an innocuous sounding label."

Salina frowned. "Did Claire approve this—this blood contains the keys to the kingdom?"

Dev nodded. "It was Claire's idea, partly for health, and partly . . ." he paused, before continuing softly ". . . partly to prepare for a worst-case scenario."

Salina thought about this. "What do we do about customs or airport security?"

Before answering, Dev picked up the cardboard with the now-dried blood and put each splotch into separate white Mylar envelopes, which he sealed and put in his briefcase. "The dried blood won't trigger any-thing, and I'll put this sample in with my toiletries." He gave a crooked grin. "As long as I don't stumble onto a crime scene with blood-sniffing dogs, I should be OK."

# THE REAL WORLD INTRUDES

# 31 CHANGE OF PLANS



ZOE, KEERBROCK, AND CLAIRE WAITED IN BOISBEAUX FOR DEV to return from picking up Katie at the airport. Claire was there with Sofia (Sergei was growing exasperated at Claire's protracted absences, not because he minded parental duties—he loved being a dad—but because he felt Sofia, now fifteen, really needed more time with her mother). Keerbrock didn't know why Claire had insisted that they meet, but her plan was that once Katie arrived, they would brief him on what had transpired with Bart and the jadeite (and she steeled herself for a potential Plinian-scale volcanic eruption of Mount Keerbrock) and talk about next steps.

Keerbrock and Claire were sitting on Zoe's porch when a cloud of dust in the distance signaled the return of Dev. Sofia had gone off with Zoe to help feed the elephants. Claire felt a surge of adrenaline when Dev got out of the truck looking very worried. He was alone. He strode over to the porch, distraught.

"She wasn't on the plane; she never checked in for the flight. When did you last see her?"

In the ensuing silence, dread slowly crowded out every other feeling. Claire knew nothing, but knew everything. She also knew that the world had changed, and that she and the others were going to face an awful choice.

She turned to Dev. "We split up in New Delhi; different flights."

Keerbrock looked at Claire with amazement. "New Delhi?"

Claire didn't want to go into that now. "That's why I asked you to come here—to tell you about that trip." She shook her head. "But that's a long story. Right now, let's figure out what happened to Katie."

Dev was thinking aloud. "She didn't take her phone, right? But if she got delayed or diverted, she could have bought a burner phone or gotten someone to send us a message."

Claire asked Zoe if she could borrow her computer—in keeping with protocol she had left all electronic devices at home. "I'm sending an emergency flare to Rob. I'm also going to see how fast Sergei can get down here."

Zoe and Sofia were returning. Claire got up to intercept them. She turned to Sofia, who had her mother's blonde hair and her father's penetrating, studious eyes. "I've got a problem that needs sorting out." She winced inwardly when she saw Sofia's disappointed expression. Sofia knew nothing about Bart, and while Claire yearned to tell her about him, she knew it was best for both Bart and Sofia's security. Sofia was an intelligent confident young woman, but she was also a teenage girl with a lot of friends from school, sports, and dance, and she was increasingly interested in the boys in her class. Telling Sofia about Bart and swearing her to secrecy was a nonstarter. She certainly could, and was capable of keeping a secret from her parents (thought Claire, ruefully remembering her teenage days), but could she keep such an explosive secret from her friends? Given the warp speed of social media, once out it would be everywhere, and it would be game over for Bart. Claire rationalized her secrecy by comparing her situation to a family where the parents worked on the clandestine side of the CIA.

Sofia studied her mother's face. "You're always doing this, Mom. Maybe I can help. Dad's been teaching me chess. He says I have a strategic mind."

"I'm sure you could help Sofia, but issues relating to donors have to remain confidential." Claire prayed this lie would be credible. "But you can help. How about trying to catch some catfish for dinner?"

Sofia had a spent a lot of time on her own given her mom's frequent absences, and she knew when she was being manipulated—fishing being one of her favorite activities. On the other hand, this was her first trip to Boisbeaux, and she knew she had to be a team player if she wanted to be included on more of her mother's trips. She turned to Zoe. "OK then, where's the fishing rod?"

Claire decided to sweeten the pot. "Dad's coming tomorrow."

At this Sofia brightened considerably. She didn't break a smile, but she gave Claire a thumbs up.

As Zoe walked off with Sofia, Claire called out, "We'll be on the porch. Please bring your computer."

Claire walked back to the porch lost in thought. She clenched her stomach as she realized that not only had all their efforts to avoid electronics not maintained the secrecy and security as intended—in her heart, she knew there was no innocuous explanation for Katie's failure to get on that plane—but that decision now made it much more difficult to figure out what was going on, much less try to mount a rescue. She thought back to the aborted attempt by mercenaries to snatch Bart from Mbembe. Mounting that kind of an operation suggested very deep pockets. Kidnapping Katie, if that's what had happened, suggested long term surveillance and access to major resources. Again, very deep pockets; most likely a government. A cloudy image passed through her mind. She frowned, why was that popping up now. It was a fleeting memory from several years earlier of seeing that Russian at the paleontological conference at Dinosaur National Monument in conversation with someone who looked like a cop. What was that about?

She rejoined Dev and Keerbrock on the porch. Dev was pacing. Keerbrock was deep in thought. Zoe rejoined the group, carrying her laptop. "Can I use that please," asked Claire, "We're going to have to break protocol. First let's pool our thoughts."

"If we're going to pool our thoughts, I need to catch up. What's this about New Delhi."

Zoe and Dev looked at Claire, who sighed and turned to Keerbrock.

"These are not the best circumstances for telling you what we've been doing, but here goes." She then told him about Katie's idea for how best to learn what was encoded in the jadeite, how they implemented the plan, and the results. As she unwound the story a montage of expressions passed across Keerbrock's face, most of them being variations on puzzlement and consternation, rounding out with amazement.

"You're just telling me this now?"

"Katie . . . we felt that this was so far outside your realm, and it was such a long shot, that it was best to just do it."

Keerbrock nearly exploded. "You should give me more credit . . . I want to hear every detail of the experience!" He calmed himself down. "But now let's figure out what happened to Katie."

"I'll lead off," said Claire. "I give it ninety percent likelihood that she's been kidnapped, and, if she was kidnapped, I give it another ninety percent likelihood that it was because of Bart. That means that we'll hear from someone who will offer to trade Katie for Bart."

"Will we?" Dev's voice was level, but his eyes blazed with intensity.

Claire felt helpless to answer. "How can I answer that?"

Keerbrock stepped in. "That's a choice I can't imagine making either. No one's asked anything of us yet, so the best use of our time is to try to figure out a way that we don't have to make that choice. Agreed?" He looked directly at Dev.

Dev nodded.

"OK then, what do we know? We know—using Claire's ninety percent likelihood—that someone figured out that we brought back Bart. We already guessed that from the abortive snatch attempt." Keerbrock thought a bit. "Question is, did they just figure that out, or did they know all along and wait until Bart matured a bit. Anyone who knew about Bart in Mbembe would also know that we were keeping his existence secret from all parties. That means that they also knew that it was in their interest for Bart to grow up in Mbembe—until they were ready to take him."

Claire jumped in. "I thought of that too; both the raid and taking Katie imply deep pockets, and patience. Also, neither of us had electronic devices when we went to Tibet so they must have been able to track Katie, either by hacking or by putting some device on Katie's clothes or luggage."

"What about bringing in the authorities. Maybe they could get access to the New Delhi airport security footage?"

Claire looked at Dev. "We could do that, but it would be game over for Bart.

Dev bridled at this answer, "We don't do that, and it might be game over for Katie."

Keerbrock quickly stepped in. "Claire's right. Also, there might be ways we can get access to that footage without bringing in the authorities . . . Anyway, we're not there yet."

Dev sat down and brooded. Then he looked up. "Bart."

"Bart?" Claire was confused.

"Maybe Bart can help. We've seen and experienced his powers. If he could connect with Rencho, he can connect with Katie, particularly since they spent time together. If he could put mercenaries to sleep, maybe he could do that with her captors . . . or somehow disable them?"

Everybody thought about this.

Claire spoke up first. "It takes time to get to Mbembe."

"Salina is already there," Dev responded.

"I haven't seen these powers," Keerbrock added, "but wouldn't Bart have to know who her captors were and where they are?"

"Maybe one or the other—he didn't know who the mercenaries were until he sensed their presence," Claire responded, and then took a few moments to consider the who portion of Keerbrock's question. "Long shot, but way back when we used Francisco's paper as a red herring to distract attention while we moved Flo to Mbembe, there was a weird Russian at the conference. Wait a minute." Claire did a quick search on Zoe's computer. "The guy at the conference was . . ." She clicked through the participants. "Dimitri Medvedev. Hold on." She did a quick search. ". . . has impressive academic credentials, but few publications, no internet presence at all. Supposed to be affiliated with the Yakutsk Mammoth Museum . . . have to wait for Sergei to see if there's more, but he's not listed in the English language version of the website."

Keerbrock shook his head. "If this dates back that far, we're up against someone or *someones* very powerful, patient, and determined."

At that point, Zoe's computer pinged. Rob had gotten the flare and set up a secure videoconference and was inviting them to enter. As she clicked on the icon, Claire saw Sofia trudging toward them with a bucket and fishing rod. Two fish tails were sticking out of the bucket. Claire whispered to Zoe, "Can you divert her?"

Zoe got up, clapping her hands. "Dinner! Thank you, Sofia!"

Zoe met her in the front yard. "Look Mom!" Sofia said, holding up the bucket.

"Wow, we're going to dine in style!" When Sofia wasn't looking, Claire caught Zoe's eye.

She got the message. "OK Sofi, Let's take these to the kitchen, then how about a horseback ride and a visit with the elephants before we start cooking?"

Sofia gave a long look at the group before nodding and following Zoe.

As the two headed to the kitchen door, Claire and the others turned their attention to Rob. Claire quickly briefed him on Katie, and what they were thinking.

"Thoughts?"

Rob had heard about what Bart did to the mercenaries. "Would he be willing to do this, even if we find out what he needs to know?"

"That's the question—I get the sense he's something of a pacifist," said Claire, "but since he knows that some group has already tried to kidnap him, I think so. We're his family as much as Flo and the herd." She looked at Dev. "And I regard Bart as family."

Rob pondered this, wondering what he'd missed. "I'll get my cyber security team on this Medvedev—though I agree it's a long shot. Anything else about the conference that was off?"

Claire thought. "Yeah, my memory is of Medvedev talking to a guy who looked like a cop."

"A cop? At a paleontological conference?"

"I know, weird, but that's just my impression, and probably why it stuck in my memory. There were two spooks there from DARPA, but they approached me openly, offering research money. They never followed up."

"I'll add it to the list."

"One last thing," said Claire. "We need to talk to Salina, but only if we get confirmation that . . . that we've got a real problem. Can you be prepared to set up a secure conference on short notice?"

"Do my best, but, as we've learned, nothing is completely secure."

After getting off the call, Claire dove into her own research on Medvedev using Zoe's computer, Keerbrock and Dev took walks in different directions, and Zoe and a sullen Sofia served fried catfish for dinner. There was conversation, and everyone praised Zoe and Sofia their cuisine.

"I used to have the metabolism of a hummingbird; now it's more like a Galapagos tortoise. This could sustain me for a month." Keerbrock said as he picked at the catfish, corn, and bread.

After dinner everybody went to bed early, Claire and Sofia to a bunkhouse they would share with Sergei when he arrived the next day. Claire wanted to get up early—Rob was eight hours ahead of them and they wanted to be awake when he reported back on his findings. They also wanted to be ready if a message came in from the kidnappers—if there had been a kidnapping. Intentions aside, nobody, with the exception of Sofia, caught more than isolated minutes of sleep.

# 32 WORKING IN THE BLIND



THE GROUP STARTED STRAGGLING INTO THE KITCHEN AT 5:00 a.m. Claire was the last to arrive, having to get out of bed and get dressed without waking Sofia. In the heart of her teenage years, Sofia would sleep until eleven, given the chance. Zoe was already up and had made coffee. The pre-dawn was warm and humid, but the air was fresh, so they moved to the porch.

Keerbrock wasted no time. "I know we've all been turning this over. Here're a couple of thoughts. Kidnapping seems like a rash step, but, if—and I know it's a big if—their awareness of Bart dates back to that conference, this is not a rash group. They, again it's probably the same group, took a shot at snatching Bart, but didn't try again after their abortive first try. Then they take one of our core group, probably to set up a trade. What can we infer from this? One: they know a lot about us, and have been following our project for a long time. They know about Katie, about Mbembe, and about Bart. They had the resources to mount a raid, and then, later, to track and intercept Katie. Two: they're as interested in keeping this secret as we are. They've had every opportunity to blow our cover, but haven't done so.

"So, what can we infer from these two postulates? One is that they want Bart for some purpose, not for the glory of the most spectacular discovery of all time. That purpose is probably ground-breaking technology with commercial, military, and intelligence purposes. That makes it more likely than not we're dealing with a government, or some government-private partnership." Keerbrock sat upright as a thought just hit him. "Or it's possible that we're dealing with a group that wants to sell Bart to a government . . . The second thing is that because they need to maintain secrecy, they are unlikely to do something so rash and so brutal that we will bring in the authorities, particularly the American government." Here he looked at Dev, who nodded. "So, I expect, their approach will come in stages, with them gradually upping the pressure." He looked around the porch. "Agree, disagree?"

Claire spoke up, "Thanks Will, that sums it up well—and I agree with the caveats. There's one more thing." She looked at Dev. "Katie is not a shrinking violet tied to the tracks. I don't know if she told you about this Dev, but during her days as an undercover animal activist, she sometimes found herself hostage to some particularly brutal men. If there's a crack in their armor, Katie will find it. Right Zoe?"

Zoe, one of Katie's copains from those days, nodded vigorously, "Hard core. Never seen anyone better." Zoe squinted. "I probably shouldn't tell you this, but one time in Mexico, she got caught filming a roadside zoo guy using powerful electric prods connected to a generator to get tigers to roar. She was tied up and the asshole was going to use the prod on her—and clearly had worse planned. Her legs weren't tied up as part of the worse part. As he approached her, she flipped the chair sideways and scissored her legs, flipping him into a water tub where he was electrocuted. She'd also use her looks . . ."

She was interrupted by Dev who held up his hand with a pained expression. "Thanks Zoe, we get the picture. As you might imagine I have mixed feelings hearing these stories." Dev got up and started pacing. "But your point is well taken. I'm thinking about when Salina and I brought the jadeite to Bart. Before we arrived, a leopard and her cubs were sitting with Bart. Salina asked him about the leopard family, and Bart said that the leopard was 'his eyes.'"

Claire jumped in, "You're thinking that if connected to Katie somehow, she could be his eyes." As she said this, she caught a glimpse of Keerbrock grimacing, but she also noticed that he held his tongue.

Keerbrock waved a hand. "I haven't had the experience of Bart's powers as you have, but since both of you experienced the same thing six thousand miles apart, I'll *try* to keep an open mind. But I'm assuming that you're thinking dual track—traditional gumshoe with a New Age kicker?"

Claire smiled for the first time since Katie failed to show—Keerbrock wasn't known for his sense of humor. "Yeah, bringing Bart in will either work or it won't." Zoe's computer pinged. "Speaking of gumshoe, here's Rob." They gathered around Zoe's computer.

Rob wasted no time. "For a guy with his credentials, Dimitri is almost invisible. He may or may not be a legendary hacker. I think the way into him may be through that cop—turns out he's a retired FBI agent—excellent job, Claire! His presence at the conference is almost as mysterious as Dimitri's. Name's Roznik, and it turns out he's been living quite well for a divorced FBI agent. I'm going to brace him and if I get a contact for Dimitri out of him, I'll put the screws to Dimitri, big time!"

He paused. "Still no word from kidnappers?"

"Nope."

Keerbrock jumped in. "Could that indicate dissent in the ranks?"

"Maybe, but if it's a kidnapping, these guys are playing a long game."

Keerbrock thought about this. "Shouldn't we wait to contact Roznik? Maybe Katie yelled at an airport security guy; maybe someone's holding her temporarily, just to try to flush us out? Maybe . . ." he decided not to voice this other maybe.

"Good points," Rob responded, "but we don't want to lose another day. I'll hold off for a few hours. In the meantime, there's no reason to wait to see if Bart can help. I've sent a message to Andre, the legionnaire. He's going to bring the encrypted sat phone to Salina in Mbembe. Zoe? You have one at Boisbeaux, yes?"

"I'll get it."

"Good, Claire should try Salina in a couple of hours. OK, I'll sign off for now. If you get any message, ping me. For now, we wait."

Zoe went to get the phone. Claire went off to get Sofia for breakfast. She welcomed the break as it gave her time with her daughter without feeling that she was abandoning Katie.

Sofia wasn't buying Claire's cover story. "That's a lot of urgent meetings for a donor problem, Mom."

Claire sighed. She decided she had to tell Sofia something plausible or her daughter would make it her mission to find out. "You know about all the craziness that happened before you were born, after I went public about the ancient elephant bones?"

"Dad told me about it. Also, a couple of my friends told me that you were famous a long time ago."

Claire was intrigued. "Really what did they say?"

"Only that their parents said you were a big deal and in all the papers. But what does any of that have to do with what you're doing now?"

"We've continued the research—in secret, just to avoid another media zoo—and it's at a critical juncture. That's all I can say."

Sofia gave her mother another laser-like stare. "But you'll tell me someday, right?"

"Yes! Before anyone else outside knows. I promise!"

Sofia smiled. "OK deal." She offered a handshake. "I'll keep my distance from your 'donor' [Sofia made air quotes] discussions. When he gets here, tell Dad that I'm helping Zoe feed the elephants."

While Claire was talking with Sofia, Dev pondered their situation. He knew with certainty the third "maybe" that Keerbrock didn't voice. He knew the odds of a benign explanation for her disappearance were vanishingly small. At this point, he had to hope that Katie had been kidnapped, and by rational people.

## 33 THE CLOCK TICKS DOWN

THE FIRST MESSAGE FROM KATIE'S CAPTORS ARRIVED AT THE same time as Sergei. Zoe went out to the mailbox to retrieve the mail just as Sergei was driving up in a rental car. Zoe silently waved a plain brown envelope. No address, no stamps.

Claire walked over to Sergei and also gave him a hug, whispering in his ear, "When Sofia gets back from feeding the elephants, let here show you around for a bit and then join us."

As they walked off, he looked back and mouthed, "How bad?"

Claire shook her head.

On the porch, the group gathered around Zoe. "Should I use rubber gloves?" she asked.

"We probably should," said Keerbrock, "but an operation big enough to get an envelope here, is also run by people smart enough not to leave fingerprints. We're not going to the authorities anyway," he glanced at Dev, ". . . yet."

The envelope contained a thumb drive. Zoe was about to plug it in to her laptop when Claire held up a hand. "We don't know what's on this. Do you have an old expendable laptop?"

"Got a bunch," said Zoe, heading back into the house. "I'll find one that still fires up." She returned with a MacBook that was at least three generations old.

They plugged in the thumb drive, and on it was a photo of a one-page document. At the top of the page was a photo of Katie. She was sitting at a table in a spare, white-walled room. Her expression was flat.

Her hands were on the table, fingertips touching. On the table was a meal and a glass of water. Below the photo was a succinct note that looked as though it was from Katie, though they knew it was not. It read, "All fine here. My friends want to know if we have a deal. If so, we should announce the happy news on the Boisbeaux website. Why not a photo with elephants and balloons?"

"This tells us a lot," said Keerbrock. "It confirms that they are doing this in stages. They want to make it as easy as possible for us to comply. They don't need to make demands because they know that we know what they want. And their demands are going to be simple. My guess is that when it comes, the demand will be that we pull everybody from around the concession for some period of time." He paused. "And let them take Bart."

Voicing it aloud made the choice they faced seem all the more impossible.

Dev was staring intently at the photo. "Look at Katie's hands. The way her fingertips are overlapping on the table looks awkward. She's trying to tell us something." They all took a fresh look at the photo. Zoe zoomed in on her hands.

Keerbrock saw it first. "The way her index finger of her left hand overlaps with the first two fingers of her right hand looks like the letter Z."

Sergei had returned after setting Sofia up for some more fishing. He peered at the photo (Rob had brought him up to speed before his flight). "She's telling us her captors are Russian. Z is the letter the Russians used so their troops could distinguish between Russian armor and Ukrainian armor during the invasion."

Claire squinted again. "If that's the case, we should ping Rob to see what he can get from Roznik."

"What if Roznik has nothing to do with any of this?"

"It's a gamble, but the alternative is making an impossible choice, a choice that none of us wants to make. I'm sending Rob a green light—we've got to act fast.

Dev brooded, remembering his glimpse of the Wagner Group mercenaries at the airport in Bangui. He told the group about his brief encounter. Claire shook her head, "Some mercenaries tried to snatch Bart long before you went to CAR."

While they waited for messages from Rob and Salina, Sergei went off to spend some time with Sofia. When he got back to the cabin, Sofia gave him a direct look, "Dad, what's going on?"

Sergei knew this moment was coming and dreaded it. He didn't know that Sofia had earlier probed Claire. Much as he wanted for Sofia to spend more time with Claire, he also knew that going on a trip with Claire increased the odds of her seeing things and asking questions that neither he nor Claire could answer. "Sofia, your mom's consulting on a top-secret project and something's come up that she has to sort out."

"Is she CIA?"

Sergei laughed. "Far from it."

Sofia looked thoughtful. "KGB?" (She liked spy novels.)

Sergei smiled, "Not since glasnost." He turned stern, and using his thickest Russian accent added, "These matters are not to be discussed!"

Sofia giggled. "SPECTRE? Oh my God," she affected a gasp, "SMERSH!" (She really liked early Bond movies.)

Sergei put his hand to his chin, worried. "You may be on to something . . . I'll make discreet inquiries to Blofeld."

Always delighted with her dad's ability to turn things light, Sofia, however, was not about to give up. "Is it related to those bones you found?"

Sergei absolutely hated lying to his daughter. "Even I don't know what this project is about, but Mom is one of the good guys, and would never do anything that might hurt somebody. Please trust that this secrecy is important. I do."

Sofia gave Sergei a long look. "OK, Dad." She gave him another long look. "I've got some homework to do anyway."

While this conversation was going on, Keerbrock sought out Claire and Dev to get a more detailed description of what happened when they brought the jadeite to Bart, and also what they learned from the Buddhist monk, Rencho.

He listened intently as they went through the experience. When they finished, he asked a series of questions. He wanted them to go over Bart's reticence to use the synthesizer and Bart's assertion that thinking in words somehow interfered with his inherited mental powers. Did that relate to why Rencho was better able to enter the scenes encoded in the jadeite that Bart had projected into the ether? Had they shown Bart a picture of Rencho, how had he oriented himself? Keerbrock also asked for more detail about how Bart thwarted his own attempted kidnapping.

After an intense round of back and forth, Keerbrock looked abashed. "You know, I accept that his powers are real, but I don't understand them. I'm the one with the degrees and the expertise, but Katie's been ahead of me every step of the way. Her approach has been unscientific, even impulsive, but she's like a savant. Her intuitions have been pitch-perfect. Maybe I'm the prisoner in Plato's cave, mistaking shadows for reality. Maybe I'm so deep in words and math that I'm the worst person to try to understand Bart's powers."

Given Keerbrock's accomplishments and pride, Claire was astonished and discomfited by this confession. She also felt an unworthy mixture of hurt and envy that she quickly suppressed—she needed Keerbrock at his best right now. "I dunno Will, Katie can point the way to Quantum entanglement, but you're the one who understands it. Whatever powers Bart has are natural, produced by natural selection, and who better to understand them but you?"

Keerbrock chuckled hearing this. "Until you just took me through what Bart can do, I would have agreed with you. But maybe I should have studied Buddhism rather than geophysics?"

Dev had been listening quietly, his anxiety growing. The problem was, he agreed that Bart represented a natural miracle, a superior being who deserved to be cherished and protected, if not worshipped. But Katie was the one filling a hole in his soul he had not previously known was there. Whatever path they took if forced to make a choice would tear the team apart and haunt them for the rest of their lives. He needed to figure a way out of this Sophie's Choice. He needed to think of a plan B.

They had been sitting at the picnic table on Zoe's porch. Putting his hand on the bench to get up, Dev punctured his palm with a splinter. He looked at the drop of blood the splinter produced, and lurched upright as it hit him. Plan B unfurled before him. Worse comes to worst, Dev knew he had an ace in the hole. He squinted, wondering whether he should tell the others. *Only break glass in case of emergency*, he thought. He'd keep plan B to himself for the time being and see how things developed.

# 34 A CHAT WITH PETE ROZNIK

ROB HAD A FAIRLY EASY TIME FINDING ROZNIK. NOW seventy-seven, the former FBI surveillance specialist was living in comfortable retirement. He had a modest, single-story home on the Indian River in Palm Bay, Florida and a not so modest forty-six-foot Hatteras fishing boat on his dock. Rob got his phone number, dialed it, and came at him hard. "Hello Pete, I'm going to make this brief. There're two ways this is going to go. You can keep the money you got from the Russians, and we'll keep your secret. All you've got to do is give us a contact for Dimitri Medvedev and the names of the other Russians involved. Do you want to hear the other option?" There was silence on the line. Rob went ahead. "Option two is that we find the contacts ourselves and when we do we let the Russians know we got the info from you. As you may know, they don't like loose ends. Oh, and we also let the FBI know that information you gathered from FBI surveillance and sold to the Russians led to the kidnapping of an American citizen."

This was pure bluff. If he were guessing wrong about Roznik's involvement, Roznik would simply hang up. But he didn't hang up.

After a long pause, Roznik said, "kidnapping?"

"Yes, and time is precious. Give me contacts and what names you have, and you're free and clear."

"There was nothing illegal about what I did."

"I don't care, but others might. Contact info?"

There was a long pause. "Give me a minute."

After several minutes, Roznik came back on the line. "Who are you?"

"That doesn't matter. What matters is that I could find you."

Another pause.

"I give you this and I never hear from you again?"

"Depends on what you give me."

Another long pause. "Look, I picked up something in a sweep of a mob hangout. It had nothing to do with my case, but the bug picked up a big-time scientist looking to recruit someone for a super-secret project. I ran into a Russian scientist at a conference whose buddies were willing to pay to find out about this project. They weren't government secrets and for damn sure there was nothing about a kidnapping."

"Pete. There's a direct line between your little transaction and the kidnapping. Names and contacts? Now!" On the phone, he could hear Roznik give a sigh of resignation.

"I don't know the names of his colleagues, but I guessed they were intelligence or military, not scientists. There's a digital dead drop I used to make contact, here's how it worked. It had a lot of trip wires . . ."

Something occurred to Rob. He interrupted, "Have you gotten all the money?"

Roznik hesitated.

"Simple question."

"I got half the bonus for keeping quiet five years ago. I'm overdue the rest."

"Why haven't you asked for it?"

Roznik sounded exasperated. "Should be obvious—they might send a hit squad along with the bitcoin."

Rob drummed his fingers. This was pure gold. *Thank God for cheap Russians*, thought Rob. "Well, you're going to ask for it, only we'll be hovering in the background—don't worry, the money will go to you. So, tell me: exactly how would you ask for it?"

"Dunno about this—remember, I mentioned a hit squad."

"C'mon Pete! You're a surveillance guy! FBI, for chrissakes! Besides, our guys will be monitoring you."

"You have that capability?"

"Be easier if you cooperated."

Another pause. "OK."

Roznik walked him through the set of procedures Dimitri had set up to make contact. He was impressed. They used an online chat group dedicated to classic British sports cars. If Roznik needed to make contact, he would put up an innocuous post about seeing a green 1964 Austin Healey 3000 driving through Mayfair, noting that it had a dent on the left fender. Dimitri would then put up a reply that he had seen something similar offered for a price. The price would be the exact time to expect a call on a burner phone. For instance, if the price was $14,245.00, the dollars would indicate that it was Eastern Standard Time on the 14th at 2:45. Roznik explained that he had never used the contact since the initial payment.

Before hanging up, Rob wanted to know one more thing. "As a former agent, do you think Dimitri is government?"

"Nah, he's smart as hell, but not a pro. He was sloppy about trying to blend in; I got the impression he was winging it at the conference. Probably was hired for some unique skills, but what those are, I have no idea."

"What about his colleagues."

"No clue, Dimitri was the only contact."

"Any guesses?"

Worst case scenario off the table, Roznik was loosening up. "Decades at the bureau left me somewhat cynical about bureaucracies and human nature. Someone wants this elephant badly and was willing to wait a decade to make their play. To me, that's not a government—administrations change, leadership changes, things leak, funding gets pulled—but most important, the bosses want to show their bosses results now, not ten years down the road. Not many want to wait ten years for results." Somewhat ruefully, given what he'd done himself, Roznik continued. "My guess is that this started off a legit op, greenlighted by some Russian agency, but along the way, the guys—or a guy—behind it, realized that this elephant would be immensely valuable, yes to the Russian government, but maybe also to another, more generous, government. This may have started as an official caper, but I wouldn't be surprised if they're now freelancing."

"Interesting," was Rob's response, but he was thinking "Exactly!" And that made the situation far more difficult—and dangerous.

# 35 KATIE MAKES A DECISION

IT DIDN'T TAKE LONG FOR KATIE TO TAKE STOCK OF HER situation. The good news was that she hadn't seen any of her captors. If they intended to kill her, she reasoned, they wouldn't care if she saw them. Her interrogations, such as they were, had been through an intercom. They'd been half-hearted, and her stock answer was that she helped out at a refuge for formerly captive elephants in the US.

The unwelcome news was everything else. Her captors—she'd heard traces of conversations in what she thought was Russian—seemed to know a lot about her and Claire. Worse, they knew about Mbembe, and worse yet, they knew about Bart, or at least had a strong suspicion that he existed.

Katie tried to reconstruct her abduction. Her last memory before awakening in this room was someone spraying a mist in her face in the ladies' room at the airport. She had no idea how they got her out of the country, or whether she was still in India.

Katie looked around the room. What was surprising was that it wasn't equipped either like a prison cell—she'd seen a few of those—or an interrogation room. It was more like a room in an old farmhouse. The walls were stained planks separated by ribs. There was a skylight (out of reach) but no windows, which led her to believe it was a repurposed storage room of some sort. She had a rudimentary bathroom, and the room was furnished with a mattress on the floor, and a simple table and chair. Lighting came from the skylight, an overhead fixture, and a lamp beside the table. The food they gave her was simple but adequate, and they let her keep a couple of books she had brought along. She thought ruefully that she now had the time to read Richard Powers's *Overstory*, a book that had been on her bedside table at home for several years.

Putting all this together, she came to some conclusions. She was being treated as a hostage, and not a criminal. She was probably a bargaining chip to be traded for Bart, and, as such, her captors seemed to be taking care to deliver her undamaged, should things come to an agreement. She was also fairly certain that whoever was running this plan was doing it off the books, even if they had some official role. They clearly had deep pockets and sophisticated surveillance capabilities, but the impromptu feel of her confinement suggested that someone wanted to keep the circle of knowledge really tight.

Darker thoughts intruded. She was sure that Claire and the others had figured out that she'd been abducted, and she was terribly afraid that they would make the trade. Were the situation reversed and Claire was the captive, Katie hoped that she would have the steel to resist that trade, even if the abductors upped the pressure by sending back pieces of Claire (and Katie realized that this might be on the table for her if things dragged on). Bart was a miracle; protecting him trumped everything else.

In this dark place, a thought crossed her mind. She could preempt a trade. Claire would surely demand proof that Katie was alive before making any trade, and if they couldn't provide that proof, no trade would happen. *No Katie, no Bart.*

Katie shook her head. That the thought even entered her head was absurd. She thought of Dev, of the mountains of New Hampshire, of elephants, of everything she embraced in life. Of course, she didn't want to die. But she and Claire and the others did not bring Bart back to life after five million years for him to become a freak to be studied or sold. She hoped—prayed—it wouldn't come to that, but if it did, for Katie, it wasn't even a choice. And she wasn't powerless. She needed a plan.

# 36 CLAIRE CALLS BART

IT WAS THE HEAT OF THE DAY, 3:00 P.M., WHEN SALINA unexpectedly showed up at the bai. Whether it was through his network of animal eyes, or his own extreme sensitivity to his surroundings, Bart somehow knew she was coming, and he entered the clearing from the far side, just as Salina entered from the trail. Salina waved, and Bart came across. They sheltered from the blazing sun in the shade of a giant Afrormosia tree.

Bart looked at Salina curiously. As soon as she turned on the synthesizer, Bart said, "Something is wrong. What happened?"

Salina shook her head. "How did you know?"

"Salina, you're radiating stress. What happened?"

She took a breath. *Better to dive right in.* "Katie's been kidnapped."

It's hard to read an elephant's expression, but Bart's initial silence conveyed shock.

"Taken, like those men tried to do with me?"

"Yes, this is another way they are trying to get you."

Bart didn't hesitate. "Then, I will go with them."

Salina reached up to pat his shoulder. "We will *never* let that happen! And Katie would not want that."

"What choice do you have?"

Salina took another breath. "That's why I'm here." She reached into her pocket and brought out the satellite phone that had been delivered to her by Andre. She turned it on. "Claire thinks you can help. She wants to talk to you."

Bart peered at Salina as she hooked the phone up to the speaker on the synthesizer. "What is that?"

"It's called a sat phone—it's a way we humans can talk to each other at great distances."

Bart paused for a moment. "I can feel its energy; it's very crude, grating, and disruptive."

This was new. With a flood of gratitude, Salina realized what a stroke of good fortune it had been to raise Bart in Mbembe where there were no microwaves whatsoever. On the other hand, she didn't want the medium to interfere with the message from Claire. "If it's too irritating, I can turn this off and tell you what Claire wants to say later?"

"If Mom thinks it's so urgent that she is using this thing, what she wants to say must be important. We can talk."

"She should be calling soon." Salina looked at her watch. For a moment or two, there was nothing but the sounds of the rainforest. Then the phone buzzed. Salina accepted the call and Claire's voice came through the speaker. "Hi Bart, it's Claire."

Bart cocked his head at the phone. "Hi Mom. You used to be larger."

Salina and Claire both realized that this was an attempt at humor and laughed.

"I'm sorry I couldn't come in person, but this is urgent, and there wasn't time."

"I understand. Salina told me what happened, and I told her you should give me to those men. I owe my life to all of you, and I'm willing to go.

"That will *never* happen, and I'm calling because I think you can help us avoid facing that choice."

"What do you mean?"

"Remember when you reached out to Rencho? Me and Katie experienced it too, though not as fully. Were you trying to reach us too?"

"Yes, once I have a connection with a person or animal, I can reach them again. It helps though if they are open and expecting it. Also, you were my eyes. When I was projecting what I experienced through the stone that took all my energy, but afterward I could see the scene through your eyes."

Seven thousand miles away, Claire held her breath for a minute. "Do you think you could reach out to Katie?"

Bart was silent for a moment.

"Of course. But I need a sense of where she is in relation to me, and it would help if Katie knew I was trying to reach her."

Claire's hopes faded a bit. "Let's see what we can do to help you. We don't have much time. Salina? Let's connect same time tomorrow."

# 37 THE COLONEL WAITS AND WORRIES

THE COLONEL GOT UP FROM HIS WELL-WORN WOODEN CHAIR. Nominally attached to the GRU—Russia's military intelligence unit—the Colonel's office was decorated in a vaguely modern, not unpleasant building in Zelenograd, Moscow. Zelenograd was Russia's attempt at replicating Silicon Valley, and his office lay about twenty miles from the city center. He went to the window. In the distance he could see the campus of the Moscow Institute of Electronic Technology. The Colonel's office was far away from GRU headquarters. This provided some insulation for the GRU given the types of activities his office sponsored, and also allowed the hackers he recruited to pretend they weren't working for military intelligence. The Colonel was well aware of the need for cutouts, but he also knew that cutouts cut more than one way, and right now he was troubled.

The Colonel's career longevity evidenced his survival instincts. He'd been a junior KGB officer in the last days of the Soviet Union, and had negotiated the shark tank of oligarchs and former KGB agents that surfaced after the collapse to carve up the carcass of the fallen empire. Then, early on, he saw the potential of cyber operations. Now his decoder ring was flashing red.

Long games, such as the play brought to them by Dimitri and then taken over by Grigory, required continuity at the top. In a country ruled by paranoia, for someone who had successively narrowed the circle of people he trusted, that continuity didn't exist. Top lieutenants disappeared, and long-term projects were forgotten—or redirected for profit by the *siloviki* who populated the Russian deep state.

The Colonel was well aware of the purge at the top of the intelligence services that had occurred after Putin learned that the analysts and agents in charge had pocketed the billions that had been designated to buy off Ukrainian officials and politicians before the invasion. They were too smart for their own good, as their analysis had convinced them that Putin would never be dumb enough to invade and his fifth column would thus never be called upon to support his crackpot plan. Now many of these geniuses were having a not-so-great time in Russian prisons, while legions more were waiting for a knock on the door.

Given the tight circle that knew about this mysterious elephant, and given the decade that had passed since the caper's launch, the Colonel felt that Operation Dumbo (the Colonel's private name for the project, one which displayed a rare sense of irony because if their suspicions were correct, the elephant might be the smartest sentient being on the planet) offered a tempting target for diversion. A number of signs bolstered that suspicion. For one thing, he hadn't heard from Grigory since that conversation with Dimitri when the idea of snatching Katie came up.

A number of possibilities flowed from this. Most likely, Grigory had evidence that this mysterious elephant's powers were real and immensely valuable. If there was nothing there, the Colonel was sure that he would have already been blamed for a waste of time and resources. Grigory's going dark suggested further that Grigory wanted to benefit from that immense value. The idea that Grigory was protecting the Colonel by keeping him in the dark was laughable.

The Colonel clenched his fists. There was so much he didn't know: whether the kidnapping had taken place, and if it had, he didn't know where Katie was being held. Worse, he really didn't know that much about Grigory. He *did* know that Grigory seemed to have serious juice, and the big discretionary budget that came with such influence.

If he took his suspicions up the chain, he risked tipping off Grigory, and, even if Grigory had gone rogue, the Colonel didn't know whether other higher ups were involved. On the other hand, if Grigory was legit, then the Colonel would have made himself a powerful enemy for no reason.

Of course, there was the option of simply getting in on whatever was going on. If it was legit, fine; if it had turned into a freelance operation, Grigory would have to cut him in if he was on the scene. *Or would he?*

The Colonel grimaced. More likely, Grigory would have him eliminated—that's what the Colonel would do (and had done). He sat back down at his desk. Putting it all together, he realized that if Grigory had privatized this operation, there was no safe option. Even if he played along, as long as he was alive, the Colonel posed a threat to Grigory if only because he knew about the project's official beginnings. So, the Colonel's future depended on the answer to one simple question: was Operation Dumbo still an official op? The problem was, the Colonel couldn't go to any official for an answer. He could go, however, to his contract hacker, the annoying prodigy whose phone call first brought Claire Knowland's discovery to the Colonel's attention.

The Colonel reached into his briefcase and brought out a burner phone. He sent a straightforward text message. "Status update?"

# 38 DIMITRI IN A VICE

DIMITRI, A BEDRAGGLED AND INCONGRUOUS PRESENCE IN HIS austere penthouse, took a sip of coffee and looked at the text from the Colonel. He shook his head; the vise was closing in on him. Ever since Grigory had raised the issue of kidnapping Katie, Dimitri had been obsessing over ways to extricate himself from the project. The last thing he wanted was a new assignment, particularly if it had anything to do with the kidnapping. He'd studiously remained ignorant of whether the kidnapping had even taken place, and he wished he'd never called the Colonel all those years ago.

Dimitri was back in Nur-Sultan, in upgraded living quarters. He opened the glass doors to the terrace, and stepped out into the heat. The modern, soulless city with its triumphal monuments and plazas, spread out before him, a vista that screamed out dreamscape of a narcissistic dictator for life. He stepped back into the apartment. Looking around his living room with its wood furnishings and chairs that could have come out of the office lobby of a law firm, Dimitri had to admit there wasn't a lot of soul in his penthouse either.

He picked up his coffee cup and took another sip, assessing the pros and cons of not responding and simply disappearing. Where could he go? Did he really want to be on the shit list of the GRU and whatever other organizations and persons Grigory worked for?

With a sigh Dimitri headed for the door. He had kept his old, shabby apartment as a workspace. Nobody knew about it, and he didn't dare keep any work-related equipment in his penthouse.

The inconspicuous hair he had placed across the door and the jamb was still there. After turning on the lights, he sat down at his desk and brought his various systems back to life. He was about to pick up a burner phone when he noticed that he had an alert from one of the bland chatrooms he used to send and receive messages. He looked at the message. Roznik needed to talk.

*Roznik!* Dimitri hadn't heard from him in years. This was getting out of hand. Once again, he thought about ignoring the message. Trouble was, Roznik had met him; knew who he was, and could connect him to Claire Knowland. He set up the conversation for the next day.

Dimitri picked up the burner phone and called the Colonel who answered with his usual abruptness. "Time for you to earn your retainer."

Dimitri mustered his courage. "This project is going in a direction I didn't sign on for."

There was silence on the other side of the line. "And what direction is that?" There was a warning in the Colonel's voice.

Dimitri couldn't back down now. "The direction taken during our last conference with Grigory."

The Colonel emitted a short, cold laugh. "That's why we're talking. I need you to find out where things stand."

It was Dimitri's turn to be stunned. So long as this was an official project, Dimitri had felt a certain protection, as he was furthering the ends of the state. If Grigory had taken this private, he was suddenly exposed, not only to the wrath of the state, but to Grigory's need to tie up loose ends. "Am I hearing this right? Grigory's gone solo?"

"I don't know." It was the first time Dimitri had heard the Colonel sound anything other than self-assured. "That's what I want you to find out."

"You've vastly better contacts than me . . ."

The Colonel cut him off. "Too dangerous. This has to be done from the outside—leaving no traces."

"I don't even know his last name or where he works?"

"It's Federov. He's chief of a little-known directorate charged with strategic industrial espionage. It's an 'arm's length' outfit, and his operatives are subcontracted rather than FSB. The wife's name is Alina—supposedly has champagne tastes. Dunno about a girlfriend. I'll text you some contact info on this phone."

Sensing that the Colonel was about to hang up, Dimitri thought about mentioning that he'd been contacted by Roznik, but decided to wait. Roznik could be useful.

After hanging up, Dimitri procrastinated a bit by logging into RussianCupid, his favorite dating site. There were a few messages, but nothing that moved him to reply. He logged out and sat back and thought. Soft target might be the wife, Alina. He'd start there.

# 39 ROB IS FORCED TO PIVOT

ROB REBOLET PULLED OFF HIS HEADPHONES AND TOSSED THEM onto his desk in frustration. He had just finished listening in on Roznik's conversation with Dimitri. Rob's men had mounted a fierce, multi-pronged attack to try to locate Dimitri during the call, but had accomplished extraordinarily little toward that goal.

The conversation had been brief. Roznik, as coached, had asked Dimitri why he hadn't been paid his bonus. Dimitri had said he'd check and hung up. The call wasn't long enough for Rob's men to refine Dimitri's location beyond Central Asia.

Rob was in his command center at Transteppe in Kazakhstan. Most operations at the mining company had been suspended as the stalemate between the Russian separatists and the Kazakh government dragged on year after year. As head of security Rob had been kept on but with a very different mission. The giant mining concession was still a prize being pursued by both sides, and most of Rob's time was spent coordinating with the US special ops soldiers that had been invited by the Kazakh government to help protect the concession. Rob would have moved on long ago, but his job gave him valuable tools to help Claire, and also a position from which to protect the ongoing dig and the analysis of the finds.

Rob looked down at his desk and saw a slightly blurred image of Dimitri that his team had recovered from a YouTube video of the conference where Roznik and Dimitri had met. Random thoughts washed through his mind: *reasonably good looking, computer nerd, paleontology, Central Asia.* Then it hit him.

He reached for his phone and dialed the lab at Transteppe where Kazakh scientists and technicians were working on bones and other objects recovered from the dig. A young tech answered and he asked for Kamila. When she came to the phone, he asked her to come by his office.

A few minutes later, an attractive woman in her early thirties showed up at his door. Rob waved her in. Kamila Valikhinova was a Kazakh postdoc who'd been attached to the project since its early days. Rob pointed to a seat and squirmed a bit; this was going to be awkward.

He looked and Kamila and drummed his fingers. She really was a beauty. Best to dive right in. "Hi Kamila, thanks for coming over."

She smiled. "Of course." She was wearing dusty khakis, but any khaki maker in the world would have happily put her in an ad, dust and all.

"Here's the thing. I need your help with something urgent, but before getting into that I need to ask you some questions. That OK?"

Kamila looked puzzled, but shrugged. "OK."

"Great . . . OK then . . . how do men and women meet in Kazakhstan?"

Kamila laughed in amazement. Rob was regarded as something of a catch by all the women who came through Transteppe. She blessed him with a dazzling smile. "Are you looking for a date, Rob?"

Rob actually blushed. "No, no, not at all. I'm actually trying to find someone, and I need to do it quick."

Again, the puzzled look. "I see." Kamila thought a bit. "In the old days, most marriages were arranged. My mother had someone picked out for me by the time I was ten. Ugh!" Kamila made a sour face. "Now, particularly with professionals, it's through get-togethers and, of course, dating apps."

Rob knew Kamila was still single—she'd had a years' long relationship with Karil, another scientist on the dig, but that had ended a couple of years back. "Forgive me, but I have to ask, have you ever used a dating app?"

It was Kamila's turn to blush. She looked down. "Can I ask what this is about?"

Rob knew he was treading on thin ice. "Of course. I can't go into details, but someone on our team is in an extremely dangerous situation. I need to find a man who might help us resolve this."

Kamila was smart as a whip. "You want to use me as bait?!"

*Exactly!* "Absolutely not! You'd never have to meet him or even see him. We'd create a profile for you, and then we'd show up instead of you."

"Is he dangerous?"

"Not at all, and this might not work, but he's somewhere around here and I'm guessing he uses dating apps."

Kamila was intrigued. "Is he Kazakh?"

"Russian."

Kamila didn't say anything for a few moments. "What if he realizes he's being tricked and decides to come after me?"

Rob didn't have an answer for that. "I can't guarantee anything, and I know it's a big ask, but we have enough on him to put him in prison for life if he gets feisty."

"And you can't tell me who's in trouble." Among the many reasons Rob kept this to himself—apart from the need for absolute secrecy— was that a decade earlier Katie had a brief fling with Karil, Kamila's ex, and Rob suspected she might not be as cooperative if she learned the person in peril was Katie.

"Afraid I can't, and whatever you decide, please don't mention this conversation to anyone."

Kamila thought a bit more and then smiled. "OK, I'll do it, but on one condition."

Rob opened his hands. "Speak."

She smiled, cocked her head, and looked him right in the eye. "Afterward you take me out for a drink."

Rob blushed again. "It would be my pleasure."

Kamila lit up with another smile. "OK then, it's settled. Most people my age use RussianCupid."

"OK then, we'll get cracking. I'll need a good picture, and maybe a couple of you in the field."

"I know how it's done."

Kamila started to get up. Rob held up a finger. "I have one condition too."

Kamila cocked her head. "What's that?"

"That we have that drink whether or not he takes the bait."

Kamila rewarded him with the most devastating smile yet, and a thumbs up.

# 40 ARE WE NOT MADE OF FLESH?

THE DAY AFTER HIS BRIEF CHAT WITH ROZNIK, DIMITRI WAS back at his desk in his old apartment. So, Roznik wanted to get paid. Big surprise. He'd decided to wait to report that news to the Colonel until he had something to report on Grigory. And now he did.

After his call, he'd hacked into Alina's—Grigory's wife's—email and discovered a chatty exchange with her mother where she complained that when they went to their place in Baku on the Caspian, Grigory was always venturing off to Qobustan where there were ancient rock engravings. "Do you think that's what he's doing?" She'd asked.

"Men are very strange," her mother had replied neutrally, though she had no doubt Grigory was having an affair. After all, that's what her husband, Nickolay, had been doing when he was supposedly rebuilding his Minsk M1A motorcycle. She kept her opinion to herself, however, because she'd long ago guessed that Grigory was part of the *nomenklatura*.

Reading this exchange, Dimitri also was willing to bet that Grigory wasn't going to Qobustan for the rock engravings, and Dimitri was also certain he wasn't going there for an affair. He sent a signal to the Colonel that they needed to talk. He didn't have to wait long.

"You have something?" The Colonel was back to his gruff, peremptory manner.

Dimitri told him about Alina's email exchange with her mother. "If he's got her, it's probably within a couple of hour radius of Baku."

The Colonel digested this. "Anything else?"

Dimitri told him about his conversation with Roznik. The Colonel grunted. "That gives me a reason to contact Grigory. Can you shadow the conversation?"

*Yes, and I can also jump into an erupting volcano*, thought Dimitri. "Hard to do remotely. I'm not the FAPSI," said Dimitri, referring to the Russia equivalent of the National Security Agency.

"Well, I'm sure you're going to try to do your level best."

*Trapped!* "OK, I'll give it a shot, but I'll need your help. I'm going to send you a text with Roznik's burner phone number. Tell Grigory that Roznik needs to be either scared or paid and that you're texting him the number since Roznik's now his problem. Then send the text before he has a chance to stop you. Even if Grigory doesn't phone Roznik, if he opens the text, it will contain a tracker that will hide on his phone."

"Can he find the tracker?"

"You can find anything if you try hard enough, but he's not going to look because he's going to think that you're just washing your hands of a project that you're no longer involved in."

There was a long silence as the Colonel weighed the pros and cons. "OK, send it,"

"Give me an hour."

After they hung up, Dimitri got to work. He'd done his own weighing of pros and cons, and realized that some leverage had shifted to him since the Colonel now needed him. Even better, he now had something to trade in a pinch. *Insurance!*

After he had located and uploaded the tracker and sent the text to the Colonel, Dimitri set up a monitor. The tracker would activate once Grigory opened the text.

He settled down to wait. He was used to waiting, and he returned to his habit of killing time by perusing the various dating sites where he maintained profiles.

After cycling through a few, he turned to RussianCupid. Anything new? After sorting through a few potential matches, Kamila popped up.

Absolutely beautiful. Advanced degree. Not sure what she was looking for, maybe a relationship, but mostly someone who she could talk to.

Dimitri tried to think of an intro that might catch her attention. Knowing a bit about the game, he sent her a message. "For me, the past is an endlessly fascinating refuge. The longer ago the better. Also, I promise I will never send you a picture of me holding a big fish!"

Dimitri continued his research into Alina's online presence, but then was interrupted by a ping. Kamila had responded. "Can I hold you to that promise about the fish?"

Thrilled, Dimitri responded in the affirmative (noting that it would take a heroic degree of self-control), and for the next few minutes, they messaged back and forth, flirting and filling out the picture on each other. Dimitri, a polymath, raided his prodigious memory bank and told her about new tomographic investigations of the 30,000-year-old Venus figurine found on the banks of the Danube in Willendorf, Austria. She avoided talking about anything relating to the Transteppe dig, but mentioned how tomography had helped determine how ancient Americans had killed and butchered Mammoths. In all, it was a glorious example of verbal foreplay, ultra-nerd division, and it ended when Kamila agreed to have coffee with him the next day.

Dimitri had proposed a café, but she had responded that she was stuck inside all day and would love to meet someplace outside. Respecting that she wanted a place where she could not be trapped, Dimitri offered another option. *What about that coffee kiosk in Presidential Park, at 4 p.m.?*

Kamila quickly responded, *Done!*

# 41 KATIE MAKES A PLAN

IT CAME TO HER FULLY FORMED IN THE PRE-DAWN, INGMAR Bergman's hour of the wolf, that hallucinatory time when the unconscious and conscious comingle, when most babies are born, and when most people die. The plan was simplicity itself. She figured out that the guards watched her in shifts. She would seduce one of her guards, get his weapon, and force the other guards to shoot her, either by threatening to shoot her victim, or actually shooting him. She liked the idea because it offered the glimmer of hope that she might actually be able to shoot her way out and escape. There were exceedingly low odds of being successful, but in her hours of brooding over what to do, Katie had recognized that the fire deep within her—the fire that had earlier made her a warrior for captive animals, and that drove her to help bring Bart back from a five-million-year slumber—wouldn't consider the thought of suicide. That fire could, however, propel her to go out guns blazing.

From her days in animal rights activism, Katie had always been a "ready, fire, aim," kind of girl. Now, in her thirties, implications and consequences intruded more easily than in her early twenties, when hormones and adrenaline ruled the roost. She didn't worry about disappointing her family. Her father, a well-travelled rocker, had died in a car crash when she was twelve, and long before that her mother had already gone off the rails on drugs and alcohol. She'd left what passed for home at seventeen, and found a substitute for family in her network of like-minded activists. However, as a result of meeting Dev, the idea of having a kid was released from the dungeon to which she had consigned the prospect, given her views on the state of the planet and society—Katie regarded humanity as an invasive species. And, of course, she was a member of that species, setting up a cognitive dissonance that expressed itself as a discordant thrum at the edge of her consciousness that had haunted her and alienated her since she'd arrived at that conclusion in her early teens. What the world had encountered was a beautiful woman who always seemed a bit remote. But then Dev came along.

Ah Dev . . . She'd picked Dev on a whim. She hadn't been with a man in years, and then he turned up. Better yet, he became one of the fold. He was a good-looking guy with a brain, wit, and a conscience—and single. Why not? But now it was no longer a lark. She opened her heart to very few men, and none in years, but she discovered in Dev something of a kindred spirit, another lost soul who saw the world—and himself—too clearly for his own good. Dev was the missing piece in her life; could she give that up now that she'd just found him? Her thoughts wheeled to Bart, her five-thousand-pound, genius stepson, attuned to a world she couldn't access. Bart, who hadn't asked to be brought into this world, but who opened a window on how an intelligence might work in harmony with the natural order. Her resolve stiffened; he was everything to her, and protecting him trumped everything.

She needed to move fast. If a deal had been made, her sacrifice would be a waste. If that happened, trading Bart for her life would ruin the lives of everyone ever connected to bringing Bart to life. In that sense she would be acting not just for Bart, but for all of them.

She heard the door being unlocked as the guard brought her breakfast. She was propped up on her mattress when he came in. She checked to make sure he was armed. He was. Good. The guard, a fit young Moldovan named Mihail, glanced over at her. Even though his face was covered with a kerchief, Katie could see his eyes. She held his gaze with a long look. Her message was unmistakable. He'd be back.

# 42 NOT WHAT HE EXPECTED

THIS WAS DECIDEDLY NOT HOW DIMITRI EXPECTED THE afternoon to go. In his mind, he'd meet Kamila at the coffee kiosk in Presidential Park, they'd walk over to the splendid fountain in the shape of a Samruk, the mythical bird that symbolizes freedom in Kazakhstan, and get to know each other. After experiencing firsthand Dimitri's charm and erudition, perhaps Kamila would reward him with a long glance and give him the answer every man longs to hear when asking a lovely woman when they might see each other again: "Whenever you'd like." He wouldn't tell her about his wealth (and definitely not how he'd gotten it!); he wanted the relationship to be a meeting of minds and hearts, unpolluted by money. Who knows, he'd speculated, maybe this would open a new chapter in his life, a movement out of the shadows and, maybe, even toward normalcy—couple of kids, teaching the little ones how to ride bicycles and swim, with Kamila emerging from the house, smiling patiently, and calling them to dinner.

For her part, Kamila was thinking none of these things.

And now, instead of a romantic first meeting with Kamila, he'd gotten a text saying that she had to postpone their meeting because her mother had fallen, and she had to help her around her flat.

From there things went downhill fast. When he had returned, disconsolate, to his office, he'd been rushed by two extremely rough-looking men with dead eyes, shoved into his office, and tied to his desk chair. They'd gagged him and said nothing. Then, a tall man arrived, wearing a ski mask. The two thugs had departed, and the man had casually looked around the office before grabbing a chair and seating himself in front of Dimitri. The man took out a pistol and screwed in a silencer. Then he said in English, "I don't have much time."

On the one hand, Dimitri was relieved the man wasn't Russian, but then again, there was that pistol with a silencer. Struggling to control his voice Dimitri ventured a question. "What's this about?"

"Dimitri Medvedev, you know what this is about. Katie."

*He knew his name!* Dimitri thought furiously. American accent. *Americans aren't going to assassinate someone over an elephant. Are they?* The tall man seemed to sense that Dimitri was about to stall.

"Don't waste my time. We're working against the clock. If I don't get what I want, those two guys will come back, knock you out—if I haven't already put a couple of bullets into you—and then take you away after dark. One-way trip."

"I'm also a dead man if I talk to you."

"No, the Russians won't know it. And if you're helpful, we'll get you out of Kazakhstan."

"I had no part in the kidnapping."

"That's a start. Tell me all you know."

Dimitri tried to think of a story he could sell, but he didn't know what this man knew—and, again, there was that gun with a silencer. So, he spilled. He told Rob about how Grigory had taken control, about how the Colonel feared that Grigory had gone rogue, and about how he had figured that Katie was held somewhere in the vicinity of Baku. He didn't mention the tracker.

Rob digested all this in silence. He started to get up. "Not good enough." He went to the door and rapped twice. His men answered the rap.

Dimitri panicked. "Wait!"

Dimitri cracked the door and held up his hand. He turned back to Dimitri.

"I told you I don't have time."

"Through the Colonel, I put a tracker on Grigory's phone. It's still there. I can shadow it."

Rob pulled out a knife, and while holding the pistol on Dimitri, he cut the ties binding one of Dimitri's hands. "Let's see what you've got." He handed Dimitri his phone which his men had retrieved before tying him up. "I don't think I have to tell you," started Rob in his most menacing voice, "what will happen if you try anything cute." He kept the pistol trained on Dimitri as the hacker plowed through various firewalls to get to the tracker. He pulled up the history, and showed it to Rob. It showed the movements of Grigory's phone against a map, but the names of the towns were in Russian. Rob studied the phone's movements. He pointed to a spot Grigory visited a couple of times just West of the Caspian Sea. "Translate."

Dimitri peered at the phone. "It's a small village in Qobustan called Oghuz."

Can you pull up the exact position of the destination of the phone when he's visited that town?"

Dimitri went back to work. After about a minute he showed the phone to Rob, who wrote down the coordinates. He also wrote down Grigory's name and what Dimitri knew about the Colonel. "OK, you did good. By the way, you now work for me. Welcome! Call me Stan. If I need to, I'll contact you through that British classic car mag." Dimitri went bug-eyed hearing this. Rob smiled. He went to the door and waited while his men reappeared from the stairwell where they had been keeping out of sight. He spoke rapidly to the two men, and then came back inside with one of them. "I'm leaving now. He's . . ." Rob nodded his head toward the guard now inside the apartment, ". . . staying for another twenty minutes. He'll untie you, but wait another ten minutes before leaving. The other guard will make sure you keep to that. Try anything, and you'll have both your Russian buddies and my pals going after you. And, by the way, in that case, decades in prison for being accessory to kidnapping is your best-case scenario. Play ball and I'll keep to my promise."

Dimitri couldn't find a way to disagree with that analysis, but now, fairly sure that he wasn't going to die imminently, he recovered some of his poise. As Rob walked to the door, Dimitri said, "I can be useful."

Rob nodded and left.

# 43 BETTING EVERYTHING ON BLACK

IT WAS SEVEN P.M. BY THE TIME THE HELICOPTER DROPPED ROB off at Transteppe, which meant it was eight a.m. in Boisbeaux. It was also beginning on three days since Katie had been kidnapped. Rob wasted no time and set up a call to commence in ten minutes. While he waited, Rob thought about the best way to go forward. A former Army Ranger, Rob was no-nonsense to the core. The idea of trusting Katie's fate to the woo-woo abilities of an elephant just about exploded his central nervous system. But he'd seen what Bart could do when the Russians had attempted to kidnap him, and also knew that Bart had an otherworldly ability to reach into the consciousness of someone thousands of miles away. *Give Bart a shot*, he thought. *And then send in a team.*

He thought back to missions in Iraq and Syria. There was always something they were missing. He quickly ran through the list of players, the Russians, the team in Boisbeaux, and then it hit him . . . *Katie.* The least likely word anyone would apply to Katie was "passive." *What might she do?* He thought about her passion and devotion to Bart, and looked at his watch. The call was in three minutes. He sent a message to Claire. "Make sure Dev is not on this call."

He immediately got back a simple one letter message, "?"

"Please, it will become obvious. And let me know if he's on."

"OK, better hop in that case."

When he joined the encrypted call a few minutes later, Claire took over. "You're on with me, Will Keerbrock, and Sergei."

"Where's Dev?"

"Running a quick errand, he'll be on in about ten minutes. Also, I've teed up a call with Salina after this call."

"Good. I've got some info, and given what I'm about to tell you, it's kind of urgent that Bart try to reach out to Katie. If he does make a connection, we can talk about what's next."

"I think I know where this is going," said Keerbrock.

"It's why I didn't want Dev on this part of the call. Bottom line, Katie's not going to let Bart fall into the Russians' hands, and, when you think about it, there's only one sure way she can stop it." He paused to let that sink in.

There was a stunned silence. Claire was the first to speak. "There's no telling what he'd do if he thought she'd take that route."

Rob then filled in the group on what he had gotten from Dimitri. "The coordinates are more exact than what we had for Rencho. Claire, can you reach out to Salina immediately? Tell her it's urgent that Bart try to reach Katie now. Maybe Bart can let Katie know somehow that she's not alone; maybe there's some magic he can perform through her eyes. I'm preparing a team, but if Bart can reach Katie now it would be immensely helpful." He paused, "And maybe help prevent a tragedy. Let's reconvene as soon as you know whether it worked."

They signed off, and Claire immediately reached out to Salina.

# 44 ACROSS TIME AND SPACE

KATIE FELT A RENEWED WASH OF EMOTIONS AS SHE THOUGHT about her date with destiny—if Mihail showed up. If he did, the probability was that these would be her last few hours. Lying on her mattress earlier, she'd thought she'd settled that score, but now she recognized that there was no way she could process the prospect of purposefully marching toward an endpoint of her life. Adrenaline, anxiety, purpose, anticipatory sadness at what might have been, all swept through her anew. The one thing she didn't feel was sexy. Unless she could summon sexy, this wasn't going to work. Her throat was dry, and there was a hollow in the pit of her stomach.

She guessed it was around three in the afternoon. She had a few hours to get it together. She slowed her breathing and tried to settle her feelings and get her heart rate down. She felt a tremor run through her. *Wow, meditation really does work*, she thought. Then she recognized the feeling for what it was. As the tremors coursed through her veins, her heart soared for the first time since she'd been taken as a new thought came to mind like a banner headline: Bart was going to save her!

Every sense came alive, and time slowed. She felt an urge to stand up and look around as she slowly panned her eyes around the room. Even as she was overwhelmed by Bart's magic, she wondered, *how can I help*? She sensed that Bart was using her as his eyes, and she remembered that when Bart reached out to Rencho, she and Claire knew what Bart wanted them to do even though no words passed between them. Could she send a message to Bart?

There was a small mirror in what passed for her bathroom. Katie walked up to the mirror, breathed on it, and then wrote "9 p.m." She stared at the mirror, and then, wondering whether the image would reverse when Bart saw it through her eyes, she breathed again, and quickly drew a moon and stars.

She could do more. In front of the mirror, she held up four fingers and then pretended to shoot a gun, trying to convey that there were four guards. She erased that image and drew two stick figures holding hands with a moon overhead. She erased that, breathed, and wrote the word "fake." She quickly erased that, drew a big heart, and wrote the word Dev. Then looking into the mirror, she smiled and held her hands over her heart. She felt the tremors begin to subside and waved goodbye into the mirror.

She couldn't imagine the amount of energy it took for Bart to reach out to her, nor how long he could sustain it. She also wondered whether her taking over the messaging somehow interfered with Bart's connection. She prayed that Bart received at least some of it, that he had the vocabulary to describe it.

# 45 HOPE AND A QUESTION

IMMEDIATELY, AFTER BART HAD TRANSLATED WHAT HE HAD seen through Katie's eyes, Salina called Claire and relayed what had transpired. Claire took notes, and then sent out a message convening a conference call. She felt some hope for the first time since Katie's disappearance, and the five minutes to the start of the call seemed to expand into hours. This time they were joined by Zoe and Dev (as murder/suicide seemed to be off the table). Claire recounted what Bart had seen.

Keerbrock looked stunned. "I tell you; Katie is an improvisational genius. Salina really said that Bart could see what she wrote on a fogged mirror?"

Claire couldn't help smiling, Keerbrock was rarely flustered. "Yup."

Keerbrock shook his head, "We now have proof of Arthur C. Clarke's third law: 'Any sufficiently advanced technology is indistinguishable from magic.'"

Claire nodded vigorously, "Except it's not a technology but a natural ability." She then went on to sum up what Katie seemed to be trying to convey, decorously rephrasing a few words as she realized how what she was going to say might affect Dev. "Seems like she's going to convince a guard to take her outside at 9:00 p.m., and wants Bart to try and reconnect then, so he can see the setup beyond the room."

"Or," said Keerbrock, who knew nothing of Dev and Katie's relationship, "She's fallen in love with a guard, goes for romantic moonlight walks, and wants us all to share her happiness."

Claire gave Keerbrock a look that in ancient times would have condemned him to eternal torment in the foulest circle of Hell. He held up his hands in surrender. Dev, elated on hearing Katie's message to him, put out his hands in a calming gesture. "Dr. Keerbrock's just trying to keep things light." Keerbrock smiled and mouthed "Thank you!"

Rob jumped in. "Me and my team will be there tomorrow, lying low, until we get more intel."

"I've got to call Salina," said Claire, "and make sure that Bart's prepared to try and reach out again at 4:00 p.m."

As they began to wrap up the call, Keerbrock said, "Could the rest of you stay on a sec, there's one more thing."

"Go ahead," said Rob.

"I haven't been party to any of these experiences, but I keep thinking about the stone. Here's the thing: when we pick it up it becomes too intense for us to hold. My guess is that it's a byproduct of the interference pattern that conveys the messages encoded within. But the messages come from Bart's ancestors' genius at manipulating wave lengths. Heat can also be generated from wave lengths—think about a microwave, or millimeter wave beams that can be used to vaporize rock."

Dev jumped in, excitedly. "Yes, Claire said that one of Rencho's drawings showed a smoldering stone, very much like the yam stone I took to Bart."

Keerbrock nodded approvingly. "So, we know that Bart has the power to generate intense heat."

The group was silent as they absorbed it.

"And that leads to two questions. One: can Bart do this at a distance?"

Dev's eyes widened as he realized where Keerbrock was heading. "And the other," Dev finished for Keerbrock, "is why hasn't he told us?"

"Exactly!"

Dev wasn't finished. "When Salina and I were with Bart and the stone, we both had the sense that he had seen something that he didn't pass on to us."

"Something to think about," said Keerbrock, "a power like that could be critical in helping to rescue Katie."

# 46 NO MORE HYPOTHETICALS

AT ABOUT 8:30 KATIE HEARD HER DOOR BEING OPENED. SHE knew it was Mihail. Her kidnappers had brought her knapsack, and she had a couple of changes of clothes. She didn't know where she was, but it was hot as blazes. For her meet-up with Mihail she had donned shorts and a short-sleeved buttoned blouse. Katie had never based her identity on her looks, but she knew men liked what they saw. She also knew that casual translated in men's minds to accessible—which was good because casual was all she had with her.

Katie had no ability to speak Russian, and Mihail's English vocabulary would compare unfavorably to that of a moderately intelligent parrot. As Mihail entered holding a bottle of vodka and a hunk of cheese, he made gestures—using his fingers to suggest walking and miming shoveling food into his mouth—and words—"back later"—to get across that he'd waited until the other guards had taken off. Getting into the spirit of mime, Katie opened her hands in a panoramic gesture, trying to get across that she hadn't seen anything beyond the four walls of her windowless room, and that she would love to go outside, even for a few minutes. Mihail seemed to consider this. To short-circuit any doubts, Katie gave him the kind of meaningful look that Dimitri had dreamed of getting from Kamila.

Mihail held up a finger—"wait"—and went out of the room. A minute later he opened her door and gestured for her to follow. As they passed the kitchen he grabbed a couple of glasses. Katie mimed asking for a glass and filled it with water from the sink. Given what she hoped was going to happen, she did not want alcohol to interfere. Mihail looked a little disappointed, but gestured for her to head for the door, and then outside. It was near sunset and still hot, but the wind had died. Katie breathed deeply and beamed. She wasn't faking; a few hours earlier, she'd been facing the prospect of never seeing the sun again. Now she found herself looking at a vast landscape of semi-desert scrub and grass.

Mihail pointed toward a small copse of thick-trunked pistachio trees which shaded a simple table and a couple of beaten-up plastic chairs. Walking over, Katie scanned the horizon. She couldn't see any other dwellings. Once they sat down, Mihail poured himself a vodka and pointed the bottle toward Katie. She smiled and pointed to her water. Mihail took a sip of vodka and looked at her, cocking his head. Katie realized she needed to stall, so she pointed toward the hunk of cheese. Mihail took out a military knife, cut a chunk, speared it, and handed it to Katie. It tasted to Katie like it was some type of peasant goat cheese, but she found it delicious and smiled at the guard in gratitude.

Mihail took another sip of vodka. Katie sensed that he was gathering his courage. Mihail leaned back in his chair, smiled, and pointed at Katie's chest and then mimed unbuttoning her shirt. This was pretty unambiguous, and if Bart didn't act soon, plan A was going to be back in full force. Katie smiled, gestured around her, and took a couple of deep breaths, trying to get across the message, "let's take our time." Mihail frowned, but didn't say anything. He took another sip of vodka.

*OK*, thought Katie. *Better make a game out of this.* She unbuttoned the top of her blouse and pointed to the cheese. To her relief, Mihail got it. He cut another piece, speared it, and once again handed it to her. Katie took it, and slowly ate it with one hand while opening one more button. She kept a lazy smile on her face, but there was a knot in her stomach. She was running out of buttons, and she was pretty certain that Mihail had come for more than a PG-rated peep show.

She saw and felt it simultaneously. The water in the glass in her hand began to ripple, and she felt the tremors that she now recognized were a sign that Bart was here. Katie let Bart's waves wash over her, letting him take control. She slowly looked around at her surroundings before focusing on Mihail. She knew what she hoped Bart would do, and also knew that she had better put more distance between her and Mihail. She stretched and stood up from her chair and took a few steps back while keeping her gaze trained on Mihail. He looked at her curiously. Katie felt a powerful pulse; Bart was doing something. She took a couple more steps backward. Mihail started to get up, but then sat down and yawned. His head dropped on his chest. Katie quickly stepped back farther—a nice nap was the last thing she needed at the moment. Mihail leaned onto the table, dropping his head onto his arms. He was in a deep sleep. Katie stared at Mihail, hoping that Bart would see that he had put him out.

Katie felt Bart's presence subside, and quickly moved to Mihail. She took his pistol and knife; she might yet have to resort to plan A if she became cornered. She searched through Mihail's pockets and found a cell phone. His wallet contained several bills of what looked like currency. The lettering on the bills said Azerbaijani Manat. *So that's where I am!* She took the bills. Then she used the knife to cut strips from the guard's trousers and used those strips to tie his legs to the legs of the chair. She carefully bound his wrists together with another strip. In a pocket she found keys to a motorcycle, which she also took, and he had a radio on his belt.

She grabbed the radio and the remainder of the cheese, and moved quickly toward the farmhouse, where she saw the guard's motorcycle— which turned out to be a dirt bike. *That's good!* The bike had a small container on a rack, located over the rear wheel, and she managed to get the pistol to fit snuggly inside. She was about to hop on the bike when she had a thought. She ducked inside the farmhouse and saw a large plastic bottle of water. She raced into her room, grabbed her knapsack, and stuffed the water bottle into it. On the way out, she saw binoculars hanging from a peg inside the door. She put those in her knapsack along with a loaf of bread from the kitchen counter.

Back outside, she hopped on the dirt bike and turned the key. She held her breath as the bike coughed a couple of times, but then roared to life. She hadn't driven a motorcycle in years, but managed to kick it into gear and off she went, wobbling a bit at first. She drove a hundred yards toward what she thought was west, and then she tossed the radio, leaving it turned on, with the volume turned up, to make it easier for the kidnappers to find. Katie then drove a bit further, continuing in the same direction, before doubling back, and heading east on the small, paved road that passed the farmhouse.

She was getting nervous. Whoever was relieving Mihail would undoubtedly be taking that same road, and she didn't know from which direction. To boot, it was getting dark. She made a point of noting the landmark where the sun was setting, and took the first turnoff she could, which turned out to be a dirt path heading what she thought would be north. After continuing for a mile or so, she pulled over and killed the engine.

Katie pulled Mihail's cell phone out of her pocket and scrolled through the unlocked phone's apps, discovering that the guard had WhatsApp installed. *That will work!* Katie and Claire frequently used WhatsApp when communicating on non-sensitive matters. She was quite sure Mihail's communications were monitored, but she needed to get word to Claire, or anyone. There was no cell service where she was, but if she sent a message from Mihail's account it would go into a queue, and be sent once she (or the phone) once again had service. So, she wrote: *Out. Looking forward to the party, but staying close—need a ride.* She hit send. Then she turned the phone off; no need to make herself easier to track.

Katie scanned the horizon, looking for lights that signaled a town, but saw nothing. She didn't know much about Azerbaijan, but she knew it was on the Caspian, which meant that if she went east, eventually she would hit the sea; or run out of gas, be arrested, or be recaptured. Would arrest be bad? *Yes!* There'd be too many questions about why she had been taken.

She thought about Bart. He was her best hope, but could he follow her as she travelled? How did he find her? Did someone point him in the general direction, or could he find her anywhere? She thought about Rencho, remembering that they had taken pains to orient Bart to where Rencho was. So, somehow, the team had found out where she was being held. And, if they could orient Bart, they could also tell Rob, who might be sending help. That did it, despite the danger it definitely would be better to find a hiding place near where she had been held.

The night sky was filled with the light of the moon and a million stars, enabling Katie to see the hilly, arid, rock-strewn landscape without using the headlight on the bike. She knew that she couldn't return along the same road, but figured that it may be possible for her to bushwack a path and drive slowly parallel to the road, and keep the bike noise from carrying to it.

So, Katie slowly made her way through the clear desert night, dodging scrub, rocks, and the occasional copse of trees. At one point, she stopped on a rise, and scanned the night air in the direction of the road. Nothing. And so, she drove on until she thought she was approximately a mile inland from where she had been held. Katie retrieved a sweater from her knapsack that she'd brought along for the trip to Tibet. The temperature was dropping fast, so she looked for some high ground.

How would they search for her? The next shift must have returned by now and discovered Mihail. Dogs? She hadn't seen or heard any, but that didn't mean they couldn't get them. But that would take some time and cause a commotion, and they certainly didn't want to cause a commotion. They weren't on Russian soil.

She thought back to the earlier, failed, attempt to grab Bart. If she remembered correctly, the kidnappers had some sort of drone which used thermal imaging. If these guys had another drone, she was a sitting duck. Maybe they'd fall for her misdirection ploy in dropping the radio to the west and waste some time. They'd also likely assume that she would try to get as far away as possible. Ahead of her, she saw a rock outcropping. She wheeled the bike to its north side, which afforded some shielding if they were directing the search from the farmhouse. She changed into her one pair of field trousers with outer pockets, and donned a few layers against the rapidly cooling temperatures. Then she ate some bread and cheese and had a drink of water. She put the remainder of the bread, cheese, and water back into her knapsack, and zipped it up, propping the knapsack between the dirt bike and the rock.

Katie sat back against the rock and tried to make sense of everything. She now had a real shot at escaping . . . if Rob or his team got to her in time, if Bart had some more magic in his quiver, and if she wasn't recaptured. That prospect brought plan A back to mind, along with its travelling companion, existential dread. Before Bart had reached out, her absolute determination to prevent Bart from falling into their hands had allowed her to keep that dread at bay. Now, with new hope and some control of her destiny, plan A had become an unwelcome and insistent *memento mori*. It was no longer a hypothetical. She had the pistol. She hadn't shot a gun in years either, and hoped she wouldn't have to now. Would she go out guns blazing? If cornered, she would have to.

At last, deciding that she needed to act, she got up, slung the binoculars around her neck, and retrieved the pistol. After studying the gun and locating the safety, she put it into an outer pocket of her trousers. She thought a second and then picked up the cell phone. Could they track it if it was off? She weighed the risks and then put the cell phone in her hip pocket—maybe there was service at the farmhouse. Maybe Bart would reach out to her again; certainly, Bart would reach out to her again.

Katie looked around, memorizing the landmarks surrounding the outcropping, and then started walking in what she thought was the direction of the farmhouse. Better to reconnoiter at night. Her plan was to figure out where the farmhouse was, get a sense of the activity, and then return for a couple of hours sleep. However, tomorrow unfolded, it was going to be a long day.

# 47 TROUBLE ON THE FARM

IT WAS THE THIRD NIGHT AFTER THE KIDNAPPING, AND TIME TO get a response from Boisbeaux. They'd had plenty of time to consider their options and Grigory had no doubt they would trade their elephant for the woman, Katie. Americans were sentimentalists, and Claire Knowland was a scientist, and probably a liberal. What did they call them in the states, "Bleeding hearts?" He was in Baku and about to arrange for the message to be delivered when he saw an urgent message flash on his screen. In Russian it read, "Trouble on the farm." Grigory immediately responded, "On my way," he wrote through the encrypted app, "No action until I get there." He headed for his car.

On his way to the hideout, Grigory considered his options. He was not one to lose his cool. This is the price for going solo, he thought. When he took on this operation ten years earlier, he had access to all manner of surveillance and labor. As the years passed, higher ups were replaced, and workforce turned over, and the extreme compartmentalization of his office meant that fewer and fewer people knew about this extraordinary find. After seven years only he, the Colonel, and the hacker Dimitri knew about the project. He thought about taking this project private for another year before he did anything, and even after he assembled his teams of mercenaries and contractors, he maintained his job. He still had access to the FSB's vast arsenal of technology, but for labor he now had to find people completely separate from past associations with any agency or military group, and that meant a steep decline in quality. As for access to technology, deploying any of it involved making requests that might provoke questions he didn't want to answer. Bring the Colonel back into the loop, and ask him for monitoring? Bad idea; Grigory hadn't liked the direction of their last conversation. Better to use the drone.

He considered options. If she had escaped, that was bad, but not the end of the game. He could mount another operation, and he'd figured out that Knowland and her colleagues were keeping this secret from everyone, including the Americans. The worst outcomes would be if either his government or the Americans found out about the elephant. Next worst was if a hothead on his team killed Katie. He'd lose his bargaining chip, and it might provoke Claire Knowland to go to the authorities. If she'd escaped; he'd find her—she wasn't an agent; she wasn't trained.

Grigory snorted grimly. She wasn't an agent, but she was a real looker. He should have considered that after a couple of days, discipline might break down in the mercs he'd hired. As he pulled in, he saw that Mihail was in handcuffs, sitting on a bench in front of the hideout, and illuminated by a light fixture over the door. He saw another guard working the joystick on the drone and looking at a screen. There was a lot of ground to cover.

He gestured to Andrei, his team leader, and they walked over to the table where the bottle of vodka still sat, along with Mihail's empty glass. Wordlessly, Andrei pointed his flashlight at the scene. Grigory glanced over and rolled his eyes. Andrei filled him in, and pointed to the spot up the road where they'd found Mihail's radio.

"Wasn't he armed?"

Andrei shook his head. "We're still trying to figure this out. He says he suddenly felt this overwhelming desire to sleep and passed out. She must have slipped him a Mickey Finn," (clonidine was the drug of choice for robbing tourists in Moscow, and gangsters adopted the American nickname). "We'd searched her knapsack. Don't know how she got it."

Grigory nodded. He knew exactly what had happened, and it had happened from seven thousand miles away! *What else can that elephant do?!* He had to get his hands on it. Then other thoughts intruded. *How had the elephant known Katie's location? Was there a leak? Did the animal have some uncanny ability to connect with someone anywhere in the world?*

He thought about the leak possibility. He immediately thought of Dimitri. At this point, he couldn't worry about that because he simply didn't have the workforce. He had money from a secret black ops budget he'd diverted, but it was not infinite. That Russian helicopter was expensive, and apart from this team of kidnappers, he had one man in the US who could deliver messages, and the small team stationed in central Africa that he had used in his earlier attempt to grab Bart. Even the team in Africa didn't know the importance of the elephant. He'd told them that the elephant was immensely valuable because it turned out to be immune to tuberculosis that had decimated its herd.

Grigory looked over at Mihail. He was burned, and Grigory needed to *encourager les autres*. He looked at Andrei who kept his face expressionless but nodded. Grigory walked over to Mihail, who looked up in fear and looked like he was about to speak. He didn't get a chance. Grigory pulled out a pistol and shot him twice in the head. Blood and brain matter hit the wall of the farmhouse. Mihail, eyes wide open, fell off the bench onto his face. Grigory then looked each of the remaining men in the eye. None held his gaze. "The three of you should be able to handle one woman."

He then went over to the mercenary working the drone. "Where have you looked?"

# 48 THE SHOTS HEARD ROUND THE WORLD

KATIE, BUSHWHACKING BY MOONLIGHT, AND TRYING TO GUESS how far away she was from the kidnappers' hideout, heard the shots. She was remarkably close. She instantly knew what it meant and felt a pang of guilt. Even though plan A would have resulted in her shooting at her kidnappers, she felt bad about Mihail. She'd led him on, and she'd known Mihail's boss, whoever that was, would not let such an egregious breach go without consequences. No court would ever convict her, much less try her, but she knew she might as well have pulled the trigger. She shook her head; this was not the time for recrimination. She had to be decisive and cold, or Bart would likely end up in these Russians' hands.

She looked in the direction of the gunshot, and memorized the landmarks. She guessed she was about a quarter mile away from the farmhouse. She made a small cairn of stones to mark the spot, arranged some more stones into an arrow pointing in the direction of the gunshot. She pulled out Mihail's cell phone and turned it on. Still no signal. She quickly turned it off. She had to get closer. Too dangerous to do that right now. She began retracing her steps back to her rock hideout. She would return at first light.

Rob also heard the shots. He, and two trusted contract security guards—former Army rangers from Rob's tours in Iraq—were encamped behind a small hillock off the road a mile from the farmhouse. Helen had agreed immediately to compensate Transteppe for time and fuel and Rob requisitioned a Transteppe jet to fly the 1200 miles to Baku that morning. Sergei arranged for Rob to bring along a Transteppe drone equipped with thermal imaging technology. Aware that the kidnappers had used a drone in their prior attempt at Bart, Rob had covered the van with a large, desert camouflaged mylar blanket to hide the van and their heat signatures.

*What did those shots mean?* Claire had relayed reports from Salina about what Bart saw and did earlier that evening, and knew that Katie had likely escaped. He didn't know whether the shots indicated that the kidnappers were firing at Katie, Katie at the kidnappers, or something else. Rob felt a surge of pure anger. If the kidnappers had shot Katie, they were dead men. But that didn't make sense. They wouldn't kill Katie, not if they wanted to trade her for Bart. He thought about the shots. Two shots fired in tight succession. More like an execution. If not Katie, who? Most likely the guard who had let Katie escape.

Immediately after hearing the shots, he'd sent the drone in the direction of the sound. He couldn't send it too close lest it be discovered, but didn't need to because the drone could read heat signatures from two thousand feet away. From the readings, Rob could see there was a lot of activity right around the farmhouse.

The straightforward thing to do would be to neutralize the remaining kidnappers and then search for Katie—Rob had the advantage of the element of surprise because Katie had escaped on her own and the kidnappers didn't know that Rob's team was nearby. That was off the table, because, if Bart was going to remain secret, Rob couldn't risk being identified and connected to Transteppe. The best thing would be to somehow find Katie and spirit her away without being seen. So, where would Katie go, once she escaped?

Rob looked at a topographic map of the area. The drone had about thirty minutes more airtime before it needed to come in for recharging. She wouldn't try to find another house; he assumed she had no identification and also wouldn't want to be answering questions about why she'd been kidnapped. He also assumed she'd stay close to the site if only because she knew she needed to be somewhere where Bart could find her. The search was made more difficult because while there were few people in the region, there was plenty of wildlife. Apart from goats, there were foxes, feral cats, hares, even the occasional jackal. Even the land emitted heat signatures as Qobustan was famous for its mud volcanos. Rob told the drone operator to bring the machine back in for recharging. "Let's be ready at first light. We'll see what they're up to, and figure from there."

Across the globe, Claire heard about the shots. Rob had sent an encrypted message. "Think Katie's still free, but don't know where. Shots fired, but probably not about Katie. We'll find her."

The message precipitated a mixture of anxiety and elation in Boisbeaux. Claire was pretty certain that Katie would not let herself be recaptured alive (though he didn't share this with Dev), which made it imperative that Rob find Katie before the kidnappers. Could Bart help? Rob's message came in about 1:00 p.m., which made it 10:00 p.m. in Qobustan and 7:00 p.m. in Mbembe. Claire wasn't sure how much Bart's efforts took out of him, and whether he could establish contact with her if she had moved too far from where she had been held.

After talking things over with the group, she called Salina. Briefing her on where things stood, Claire moved on to her main concern. "Do you have a sense of how far Bart is willing to go to save Katie, and how much this is taking out of him?"

At first there was silence, then Salina was back on the line. "I honestly don't know. He's hard to read and he's stoic. So far, he's done everything we've asked, but I do think that he expends a lot of energy in reaching out over long distances, much less influencing things, like he did with Katie's captor."

Claire weighed this—it was clear Salina was being incredibly careful in what she said. "Unfortunately, if we're going to save Katie, we'll have to ask Bart to reach out to her again, tomorrow at first light. Can you do that?"

"Of course, and I'm sure Bart will cooperate—if he can find her."

The others at Boisbeaux had been listening to the conversation. Keerbrock raised a hand. "Please ask Salina if she will ask whether Bart can generate heat at a distance?"

Claire looked at Keerbrock in puzzlement, then she got it. She said to Salina, "Hold on a sec," and then turned to Keerbrock. "Might be best to ask him that once he's made contact with Katie."

"Agreed."

Claire put the question to Salina. There was a long silence, then Salina said, "Why?"

Claire knew how protective Salina was of Bart, but they all were. She wanted to say, "Because it might be the only way to save Katie's life." Instead, she said, "If it comes to that, Bart will know why."

There was another silence. Then, again choosing her words carefully, "He's never said this explicitly, but I've got a strong sense that Bart does not want to be used as a weapon."

Claire felt exasperated, but took a few breaths to hide it. "I completely understand, which is why it should be posed as a question. Salina, all any of us want is to keep Bart safe and rescue Katie. If Bart has the ability to project heat, it might prevent weapons from being used, and I think Bart will understand that."

"I get it too, but I don't want to do anything that would have Bart questioning my motives."

Claire thought about this. Salina was right. "Why don't I call in and ask the question?"

"Won't work. Bart finds the microwaves of a sat phone grating, and they might interfere with his efforts to reach Katie." Another pause. "OK, he'll probably figure it out, but if he makes contact and things get dicey, I'll ask him."

"Tell Bart that I asked you to ask him."

"No, I'll do it. I'll do it because you're right—if he has that power and uses it, it will be to prevent weapons from being used."

Claire welled up with gratitude. "Thank you, Salina."

After the call, Dev looked at Claire. "What was *that* about?"

Keerbrock chuckled. "Bart's wonders never cease to amaze. The latest seems to be that he's Sergeant York—or at least before York had his battlefield conversion."

# 49 MBEMBE AT DAWN

THE BAI WAS JUST COMING TO LIFE. IN THE SURROUNDING trees, African grey parrots commenced a chorus of indignant cross-chatter. Mangabeys, Colobus, and Blue Monkeys added their two cents, and in the distance, Salina could hear the first pant hoots of the day as a group of chimpanzees stirred in their arboreal nests. She set up the voice synthesizer in the bai as the first light bathed the bai. Bart separated from his herd at the edge of the bai and walked over. He emitted a short series of rumbles. "Something is wrong?"

Salina had been dreading this conversation, even as she knew it was necessary. She'd put on a smile, but was clenched up inside. She realized she should have known better. If Bart could diagnose Claire's hurt shoulder by sensing her aura, he could see Salina's tension. "I'm just worried about Katie."

"Is she free?"

"She's free, but not safe. Can you find her?"

"I will find her now."

Salina had no idea what he was going to do, but stayed silent. Bart turned in the direction he had taken when he last reached out to Katie. Salina felt the power of his presence and his concentration as he sent a pulse out into a world to which only he had access.

# 50 A BOLT FROM THE BLUE

THE FEMALE IMPERIAL EAGLE STIRRED IN HER NEST, A MASSIVE structure of twigs and grasses set in the middle branches of a lone cypress, some three miles from Katie. The eagle's two fledglings had left the nest a week earlier, but stayed close. The sun had been up for three hours and thermals were beginning to form as the arid land heated up. Something alerted the great bird to a threat. She launched herself from the nest, glided toward the nearest thermal and then spiraled up several hundred feet. She lazily panned the landscape. Some force guided her toward the small farmhouse. She scanned the perimeter of the farmhouse in expanding circles. Then, again as if guided by some force, the eagle focused on a human no more than fifty yards from the farmhouse.

Katie looked up and saw the eagle. She remembered the eagle that had followed their trek back from the monastery to the guesthouse and wondered, *could it be?* She didn't have time to dwell on that thought because she saw another object in the sky, a drone, hovering between her and the farmhouse. Busted. She turned on the cell phone. A signal! She left it on for 20 seconds that seemed like an eternity; hoping it was enough time for the queued message to be sent. Then, she turned the phone off and she began to move back toward her hideout in the rocks, taking a zigzag route. Unless that eagle meant that help was on the way, plan A was now the only plan.

Things were speeding up fast, and Katie found herself reassessing in real time. As she retreated, she heard stirrings and shouts from the farmhouse. She glanced up to see whether the drone was still there. Yup, but as she was about to look away, she saw the eagle fall out of its circling and dive toward the drone at extraordinary speed, talons extended. It crushed the housing and cracked the circuit boards that controlled its sensors and then dropped the wreckage, which fell into the yard in front of the farmhouse. The hubbub emanating from the farmhouse was replaced by stunned silence. Then she heard shots fired at the eagle, none of which came close.

At the farm, Grigory looked at the wreckage of the drone. He hadn't seen the eagle attack it, but the drone operator told him about it. He knew airport security forces in England had trained hawks to take out drones, but did not believe that was the case here. It was that elephant again. What else could it do? He turned to Andrei. "We don't need the drone anymore. We know where she is. Just get her—alive!" Andrei gave orders for his men to fan out and they started moving north toward Katie's last location.

Rob also saw the eagle take out the drone. Surreal, he thought; it had to be Bart's work. He already knew Katie was close. Claire had received Katie's WhatsApp message and immediately relayed it to Rob. Rob and his men then drove closer to the farm, hoping that Grigory was preoccupied with Katie. They stopped five hundred yards away and proceeded on foot. Neither he, nor his men, had arms—too short notice to get weapons into the country, but they had knives and radios. They also had flare guns, which are easy to get past customs and could be used as a weapon at close range. They also could be used to alert the others if someone got in a fix. And they had Bart, though he had no idea where Bart would draw the line as to what he would do.

That the drone was out of action was a godsend, but they were still a few hundred yards behind Grigory's men. As they moved, his drone operator monitored the heat signatures of Katie and the kidnappers on a portable screen. Two men were about two hundred yards behind Katie, while one man was back at the farmhouse. Rob figured the guy at the farmhouse was Grigory. He split up his team, detailing the two former rangers to neutralize and gag the boss, while he tried to close the gap on the two henchmen.

Not long after they split up, they heard a shot. He was too far back to see what had happened. Either Katie was shooting at Grigory's men, or they were shooting at her. *Not likely the henchmen*, thought Rob. Katie was their meal ticket. That meant it had to be Katie doing the shooting. He thought furiously. Katie's plan A unfolded in his mind in an instant—she wasn't going to be taken alive. He got on the radio, "The shots distracted Grigory. Take him now! She doesn't know we're here! I'm sending up a flare." Rob pulled out his flare gun and fired it into the air.

WHEN SHE SAW THE EAGLE TAKE OUT THE DRONE, KATIE'S hopes had soared. But nothing had happened since, and now Grigory's henchmen had tracked her down. It looked like it was going to be a High Noon at the OK Corral situation after all. Hiding behind her the rock outcropping that had become her base, she pulled the pistol out of her thigh pocket. It felt strange in her hand. She flipped off the safety. The men were approaching, guns at the ready, from two different angles. One guy was signaling the other to move forward. They didn't seem to be concerned about whether she was armed. They were about twenty feet away. Okay then. Katie darted out from behind the rock, pointed at the leader and fired. And missed. They dove for cover, but didn't fire back—confirmation that they were under orders to take her alive. *I don't have orders not to fire*, she thought. She was planning how to take her next shot when she saw the flare. *Rob?!*

The henchmen saw the flare too. The leader got on his radio and said something in Russian. Nothing back. He tried again. Nothing. He yelled over to his partner in Russian. She heard rustling as the men repositioned, but she couldn't see where. She heard a brief scuffle off to her left. She peered around to get a better look when she heard someone behind her say something that sounded like *brosit pistolet.*

Plan A or plan B; Katie had about one-tenth of a second to choose. She could end things now and they definitely would have no one to trade for Bart. But maybe the Russian would just shoot to wound her. And where was Rob—or whoever the flare guy was?

The decision was taken out of her hands. She had to put the pistol down. Something between electricity and heat was making it impossible to hold. She heard the Russian swear as he dropped his gun. As she was turning around, she saw a blur coming right at them from the sky at fantastic speed. The Russian saw it too, but even as he began to raise his arm to ward it off, the eagle hit the side of his head with his breastbone and the Russian collapsed in a heap. The eagle stood on the Russian's chest for a minute, as though mantling her prey. Then she looked up at Katie with blazing intensity that would freeze prey in its tracks. It certainly froze Katie. *There's a message there from Bart*, thought Katie. *But what?* The eagle flew off.

Rob appeared a moment later, sporting a welt on his cheek and abrasions on his knuckles. He looked at the scene, checked the Russian's pulse—he was out cold, but not dead. "Between you, the eagle, and Bart, I'm not sure I was needed."

"Oh yes you were," said Katie, "that flare saved my life." She ran to Rob and gave him a hug that nearly broke his ribs. "Thank you!"

Rob's two rangers appeared and got to work. Rob gave Katie some water and a sports bar and motioned for her to find a place to sit, but she wanted to help. She retrieved her knapsack. One of the rangers took Mihail's dirt bike and headed off toward the farmhouse.

Rob had already tied up the henchmen he had subdued. One of the rangers looked at Rob's cuts and bruises and joked that he was losing his touch. Rob tied up Andrei, and then tried to revive him. He probably had a serious concussion. They took weapons, radios, and cell phones. The ranger returned from the farmhouse with a duffle bag, and they piled all the stuff in except for the two rifles. Using the Russians' guns to prod the two henchmen, the group headed back toward the farmhouse. Before they got there, Rob donned a ski mask. He didn't want Grigory to see his face. Seeing that, the two henchmen breathed a sigh of relief—it meant that Rob didn't intend to kill them.

Which was true, but Rob intended to leave them immobilized until he, Katie, and his men were out of the country. Therein lay a dilemma. Rob had no interest in turning Grigory or his men over to the authorities. Should he tell him that or let him figure it out? When they got back to the farmhouse, they found Grigory bound to a chair. He was gagged, but not blindfolded, and he glared at Rob.

Rob's men brought the two henchmen into the house, secured them to sturdy pipes in the wall of the kitchen, and then picked up Grigory, chair and all and brought him in as well. Then they set about disabling Grigory's car, another vehicle that belonged to one of the henchmen, and the dirt bike. They then did a detailed search to make sure they'd left no weapons or communications behind. They let the men keep their wallets—again, Rob had no interest in their coming to the attention of the authorities. One of Rob's men came out holding up Katie's passport and wallet. "Yeah! Thank you, though given that passport picture I was kinda hoping it was gone." she said and stuffed both items into her knapsack.

So far nobody had said anything either to Grigory or his men. Rob motioned to his men and Katie to start heading for the van, which was off the road a few hundred yards away. Rob ducked his head into the farmhouse one last time and looked at Grigory, who looked apoplectic. "Don't make me regret not killing you," he said. Rob hesitated for a moment and then took out a piece of paper and pen. He wrote an email address on it and stuffed it into Grigory's shirt pocket. "That's a dead drop. Use PGP encryption if you want to chat." He left without waiting for a response.

When he caught up to Katie, she held her arms out, wheeled around and said, "Eleuthera!"

Rob was confused. "The island?"

"Freedom!"

Rob smiled, but then turned serious. "How close?" He didn't have to say to what.

Katie shuddered. "Too close to talk about." She changed the subject, jerking her head back toward the farmhouse. "What were you doing in there?"

"I left a note with Grigory."

Katie was puzzled. "I didn't think you two were getting along."

"Exchanging numbers."

Katie's puzzlement deepened. "Not that there's anything wrong with it, but I didn't think he was your type."

Rob laughed. "Who knows; in different circumstances . . ." Then he turned serious. "Seemed like a good idea to have a way to communicate. I left a digital dead drop address."

Katie thought about this. "He's going to try again, isn't he—now that he's seen more of what Bart can do?"

Rob grimaced. "No doubt, but that's not a problem we can solve now. We also may need to move Bart. Right now, let's get you home."

They were about to round a bend, and Katie took one last look back at the run-down farmhouse. "What's going to happen to them?"

"They'll eventually escape, but they don't have phones, weapons, or a working vehicle. By the time they get help, we'll be long gone."

# 52 RINSE AND REPEAT

KATIE WALKED IN TO A STANDING O WHEN SHE ARRIVED AT Boisbeaux from Biloxi airport (Dev insisted on picking her up), albeit the ovation was from four people (Sofia was off helping Zoe feed the elephants). Rob had flown her to Dubai on the Transteppe plane, and then escorted her right to the gate for her non-stop flight to JFK. Rob and his men then flew back to Transteppe. Met by Dev, Katie had given him a fierce embrace, but the ride to Boisbeaux took place mostly in silence. Katie even managed to nap. At Boisbeaux, Katie embraced everyone, murmuring thanks. She looked happy but exhausted. She smiled at everyone, but looked haunted. Zoe took Sofia off for a horseback ride, so that the rest of the team could discuss what happened and what might be the next steps. Over glasses of champagne, Katie told them what she could remember of the kidnapping, but there were big gaps as her last memory after splitting up with Claire in New Delhi was of stepping into a lady's room at the Delhi airport.

Rob joined the group by video conference, and after everyone voiced their appreciation, the mood turned serious. Claire started by asking Rob for his appraisal of the situation.

"OK then, the good news is that they have an equal interest in keeping Bart secret, but that ties right into the bad news, which is that they're definitely going to try again, and now they know who we are and where to find Bart. They also know that we aren't going to go to the authorities."

"Who are they?" inquired Sergei.

"Best guess is a senior intelligence operative gone rogue. That hacker, Dimitri, believes that to be the case. He originally dealt with some guy he called the Colonel, but then Grigory took over and cut the Colonel out."

Katie jumped in again. "I need to say something here. Make no mistake . . ."

Claire saw where this was going and frantically tried to make eye contact with Katie, jerking her head toward Dev.

Katie, however, was looking into the middle distance and just continued, "My gratitude to all of you for rescuing me knows no bounds. But I discovered something in that farmhouse," she made eye contact with each of them in turn, "and that is that there's no limit to what I'll do to protect Bart, absolutely none."

"I think we know that," said Claire trying to cut off Katie from going further.

But Katie wasn't finished. "Another minute . . ."

Dev watched this interchange intently. Clearly Claire did not want Katie divulging something in front of him. Then he got it. He slumped in his chair. Gone was his louche demeanor. For the first time since he joined the project, he looked vulnerable and confused. Whatever their relationship, it would always be secondary to a higher calling.

Returning to the present from whatever place she had been, Katie saw his reaction. Her expression softened and she reached for his hand. "Don't worry Dev—you're the reason I kept hoping for Rob to show up." She turned to Rob on the screen. "And when he did, he gave that thug a righteous beatdown!"

They all laughed with relief. Rob touched the bandages on his cheek. "He got in a few licks." He paused. "But you bring up a good point. I'd hate to be the one to tell Bart that we killed people to rescue Katie. Something to think about as we plan next steps."

"We didn't kill people, but I'm responsible for Mihail's death," said Katie softly. "And Bart probably knows that."

There was an uncomfortable silence. "You had no idea that the ringleader—Grigory?—would kill your guard. It was an impossible situation, and there were no easy answers," said Claire, trying to get the conversation back to next steps. "Let's focus on how we protect Bart with no more bloodshed."

Keerbrock stepped into his professorial persona. "OK then, let's sum up. Our cover's blown and they know we won't go to the US authorities. On the other hand, Grigory's got to worry that his freelancing will get discovered. That limits his ability to maneuver. So far so good?" They nodded. Claire in particular always found it thrilling to see how Keerbrock's mind untangled complex situations. Keerbrock continued. "So, we have a multi-variant decision tree. Grigory might decide whether the risks merit coming in from the cold, and tell his colleagues about this wonderful discovery he's been following for years, thereby enlisting the full power of Russian intelligence in his efforts to get Bart. Not good from our point of view. Or he might regroup and mount another effort. Or the Russian intelligence apparatus might figure out what he was doing, disappear him, and launch their own effort. There are probably other variations, but *every* single one of them involves going after Bart again. None of them involve leaving him in peace."

Keerbrock paused. "Then there's our side of the decision tree. As a postulate, I agree with Katie—protecting Bart stands above all other considerations. That means finding a way he can continue his life away from prying eyes. We could move him, but the how and where are both problematic, and he would have to agree. We could make up another adolescent elephant to look like him and arrange for sightings far from Mbembe—also difficult and problematic . . ."

Dev cut in, "Or, we could buy them off."

All eyes turned to Dev. "Continue," said Keerbrock graciously.

"We give them another Bart."

Claire suppressed her initial outrage at the suggestion, knowing that Dev would never make such a suggestion unless there was more to it. As usual, Sergei got it immediately. He nodded; Dev was a smart cookie. He let his remark sink in. Keerbrock was next to get it, "Of course, the blood sample."

Then Claire got it, and she didn't like it. "How could we live with ourselves if we let a homicidal kidnapper raise a miracle such as Bart?"

"Maybe if we help them raise him properly," said Dev.

Again, this remark was greeted by saucer-eyed stares.

Seeing the response, Dev hurried on. "If they successfully clone from the blood, we let them know that microwaves or any intrusive examination will interfere with and probably damage the elephant's abilities. In other words, we let them know that the only way to see the elephant's genius is to raise him or her the right way. Of course, it's not a perfect solution, far from it, but it could buy Bart years of peace. If anybody has a better idea, let's hear it."

Sergei jumped in. "We don't have to decide today. Grigory's going to be preoccupied with covering his tracks on the mess he created. It will take him some time to regroup. And even if we decide to do this, we can tease it out slowly." Sergei looked around the group with wide-eyed innocence. "Oh, and if we decide to go ahead, who's the lucky person who's going to tell Bart?"

# BART MAKES HIS CHOICE

*Chodron frowned as he looked at another of Rencho's strange Thangka paintings. He'd given up trying to understand what the revered lama was trying to convey. Once again, Rencho had depicted a strange elephant, but where his earlier work had depicted a scene of desolation and sadness, this painting evoked joy. Once again, there are strange creatures, unknown to the traditions of Thangka, or to Chodron for that matter. Chodron sighed. At least now, there was no longer any need for diplomacy.*

# 53 VALEDICTORY

IT WAS FIRST LIGHT IN MBEMBE. KEERBROCK, CLAIRE, AND ROB approached the bai along with Salina and the synthesizer. They could see Flo and Bart's herd but there was no sign of Bart. They made their way to the center of the bai, and Salina set down the equipment. She turned on the synthesizer to make sure it was working, and then they looked around.

Still no Bart.

Given events of the past months, Claire got worried. Keerbrock looked around, confused. Salina furrowed her brow, "He was here, I can smell him."

"Yes, so can I," said Claire, now less worried. Young male elephants have a honey-like scent, which serves as a signal to adult bull elephants that they are not a threat.

Then the synthesizer came to life. "I'm here," Bart said. They all wheeled around, seeing nothing. A few seconds later, he simply materialized, not twenty feet away.

Keerbrock was dumbstruck. He reminded himself that Bart may be some otherworldly genius, but he was also an adolescent. Rob's jaw dropped. "Take that David Copperfield."

This elicited puzzled looks, "Sergei's joke from way back when. I'll bet he never expected Bart could do it on his own."

Claire turned to Bart and clapped her hands, "Quite an entrance Bart! How did you do that?"

"I faded into the background."

Keerbrock got it immediately. "I think Bart's telling us that he affected our perceptions of what we saw. Reality isn't perceived as raw data, sensory data is processed, and visual data is often altered to fit what the brain expects to see. Something like that?"

Bart cocked his head and looked at Keerbrock with real interest, but didn't respond directly to the question, only saying, "I've been practicing."

Claire stepped forward. "Bart this is Dr. Keerbrock. He saved my career when it needed saving." She turned to Rob, "And this is Rob Rebolet. With your help he saved Katie, and, in doing so, helped protect you."

Bart nodded to both of them. "Thank you. I'm happy to meet both of you."

Claire continued. "Dr. Keerbrock is the most qualified of any of us to understand the difference between how you see the world and how we see the world. I'm hoping that we can talk about that a bit. Is that OK? I'm sure Rob has a few questions too."

"I will try, but words are not my favorite way to communicate, and my vocabulary is not large."

"Thank you, Bart," said Keerbrock, "A great scientist once said that you can only understand a complex problem if you can reduce it to a series of simpler, relationships and terms." So, I'm going to try and pose a few questions that require only simple answers in response. Is that OK?"

"I always prefer simple."

"Good. Claire has told me that you don't like the synthesizer because using words interferes with the way you prefer to think about the world around you." Keerbrock paused and took a breath, trying to think how best to phrase his next thought. "Is that because a word freezes something in a specific way, where before what that word refers to is interconnected to many circumstances and has multiple meanings and possibilities?"

Bart digested this in silence, almost as though he was reluctant to answer. "You are correct. Using a word is like dropping a rock in a river that diverts its course, a conversation is like building a dam." He stopped to let the synthesizer catch up. "Once a dam is built, the flow of water becomes constricted and everything downstream is changed. Without words, I am part of that river; part of life."

Keerbrock looked apologetic and guilty, something Claire had never seen before. "I apologize Bart, I didn't know how much it must cost you to communicate with us."

"I participate in these conversations because you brought me into this world. You brought me that stone which enabled me to see my ancestors and their life. And I use words because you are my friends. You may continue, Doctor."

"I'll only ask one more question. If you don't use words, or physics, or math, how do you plan and affect the world around you so precisely and effectively?"

By way of answer, Bart made a panoramic sweep of his head, directing their attention to the bai and the forest around it. Two serpent eagles took flight and circled overhead. They were joined by a kettle of bearded vultures that spiraled higher above them. In the distance they heard the sharp raps of gorillas drumming against their chests. Bart let the sights and sounds sink in. Then he emitted a short series of rumbles, and the synthesizer came to life. "Nature has had all the time in the world to solve every problem, and nature did so without words or physics or math." Bart paused to let the synthesizer catch up.

"Salina showed me pictures of an octopus which can match its background perfectly. Is that possible with words, physics, and math?"

Bart let that sink in too. "If everything is part of one flow, then every part of that flow might be reached." Another pause. "My distant ancestors came to have access to some of those solutions, probably by accident, and as time went by, nature endowed them with more and more access to the flow of life." He paused once more. "That is my impression, and all I want to know."

Keerbrock got the message as did Claire: Bart's power came from being part of the flow of life, not investigating or questioning it.

Keerbrock nodded at Claire, and she changed the subject. "Do you have questions for any of us?"

Bart turned to Rob. "I'm grateful that you saved Katie without hurting anyone."

"I knew that's what you wanted."

"But still, saving Katie and protecting me, led to the death of someone."

There was no way of fooling Bart. "Yes, it did," Rob acknowledged.

"And more deaths could happen if that same group tries again, or others try to find me."

Again, Rob couldn't lie. "It's possible."

Claire had dreaded this moment, but now couldn't avoid it. "We have a plan that could protect you without any more bloodshed."

Both Keerbrock and Rob looked up sharply. Rob shook his head, "Claire, this may not be the best time . . ."

Claire turned to the two men. "If not now, when?"

Bart watched this exchange with interest. "Tell me."

Claire looked once again at the two men, pleadingly. "As we agreed in Boisbeaux, we have to . . ." She turned back to Bart. She told him that if they gave the blood sample to Bart's pursuers, it could buy him several years of peace.

Bart listened. "These people are not as kind as you."

"We'll tell them that the only way to understand Bart's kind would be to raise the baby properly." Claire's voice trailed off; she knew she sounded naïve even as she said spoke the words.

"Is this happening now?"

"Not yet."

"Please do not do this. There is another way."

"Please tell us, we haven't thought of one."

"Give me time."

"Of course, Bart. Tomorrow, same time?"

"My herd is asking for me." Bart nodded toward the people, and started walking toward the edge of the forest.

The mood was solemn as they walked back to the campsite. Ndokanda and Seraphime had a fire going and were heating a pungent dish of rice and sauce.

They ate mostly in silence. Over cups of cowboy coffee Rob voiced what all of them were worried about. "When you said, 'see you tomorrow,' he never answered.

"Also," said Claire, "He's never gone on at the length he did with Will. It had the flavor of a valedictory."

"I noticed that too," said Salina. "Should we go back?"

Claire looked anguished. "We have to trust Bart. He's not rash and, as we saw, he's in full possession of his powers."

"I agree," said Keerbrock, "I've never experienced anything like meeting Bart. He knows what's in his interest better than we do."

"OK then," said Claire, "We'll see what tomorrow brings." She turned to Keerbrock. "If I can change the subject, what did you take away from your conversation with Bart?"

Keerbrock took a sip of coffee and offered a wan smile. "Well, for starters, it's hard to meet a living refutation of your entire life's work."

Claire started to say, "Oh, Will . . ." but Keerbrock waved her off.

"I was trained and celebrated as a hard-core empiricist, but Bart opened the door to an entirely different way of intelligently intervening in the world, and a way that doesn't come with the cost of climate change, desertification, and ecological collapse."

Keerbrock looked from face to face. "Look at what he can do, act at a distance, put people to sleep, heal Claire's shoulder, see through the eyes of animals and birds, make himself invisible. Science can do none of those things. He was right about the octopus. It can change to match its background in one-thirtieth of a second. It does it through changing its pigmentation. He did it through altering our perceptions. Researchers have been trying to do both for decades with minimal success."

Keerbrock took another sip of his coffee. "Specifically, he put some meat on the idea that Bart's way of thinking about things and doing things is an ultra-sophisticated application of his version of quantum mechanics. For instance, the way he talked about words reminded me of an idea that is gaining traction in semiotics, namely that words exist in a type of indeterminate haze with multiple potential meanings. Much of what we do in conversation has to do with finding a common language with whom we are conversing. In this sense, once that understanding has been established, the conversation is akin to situating those words in a specific context. Thus, speaking is analogous to measurement in quantum mechanics and conversation represents a collapse of the wave function. Bart was telling us that this very act alienates us from the powers and meanings he has access to."

Keerbrock smiled again ruefully. "I could happily spend my remaining days, observing and talking with Bart, but that's not likely to happen, is it?"

"For the sake of all of us, I wish it were Will," said Claire.

Salina spoke up. "Look, we've got a free afternoon, and Ndokanda and Seraphime who know the forest and its workings better than any botanist. I could ask them to show us around. It's shady in the forest, and the elephant trails are like boulevards."

"I'm in," said Rob.

"Me too," said Claire, "but ask them to go at something less than Pygmy pace."

"Roger that," said Keerbrock, creakily getting to his feet.

As they walked, Ndokanda pointed to different fruits on the forest floor saying, "Gorillas eat that . . . chimps eat that . . ." and so on with Salina translating. He pointed to a small berry. "That's a man's hospital," he said. Everyone looked at Salina curiously. She blushed. "Cures impotence," she said, "Feel free to grab a few. Claire and I will close our eyes."

## 54 BART'S PLAN

THEY ARRIVED AT THE BAI JUST AFTER FIRST LIGHT. AS HAD become the custom, they went to the center of the bai. Thinking that Bart might be playing another of his disappearing acts, Salina set down the synthesizer and turned it on. Silence. This time, there was no smell of honey. Nor was there any sign of Bart's herd at the edge of the forest. There were only the usual sounds of a rainforest waking up. After several minutes, Keerbrock said, "As we feared . . ."

"Let's give it some more time," said Claire, "I don't think he'd leave without saying goodbye."

"Look, an African grey parrot," said Salina, pointing to a bird flapping its way toward them. "It's unusual to see one so far from the trees."

The bird kept coming toward them and alighted on the synthesizer. It fluttered its wings and then, in exact imitation of Bart's voice on the synthesizer said, "Please don't try to find me . . . we're safe . . . I'll find you when it's safe."

They all stared at the bird dumbstruck. No one knew what to say. "Thank you, bird," said Claire lamely. The parrot fluttered again, repeated its remarks, and then started flying back toward its noisy pals at the edge of the forest.

There were tears at the edge of Claire's eyes. "We knew this was coming, long before yesterday. Let's honor his request. Agreed?"

There was silent assent. Salina was sobbing. "Bart is my life."

Claire put an arm around her.

Keerbrock, never comfortable when human emotions surfaced, remained silent, looking grimly into the middle distance.

Rob spoke up. "Bart can protect himself better than we could with an army. I'm guessing that Mihail's death tipped him over the edge, and he figured this was the only way, he could stop more loss of life. Also, he can enlist the help of the entire forest."

"Sounds right," said Keerbrock.

Rob continued, "The question is how do we help him from afar?"

Claire looked at him. "Going ahead with the diversion?"

Rob nodded.

"We need to discuss this with the group back at Boisbeaux."

Walking back to the campsite, Keerbrock asked Salina, "Where do you think they would go?"

"I wish I knew," she said, "but my guess is that he will find a route that at every point is as far away from humans as possible."

# 55 THE SHIP HAS SAILED



BACK AT BOISBEAUX, THE NEWS THAT BART AND FLO HAD disappeared paralyzed the team. Knowing what they did about Bart's maturity and powers, no one wanted to suggest that they should have launched an effort to find him, but all were bereft that he was gone. All of the ideas bandied about—putting up a drone, hiring scouts—held the implied message that they knew better than Bart what was in his best interests. Worse, these efforts would corrode the trust that had been the glue of their relationship over the years.

Claire summed it up as best she could. "I think Bart found it unbearable that people were dying or getting hurt simply because he existed, and he foresaw that this was not going to stop. He said, he'd find us again, and I have to believe that he will do that."

Keerbrock, who was approaching eighty, weighed in, "I have no doubt he will do that; I just hope he does so before I rejoin that river that only he has access to."

Rob, who was back at Transteppe, refocused the conversation. "Agreed that tracking him would be sending the wrong message, but we still can help him. The immediate question is whether we should go ahead with the plan to let Grigory have some DNA? What are the pros and cons?"

Claire jumped in immediately, "The con is that Bart asked us not to do it, probably for all the ethical reasons we've already discussed. What's the pro?"

Keerbrock jumped in. "I'm not advocating, but here's one pro: If we don't give them the blood, they'll probably launch another attempt to get him, and this time, they'll quickly figure out he's not there, and they'll have no compunctions about trying to find him. If they do find him, we won't be around to help him. The blood offers a bright, shiny object to distract them." Recognizing the weak point in his argument, he continued, "Look, I recognize that this bright shiny object will become an elephant who we'd be condemning to a miserable life. It's a compromise, and, again, I'm not advocating."

Sergei had other ideas. "No need to give them an elephant; the chess board has changed. We're still thinking about a world where we have to keep Mbembe secret at all costs. That gave Grigory leverage over us. With Bart gone, that leverage has disappeared.

"Here's two, linked, possibilities: Our hacker intercepts 'traffic' [Sergei used air quotes] that indicates that Bart has died. Grigory sends a scout to Mbembe, and that scout confirms that we've pulled out our security and Bart is not there. Second, the hacker gives that same info to that guy he calls the Colonel, along with confirming details that Grigory privatized what was originally a Russian project. That'll keep Grigory's hands full."

That produced a stunned silence. Claire looked around, "Weak points? Anyone?"

"Grigory would know that we'd have DNA, and come after that," responded Rob.

"Easy enough to hide the real stuff among plenty of blood samples that are not cloneable . . ." said Keerbrock with a speculative tone. "Also, as Sergei said, Grigory would have his hands full keeping his head attached to his shoulders."

"OK, I think we have a plan," said Rob. "So, what would we say that could be intercepted if Bart actually died."

"I don't even want to think about it," said Katie.

"Me neither, but I'll try," said Claire.

"We've got time. We don't want to put anything out for at least a month or two," said Rob, "So let's keep the security and the scouts at Mbembe to keep up appearances. Then let's get this charade going."

After Rob signed off, Sergei looked at Claire. She looked deflated and was crying. He put his arm around her, which only caused her to cry more. The others drifted away. She looked up at her husband, "I never imagined anything could hurt so much. There's just a huge hole in my life. How will I fill it?"

Sergei squeezed her shoulders, "You still have Sofia and me. We're not, how you say, diced liver."

Claire smiled through her tears. "No, you're definitely not chopped liver." She straightened up. "I've got to pull myself together. I've got to break the news to Helen. Bart was her life too."

# 56 THE CHARADE



BACK IN MOSCOW FOR THREE MONTHS, GRIGORY STARED AT AN incoming message. It was from Dimitri, and he used the code word Wrangell, which meant the message was of the utmost importance. Grigory was sure that somehow Dimitri was involved in Katie's rescuers, whoever they were, discovering her whereabouts. Indeed, Grigory had made eliminating Dimitri a top priority, something he planned to do before launching a new plan to get that elephant. He dialed the number of the burner phone.

"I'm glad you got in contact," said Grigory. "I'm hoping you can help me figure out how Katie's rescuers found us in Azerbaijan."

"What are you talking about?" said Dimitri, hoping that he sounded genuinely mystified. "You went ahead with the kidnapping?"

*Mediocre acting*, thought Grigory. *Trying too hard.* "That's another discussion. What's the urgency?"

"Something happened to that elephant, so serious they sent some messages over open lines. Elephant's name was Bart by the way."

"Was?"

"Yes, was. Sounds like he's dead. Tuberculosis. They're completely freaking out."

There was silence on the line as Grigory digested this.

Once off the call, Grigory pondered the possibilities. Obviously, it could be a legend to protect Bart, if that really was the elephant's name. Grigory was lying low, but he still had a man in Africa who could get to Mbembe. He picked up his phone and sent a text.

# 57 BAITING THE TRAP

DIMITRI'S NEXT CONVERSATION WAS WITH THE COLONEL, AND it was vastly different. He relayed the news about Bart's death (and that the elephant was called Bart). Then he asked whether the Colonel knew what happened after Grigory kidnapped Katie.

The Colonel frowned. He knew that somehow Katie had escaped, though Dimitri had been fuzzy on the details. "What am I missing?"

"Grigory killed his hired thug, Mihail."

Now *this* was interesting. "Why?"

"Because Katie got his gun and motorcycle and then escaped."

To the Colonel, this seemed like a perfectly good reason for an on-the-spot execution, but he also knew that the days that FSB people could kill their own hires with impunity were long past, and worse, Grigory had done it in an operation to line his own pockets. "Why didn't you tell me earlier?"

"Because I'm afraid of Grigory."

*Good thinking!* thought the Colonel. *So am I.* "And why are you telling me now?"

"With Bart, Grigory would have had the world's largest coin to trade. Now all he's got is a failed, rogue operation and a lot of explaining to do—if his off-the-books activities become known." This last touch was a little heavy-handed, but Dimitri wanted to be damn sure the Colonel got the hint.

He did. "I have to think about this." With typical abruptness, the Colonel hung up.

# 58 ONE LESS LOOSE END

ALINA FEDEROV LOOKED AT HER HUSBAND WITH AFFECTION and amusement. He was the most intellectually restless man she had ever met. "Darling, why are you learning Spanish?"

Grigory pulled the earbuds out and paused the language program. "Sweetheart, you're going to love Montevideo; it's the most European city in South America."

"A new assignment?"

Grigory chuckled. "In a manner of speaking. You know the rules. Not a word to anyone. Especially not your mother!"

Alina frowned. Grigory was constantly harping on her mother's indiscreetness. He called her "The Voice of Russia."

Their conversation was interrupted by a loud knock on the door. She looked at Grigory in alarm. His expression told her everything.

# 59 EDGING TOWARD THE NORMAL

ROB AND KAMILA'S FIRST MEETING WAS A BIT STIFF. THEY MET at the *Aisyt*—a watering hole frequented by the offspring of the elite in Nur-Sultan. The place was noisy and reeked of privilege. Sofi Tukker was playing in the background. The bar was both translucent and iridescent and seemed to be illuminated from within. Behind the bar, similarly backlit, was as impressive an array of spirits and *eau de vie* as might be found in Saint-Germain-des-Prés or Williamsburg, Brooklyn. The bartenders were two beautiful women with tricolor hair, tank tops, and attitude, as well as one guy wearing a black muscle T. He had attitude too. Kamila ordered a Green Chartreuse, Rob opted for a Tito's with a wedge of orange. He noticed that all of the men, and a few of the women, were eyeing Kamila who'd switched from khakis to a short black skirt and simple white T-shirt. She looked stunning. Noting the stares, Rob said, "It's dangerous to look that good. If this weren't such a posh place, I'd have to fight my way out of here—and I think I'd be fighting women as well as men."

Kamila smiled mischievously. "Did I dress wrong?"

"Just the opposite. Let's find a table out of the spotlight."

Things loosened up as the evening went on. When they parted Rob asked when he could see her again and got the answer Dimitri had been hoping for.

"Anytime."

And so, they met up again, and again and again.

By the fourth date they were a couple. Everybody at Transteppe knew it, and those few workers who hadn't had designs on one or the other of them, eagerly discussed the progress of the relationship.

Isolated in Transteppe and then by the exigencies of protecting Bart, Rob didn't really know the ropes of being in a relationship, but he was a fast learner. Even so, he wasn't going to solve the problem no person has solved since the beginning of time: how to deepen a relationship if one party has secrets that cannot be divulged.

"Are you ever going to tell me what was really going on when you used me as bait?" They were sitting on the terrace of Kamila's apartment in Nur-Sultan. They saw each other at Transteppe, but preferred to meet in Nur-Sultan—away from those eager prying eyes—on those occasions when Rob came into town.

Rob knew this question was going to come up and dreaded it. He couldn't tell her the truth yet, but he realized that he could answer truthfully. "That day will be the happiest day of my life."

Kamila took his hand and pressed it. It wasn't the answer she'd hoped for, but it was good enough.

# 60 ANOTHER REUNION

FIVE YEARS AFTER BART AND FLO DISAPPEARED, A LARGE group entered the bai at Mbembe. None of the group had received any signal from Bart. Everybody stayed connected; everybody maintained the secret. Bart entered dreams and sometimes reveries during the day, but everyone who had met Bart knew what he could do. If Bart wanted to reach them, it wouldn't be ambiguous; they would know it. Was he alive? Claire felt that she would know it if he had died.

The core group kept in touch, but people gradually returned to their pre-Bart lives. Nothing was published on Bart. As far as the world knew, he never existed.

Dev and Katie had gotten married. They exchanged vows at Boisbeaux in what may have been the first wedding ever where the elephant guests outnumbered the humans. Dev's sister had thrown herself into the planning, but discovered that most of her energy was devoted to helping prepare a feast for the elephants. Now, despite her dour view of humanity Katie found herself four months pregnant. In a story as old as time, biology once again triumphed over intellect.

It was Claire's idea to have a reunion at Mbembe. Helen, Dev, Katie, Zoe, and Salina, were all there, Helen for the first time, even though she had financed the endeavor from the beginning. Sergei was there too. Sofia, now twenty, was entering her junior year in college. Rob had come in from Transteppe (he was still with Kamila, though he had yet to tell her about Bart). Keerbrock, now in his mid-eighties made the trip too.

Mbembe was much the same, but climate change had induced the drying of Africa and brought the Sahel ever closer to its borders. There were also many more elephants as word got out among neighboring elephants that Mbembe was a safe place. The ex-legionnaires were long gone, but Ndokanda and Seraphime had been hired as permanent guards and had moved their families to the other side of the river. There was still plenty of game beyond Mbembe, and, so far, there had been no poaching.

It was early morning, before the heat became unbearable. Led by Salina, they walked to the center of the bai, the place that had been their meeting point with Bart. No one spoke much. They listened to the forest. Everyone felt deeply sad. A miracle had been in their lives, a miracle they'd help bring about, and now he was gone. Even though all had come to realize that Bart's was not only the best solution, but the only solution to the dilemma posed by his very existence, they'd all expected that somehow, he would keep in contact. The shared certainty that Bart knew best was a small consolation.

Claire waved for everyone to gather around. "I really don't know what to say, other than I'm happy that we're gathered here; this place where the most important things that ever happened in my life took place; discoveries that will probably never see the light of day, but which were momentous, nonetheless. The world needs to know that there can be an intelligence in harmony with the natural world, but we can't tell the world about it. We can't because Bart deserves a life on his terms. He didn't ask to be brought into our world, but once here, he became our responsibility. And he will be forever . . ." She trailed off. "Please, anyone who wants to say a few words. Now's the time."

Keerbrock cleared his throat. "I echo Claire's sentiments. It's strange to see unfold before me the most important discovery of my lifetime, perhaps the most important discovery in human history, and simultaneously know that it will likely never be known beyond this small group, certainly not in my lifetime." He held up a finger. "In that regard, I do think there's something we can do now that will not in any way jeopardize Bart. Among ourselves, we can put together an oral history and place it in a time capsule not to be opened until long after Bart's expected lifespan. We entrust this capsule to a worthy institution that will respect our wishes, and include in it some documentation, video, etc . . ." he paused. "And perhaps some DNA with the idea that maybe there will be a time where Bart's ilk could live and people can learn from him, not just exploit him."

"Yes!" said Katie, as renewed enthusiasm swept through the group. Maybe Bart wouldn't be lost to history after all. Amid the hubbub, no one noticed that an African grey parrot had alighted on the branch of a shrub. That is to say that no one noticed until a familiar voice said "Hello."

It was the parrot speaking, once again perfectly matching the voice of the synthesizer. Everybody froze. "Please hold hands," said the parrot. Not saying a word, everyone present moved to form a circle and joined hands. The parrot flew away, and the group waited. Claire was already trembling with excitement when the first wave of energy swept through them. She stole a glance at Helen who had never experienced Bart's power. Helen's face was lit with a million-watt smile. Bart was taking control of all their senses, their imaginations, their very beings. As she surrendered herself to whatever Bart intended, one last word flashed through her mind. Ecstasy.

# 61 A DOOR CLOSES, A DOOR OPENS

A YEAR AFTER THE REUNION IN MBEMBE, CLAIRE RECONNECTED with Chodrak at the guesthouse where they had stayed previously. Katie, nursing a six-month old boy, named Willem Segal Sinjin (it turned out that neither had any particular attachment to their family name), couldn't make the trip. Without the help of Bart, Claire had no way of letting Rencho know she was coming. After returning from Mbembe, everyone had thrown themselves with a vengeance into preparing the time capsule. Keerbrock and Katie started their oral histories. Claire, along with her own oral history, had taken it upon herself to ask Rencho to record a reminiscence of his experiences with Bart for the capsule, and to ask him to contribute his drawings, though she knew that was a long shot. Chodrak, now older and with a family, was eager to take her back to the monastery—saying that their visit with Rencho was the most extraordinary moment of his life, and also somberly proclaiming that he had told no one, not even his family, about that day. He warned Claire, however, that rumors had it that Rencho, now in his nineties, was quite frail.

No eagle monitored their progress this time, a bad sign from Claire's point of view. Claire had come straight to Tibet, and felt light-headed from the altitude. When they got to the monastery she was completely out of breath. At the entranceway, they were greeted by a young monk. When Chodrak told him why they were there the monk looked troubled. He asked for their patience for a moment, motioning for them to sit on a bench, and walked through a doorway.

A few minutes later an elderly monk appeared. He said his name was Chodron, and asked why they had come. Chodrak explained that several years earlier Claire and Rencho had an extraordinary experience and that she hoped to record Rencho's memories of that day. Chodron looked at Claire closely and asked Chodrak to again say her name. Chodron then rose and paced for a few moments. With a kindly look he told Chodrak to tell Claire that this discussion would not be possible because a few months earlier Rencho had peacefully transcended his mortal incarnation.

Crestfallen and saddened, Claire expressed her deep sadness at his passing and sympathy for the monastery's loss of this extraordinary man. She and Chodrak got up to leave. Chodron held up a finger and asked them to wait. He then said a few sentences to Chodrak and bade them sit.

"He says that before Rencho died, he told Chodron that you might return, and that when you did, Chodron was to give you some drawings he made while you were here."

Claire brightened, at least the trip would not be a total loss.

Chodron returned carrying a parchment folio under one arm, and something else, rolled up in a cloth under the other. Chodron handed her the folio, which Claire accepted, bowing thankfully. He placed the item rolled up in a cloth on the bench. Nodding toward it, he told Chodrak that the item was a painting—he didn't use the word thangka—that Rencho had done very recently, and he thought that Rencho would have wanted Claire to have that as well.

Claire had brought a large, empty backpack on the chance that Rencho might actually part with his drawings. She carefully placed the folio in the backpack and then gently fit the rolled up, cloth-covered painting into the backpack. Chodrak offered to don the backpack, but Claire waved him off with a smile.

With the backpack on, she turned and bowed to Chodron and once again expressed her sorrow at the passing of Rencho.

Once they had left, Chodron smiled with merriment. What luck—or was it fate—that this woman had showed up to take Rencho's thangka off their hands. No more agitation about whether and where it should be displayed. Now Rencho's memory could be celebrated, unsullied by this last, heretical painting.

Claire decided to wait until she got back to the guesthouse before looking at the works left to her and Katie by Rencho. Anticipation (and the fact that the walk was downhill) made the trip back a jaunt.

It became something more when Chodak excitedly pointed to the sky. "Look!"

An eagle rode the updrafts along the ridge line that followed the road. Even at a distance of hundreds of yards Claire felt the intensity of the bird of prey's gaze, though it was not fear she felt, but a blessing.

At the guesthouse she thanked Chodrak for his help. She told him that while she still needed him to maintain secrecy, he could write down his impressions of their meeting with Rencho for a collection of materials that would not be opened for many years. Chodrak expressed his gratitude, saying that it had been a struggle to keep that day secret, and that he was extremely happy that sometime in the future people might read his account. Bowing, he said that he would return with his written account the next day before she left.

Claire went up to her room. She put the backpack on her bed. Taking out the folio she leafed through the drawings, picturing how Rencho had handed them to her and Katie one by one.

Then she turned her attention to the larger painting rolled up and covered with cloth. She carefully pulled off the cloth and spread the painting out on her bed. The shock of it brought a torrent of conflicting thoughts and feelings and things clicked. Bart must have reached out to Rencho even as he blessed the reunion in Mbembe. But, while he gave those who had brought him into the world, a moment of the purest bliss, he'd sent Rencho a vivid image of both his whereabouts and his intentions. Claire felt a fleeting pang of jealousy, not for Bart's trusting Rencho more than the rest of them, but rather for the realization that Bart had sought out and found creatures on Earth that were much closer to being his peers in terms of their abilities to sense and process the myriad wavelengths that enabled his powers. That unworthy pang vanished as quickly as it came and Claire thought, *Of course!*

# 62 BART'S CALLING

THE MATRIARCH ORCA AND HER POD LOOKED TOWARD THE beach from just beyond the surf line, responding to an invitation from this strange elephant on the beach. She noticed that dolphins, and some sperm whales were also gathered. Ordinarily, they would flee from the presence of orca, but something told her that they were also there at the invitation of that elephant and that it would be bad manners to spoil the informal truce. Given their arsenal of weapons and tight social structures, orcas learn from a very young age the importance of good manners.

The matriarch was quite familiar with this remote beach in Gabon. She occasionally hunted the hippos that would surf the waves, seemingly for the sheer pleasure of it. She made this beach a regular stop on her hunting migration because there always was plenty of prey, and no humans to interfere.

The orca didn't think in words but in tableaux that laid out various scenarios triggered by the nature of the situation. She was sixty years old and had accumulated a rich portfolio of experiences and visualizations accumulated first from her mother's teaching, then from observations, and then from the memories of what worked and what didn't. She learned to hunt great white sharks by grabbing their pectoral fins while a partner would rip open the exposed belly. She learned to work with other orcas to make bubble curtains to trap schools of fish. But nothing in her experience prepared her for the message from this elephant.

Though not in words the message she received was, "We are kin." This was followed by a message in her own language, one that was impossible for her to ignore, an ancient orca song that summoned the pod to a particular destination, in this case the wild beach on the coast of Gabon.

Now, in the warm waters off the coast, the matriarch heard once again that message, "we are kin," only this time this mysterious elephant implanted another orca song, this one of celebration, typically sung following a birth. Then the matriarch heard a dolphin song, though she did not know its meaning, and this was followed by an astoundingly low frequency song of a sperm whale. Again, she did not know its meaning, but highly intelligent and with the wisdom accumulated in her decades traversing the deep blue waters, she assumed the messages the elephant was sending to the dolphins and whales were similar to that of the song she had just heard.

With the oceans once again silent, the matriarch sent a message to the elephant, not knowing whether it would receive it. Her message was, "yes, we are kin," and she then followed with a song she had never uttered before, one that expressed the highest exaltation. To her delight, she found herself inspired to improvise on that song, complicating its orca melody with deeply satisfying whistles and clicks all hewing to orca conventions that dated back thousands of generations.

She received one more message, the sense of which was, "I didn't do that, you did. There's so much more you can do."

The matriarch knew that this was the end of her first lesson. She also felt something novel for an orca, hope; hope that there would be many more such encounters.

# ACKNOWLEDGMENTS

Fiction is a new world for me, and I need all the help I can get. First and foremost, a shout-out to all those who helped bring this book to life: Brian Skulnik, who shepherded the book to publication, Art Klebanoff, who published *Deep Past* and generously offered advice on the sequel, David Wilk, the social media crew at Bobi—Sarah Hill, Spencer Greene, and Eilish Urgo—and Mary Rasenberger who gave the manuscript a close read and offered many valuable comments. I also greatly appreciate the supportive comments from Mark Rayner, as well as the advice from John Silbersack, Doug Richards, and Bill Strahan.

Thanks also to Natasha Seery, who has consistently helped me navigate the shifting rapids of the digital world.

More generally, I'd like to thank the scientists at Cibus for an extensive education on the ins and outs of gene editing. My background in quantum entanglement dates back to a series of conversations with John Clauser, whom I featured in an essay on quantum reality in *TIME* way back in 1990 ("Can We Really Understand Matter?"). I focused on his work empirically proving quantum entanglement, work that helped pave the way for quantum computing and for which Clauser shared a Nobel Prize for physics in 2022. And finally, I'd like to acknowledge the benefits I've gained from tough-minded dialogues on many matters with my friends John Koerber, Scott Donahue, and Mike and Olga Kagan.

# ABOUT THE AUTHOR

Eugene Linden is an award-winning journalist and author on science, nature, and the environment. He has written eleven books, including his celebrated works on animal intelligence and climate change: *Apes, Men, and Language*, the *New York Times* Notable Book *Silent Partners*, and the bestselling *The Parrot's Lament*. His book, *Winds of Change*, which explored the connection between climate change and the rise and fall of civilizations, was awarded the Grantham Prize Special Award of Merit. His book *Fire and Flood* was named the American Meteorological Society's book of the year for 2023. For many years, Linden wrote about nature and global environmental issues for *TIME* where he garnered several awards including the American Geophysical Union's Walter Sullivan Award. He has also contributed to the *New York Times*, *Foreign Affairs*, and *National Geographic*, among many other publications.